CHECKING OUT

OTHER BOOKS AND AUDIO BOOKS
BY CLAIR M. POULSON

Framed

I'll Find You

Relentless

Lost and Found

Conflict of Interest

Runaway

Coverup

Mirror Image

Blind Side

Evidence

Don't Cry Wolf

Dead Wrong

Deadline

Vengeance

Hunted

Switchback

Accidental Private Eye

CHECKING OUT

a novel

CLAIR M. POULSON

Covenant Communications, Inc.

Brass Bell with Holiday Tickets and Room Key © Wragg, istockphotography.com

Thumb Fingerprint © Anteromite, Shutterstock.com

Cover design copyright © 2013 by Covenant Communications, Inc.

Published by Covenant Communications, Inc.
American Fork, Utah

Printed in the United States of America
First Printing: August 2013

19 18 17 16 15 14 13   10 9 8 7 6 5 4 3 2 1

ISBN-13: 978-1-62108-454-9

To Ruth, the light of my life

ACKNOWLEDGMENTS

My family has been and continues to be a great source of help in my writing. I'd particularly like to thank my daughter Mary Hicken for her hard work in helping me get this book ready.

PROLOGUE

THE SHOT TOOK OUT THE windshield of the police car I was riding in. Glass sprayed both me and Sergeant Tom Brolin.

"Are you okay, Keene?" he shouted as he steered the car to the side of the street.

"Yeah, are you?" I asked as I gathered myself from where I had almost gone clear to the floorboard. Trying to keep from panicking, I looked over at him. There was blood pouring from his right shoulder. I don't know if he'd even felt it, but it was clearly a bullet wound. "You're hit," I said as calmly as I could, which wasn't all that calmly. "We better get you to a hospital." I didn't know how bad it was, but there was a lot of blood. I realized I was shaking.

Tom put the cruiser in park and looked at his shoulder. "Son of a gun!" he said as the color started to fade from his tanned face. "Did you see the shooter?" he asked.

"It was a blue car—I think. It was going the other way. But I can't even be sure that's where the bullet came from," I said as I grabbed the mic to the radio. In the next breath, I was reporting our situation to the dispatcher and was told to stay put, that backup and an ambulance were coming.

As I put the mic down, the dispatcher called for others to come to the scene and then told all officers in the area to be looking for a blue car. That was hopeless. After all, how many blue cars were there in Los Angeles? "You better let me look at that while we wait," I said. I jumped out of the car, ran around to Tom's side, and began removing his shirt. The bleeding was bad. I pulled a handkerchief from my pocket, applying pressure to his shoulder. The bullet, it appeared, had gone clear through. I tried to keep my breathing steady.

"*Now* it hurts," Tom mumbled, and I feared that he was going to pass out. "I didn't even feel it until you mentioned it." He tried to grin, but it didn't quite work.

Help arrived, Sergeant Brolin was taken to the hospital, and I spent several hours filling out reports and answering questions. I was a reserve officer, but I worked two or three shifts a week and knew most of the officers in the precinct quite well. I had often ridden with Tom and had learned a lot from him. He was a genuinely nice guy, a good friend and mentor, but he was a police officer, and that alone could explain why he'd been shot. Anger was quickly beginning to replace my earlier fear.

No blue car with viable suspects was located that night or in subsequent days. I worked another shift later in the week, still shook up and quite livid, but nothing out of the ordinary occurred.

At the end of that shift, I headed home, arriving shortly before one in the morning. I was in a hurry to get to bed because I had a class at the university at nine. I had taken off my shoes and placed them in my closet, and I was beginning to unbutton my shirt when I heard something thud against the front wall of my apartment.

I moved quickly to the door, pulling my police-issued 9mm handgun. I opened my door about the same time my neighbor opened his. He was a big Tongan fellow, quite a nice guy, but when he picked up the brick and read the note attached to it, he looked anything but nice. He tore the note off and hurled the brick back into the street below our second-story balcony. He angrily read me the note, which said something like, "Your family will pay dearly for not cooperating." My neighbor sputtered something about how no one better harm him or his family, and without another word to me, he went back into the apartment, carrying the note.

I glanced briefly at the spot where the brick had struck between our two apartments, leaving a dent in the siding. I shook my head and went inside, mad that innocent people were being terrorized. In the past three days, someone had shot my partner and someone else had threatened my neighbor. I was left wondering about the motivation of both events. Ten minutes later, I was asleep.

CHAPTER ONE

IF I WERE TO PICK one thing that irritated me more than anything else, it would be someone calling me a liar. I may have a lot of shortcomings, but lying is not one of them. I suppose that's why I lost my temper when my older brother Sean insisted that I had promised our very recently departed mother that I would take over the management of the Tempest Hotel after her death.

Losing my temper—especially with my three older siblings—is one of my foremost shortcomings. For years I had tried both to overcome it and to rationalize that they always brought on my tantrums. I suppose both were true. Today was no exception. I had tried to control my temper after Sean said, "You will take over the hotel, Keene. We took a vote right after the funeral today. It was unanimous. Anyway, you promised Mom you'd do it."

I ran those short sentences around in my head for a very long thirty seconds before I exploded. Considering everything, that was pretty good in my book. I would have been proud of even fifteen seconds. I was also pleased that my tantrum only lasted for a minute or two. During that short duration, I loudly explained to Sean that I had told our mother I had other plans for the rest of my life and that I didn't want to have anything to do with the Tempest Hotel. What I didn't tell him was that she had told me I was the one she trusted the most and that even though I was *working* toward a career, the others were already deeply involved in theirs.

In retrospect, I have to admit that I never fully closed the door to my mother, possibly leaving her thinking that I might do what she wanted. I suppose that I just expected her to live for many more years and that by the time she passed on, I'd also be deeply involved in my career. However, I had not *promised* her anything as Sean claimed.

When I calmed down, I looked up at Sean, all the way up from my scrawny five-foot-six to his towering six-foot-one, and said, "I suppose it was the three of you who voted."

He grinned that maddening, self-centered grin of his and replied, "That's right, little brother."

"Don't I get a vote?" I asked.

The grin expanded across his face. "Of course you do, Keene. What is your vote?"

"I vote no!" I felt my temper picking up again. "We can just sell the place and someone else can worry about it."

"Noted," he said. "And you lose, three to one. Actually, I'd say it was four to one because Mom *did* want you to take over. Maybe she didn't tell you, but she told me. You'll need to move in right away." He smiled for a moment, further infuriating me, and then he added, "We all have a stake in how well the place does, and we expect it to do well."

I didn't lose gracefully, but I did lose, mostly because Mom had wanted me to take over, not because of the vote my siblings had taken. We had buried my mother, Maude Tempest, that afternoon. I headed back to Los Angeles shortly after. Three days later, I had packed up my belongings and left my small apartment behind—way behind. You see, the Tempest Hotel was located in Hardy, Wyoming—on Highway 89, close to the Idaho border and about halfway up the state. The apartment I was leaving was in Los Angeles, where I had just finished my third year of a four-year bachelor's program in criminal justice.

I'd attended the police academy the previous summer and graduated as a fully certified police officer. I'd worked as a reserve officer for the LAPD while I was finishing my schooling. My plan—and that of the LAPD—was for me to work there full-time when I graduated. My brothers and sister told me I was too small to be a cop, but that didn't bother me. I could take care of myself—better than most, in all honesty. They knew nothing of my black belt in karate. And I had no intention of telling them—unless they tried to do what they used to when I was young and they were teenagers. Neither of my brothers would ever beat me up again!

One of the things that had helped me back down from this particular bout with my siblings was the fact that I loved my mother and felt obligated, even though I'd never promised a thing. I decided that I'd go for the summer, and by fall I hoped to have something else worked out for the small hotel so I could pursue the rest of my education and career. I didn't tell them any of that. It might have provoked the kind of battle I hoped to avoid.

Why my mother and father had purchased that hotel in Wyoming was something neither I nor my siblings understood. They had raised us in various places around the world as we followed Dad, a dedicated, hard-core army officer, on his military assignments. One by one, beginning with Sean, the oldest, and ending with me, the youngest, we migrated to various locations around the country. Los Angeles was where I had wound up and planned to stay.

Sean, on the other hand, had ended up only a hundred miles or so from our folks in Wyoming. He worked in the oil field and made good money—or so he claimed. He did drive a nice, late-model, cherry-red Corvette, which he claimed was fully paid for. I suppose that was possible. Sean had never married, so he had only himself to support.

That Thursday morning, Sean met me at the hotel in the center of Hardy. I knew my way around, having visited my mother there several times following my father's death three years ago. Of course, I'd also been there for her funeral at the local LDS chapel the previous week.

The Tempest Hotel was a two-story affair, with all guest rooms accessed from indoor hallways; it was actually a very nice place—by far the nicest in the area. It even boasted an indoor swimming pool with a large Jacuzzi beside it. My new quarters, which used to be my mother's, consisted of a two-bedroom suite on the main floor closest to the office. We had referred to it as Mom's apartment.

"You better make this place pay." Sean handed me the keys and a list of what he presumed I should do as the general manager. He gave me an intense stare before speaking again. "I'll be back to check on you from time to time. So always have a clean room available for me. You never know when I might show up."

"How do I make money if I have to keep a room empty just in case you grace me with your presence?" I asked angrily. The guy really rubbed me wrong, an art he'd perfected early in my life.

Sean gave me another stern look. "Just do as you're told, Keene. See you around." He got in his bright red Corvette and sped away. I sat down behind the registration desk and rubbed my aching head. Sean and I had met there that morning at eight and relieved the night manager. I was alone now except for the four women who were busy cleaning rooms. It was the beginning of summer and thus the beginning of the busy season for the hotel. At least that's what Sean claimed, and I supposed he was right.

I looked at the computer screen and began to check the past few days' records. The place hadn't done badly. Even my mother's sudden death hadn't kept patrons from coming in. It was a nice place—clean, neat, and well maintained. The pool was kept clean and looked quite inviting. My mother had allowed groups from the school and local churches to occasionally hold activities there. That was a big deal for a small place like Hardy.

I heard the front door open, and I looked up. A very attractive young woman with red hair every bit as bright as mine entered, dressed in neatly pressed cop blue. I quickly took in two things: how nicely she filled out the uniform and the presence of a 9mm semiautomatic handgun on her right hip. I rose to my feet, wondering why a cop was already entering the Tempest Hotel. I hoped it didn't have a reputation for living up to its name.

"Good morning," I said, glancing at the wall clock that hung above the door, making sure it was still morning. It was still fifteen minutes until noon. "Is there a problem?"

"Not that I know of," the young woman answered with a smile that seemed to come from somewhere deep inside. I took an instant liking to her. I walked around the counter as she added, "I just thought I'd meet the new manager. Chief Thompkins, Officer Kerr, and I like to know everybody in town. You're new, so I wanted to come in and get acquainted."

I offered my hand as I tried to stretch myself up enough to make myself taller than her. It didn't work. Our eyes met at exactly the same level. "Keene Tempest," I said as she accepted my hand and gave it a firm shake.

"I saw you at the funeral," she said. My mind quickly scrolled back. I did remember a stunning redhead in a knee-length black dress. This was the same girl, I was quite sure, although she looked a lot different in the uniform. I read her name tag—*Donovan*—and I knew it was the same girl. I recalled that she had pronounced her first name "Shallay," with a long *a*. It had reminded me of the French word *chalet*. I really liked the name.

"Chaille Donovan," she said, displaying some of the nicest white teeth I'd ever seen as well as two cute dimples. She spelled it for me, explaining, "I'm Irish, but you probably guessed that. I'm really sorry about your mother. She was a wonderful woman. We miss her around here."

"Me too," I responded. "Her death was totally unexpected."

She shook her head, and the smile left her face. "Heart attack," she said. "At least that's what we were told. I'm not so sure, even though she didn't look like she felt very well the past few weeks."

"She didn't feel well?" I asked, surprised. Even though Mom had spoken briefly about her eventual death, it was something she had referred to as sometime in the distant future. She was just making sure she and her family were prepared when that time came. "Mom and I talked quite often, and she didn't say a word about being ill. Her death caught me totally unprepared."

"Me too, but she seemed like she was under a lot of stress lately. We often met at the café over there," she said, nodding to the north in the direction of the small establishment that was my nearest neighbor on Main Street. I'd eaten there when I got into town that morning after driving most of the night. I'd also eaten there while I was in town for the funeral. The sign over the door said Hardy Café. Not too creative, but I guess it fit.

Chaille went on. "We'd have a cup of hot chocolate together two or three times a week. She didn't talk much about her family except for you. I gathered you were her favorite." A quick grin and a sparkle in her eyes accompanied that statement. "She said you were the smallest member of the family but the nicest."

"That doesn't say much for the rest of them," I said mildly.

"She loved you all," she said. "You're just the one she talked about the most. You're all redheaded, your mother told me. People say us redheads are hot-tempered. I don't think that's any truer of us than of people who are blonde or brunette. Your mother seemed as mild a person as I'd ever met. And I think I control my temper pretty well." She seemed thoughtful for a moment then added, "Most of the time anyway." Her eyes sparkled again.

"Did you know my father, the Colonel?" I asked. People had known him as the Colonel. Even following his retirement, he'd used the title.

She nodded her head. "I met him a few times before he died, right after I was hired by the town. Now *he* had a temper."

It was my turn to nod. "He did at that." I didn't mention my own tendency to blow off steam. I was, after all, trying to get that little problem under control and doing fairly well at it.

"I'm surprised to see you here. Your mother told me just two weeks ago that she was hoping you would take over when she died, which she pointed out was not imminent at all."

"That's what my siblings told me. When she mentioned it to me, I told her that I didn't want to take it over. I have a totally different career path planned. But my siblings decided that I would manage it even if I don't want to."

"You don't want to? Then why are you here?" she asked. "If you don't mind my asking."

I shrugged my shoulders and stepped behind the counter again. "You don't know my sister and brothers."

"I've met Sean," she said. "He came around and visited your mother quite often. He works in the oil field. I really like his car." She paused for a moment. Then she added, "I'm sorry, but frankly I don't care a lot for him."

"Join the club," I said. "He can be a real jerk." I was tired, and as much as I was drawn to the pretty officer, I wasn't in the mood to talk all day. "It was nice of you to come in," I told her in an attempt to get her to leave. I had a lot to do before I could feel like I knew enough about the hotel to run it in anything close to an acceptable manner—acceptable to myself, not to my siblings. I didn't think I could ever reach their expectations, but as long as I was doing the job, albeit for only a few months, I would give it the most I could.

"Yeah, thanks," she said. "I guess I better go." She turned to the door, but after opening it, she paused and turned back to me. "Your mother said you were a reserve officer in LA and that you were working on a degree in criminal justice. So I was surprised when she said she wanted you to come here, knowing you had a career."

"I don't think she was fond of the idea of me being a cop," I told her as I sat down behind the counter. "And none of us expected her to be gone so soon." I could still see Officer Donovan's face. A shadow seemed to cross it.

She turned as if to leave but then twisted back once more. "Chief Thompkins and the other officer in our department, Payton Kerr, say I'm wrong, but I'm not sure your mother's death was due to any kind of illness, not even a heart attack."

That got my complete attention. I stood again. "What exactly do you mean?"

"I'm sorry. I guess I shouldn't say anything, but something was going on in your mother's life. She was, like I said, under a *lot* of stress. She seemed unhappy lately, not at all like the woman I had come to know so well. When I asked her one day if everything was okay, she told me that it was, but the way she looked at me and the way her face went red, I couldn't help but think that she was hiding something. I pressed her a little on the matter, but she changed the subject and wouldn't talk about it."

"Officer Donovan," I said as I walked around the counter to look directly into her dark blue eyes. "What do you mean that you don't think she died due to illness? Are you saying she may have been—"

"Murdered," she said, cutting me off. "But I'm probably wrong. I'm sorry. I shouldn't have said anything. Please, don't mention it to the chief or Payton. They already know how I feel, and they told me I was up in the night. I should take their advice and forget it. I don't need them angry with me."

She started through the door. "Wait. I think we need to talk, Officer Donovan," I said with some urgency.

"Please just call me Chaille," she said. "Maybe we can talk later. I'm probably wrong. I shouldn't have said anything." She went through the door and left me to worry.

CHAPTER TWO

I TRIED TO FOCUS ON the hotel's finances that afternoon, but I wasn't sure what I was seeing. My mind kept going back to Officer Chaille Donovan's appalling statement about my mother's death. She looked and sounded like a bright woman. She couldn't have come to this conclusion without some kind of a reason. I wanted to know what that reason was. I couldn't imagine what could have caused her to have such a thought.

The finances, to my distracted mind, looked okay for the past couple of weeks. I believed my mother had been doing fairly well. The expenses didn't seem out of line, and the income seemed fairly good. More nights than not, most of the rooms were filled. But my mother didn't appear to be making so much money that someone might kill her for it. Not that money was a motive Officer Donovan had mentioned. She hadn't actually mentioned any motives, just that my mother was stressed and perhaps hiding something. My mother had been a strong woman. Could she have been afraid of something that she didn't even dare tell her friend, a police officer? And if that were the case, what could she have feared? I had to talk to Chaille again—soon.

I got up and stretched. I heard the door open and looked over. A young couple with a baby entered. "Good afternoon," I greeted them. "How can I help you?"

"We have a reservation for this evening. I know it's a little early," the young man began, "but we were hoping we could check in now."

"I can't see why not," I said, glancing at my watch. Our check-in time was three o'clock, and it was currently two thirty. I opened a computer screen and saw that several rooms were cleaned and ready.

That couple was the first to check in that day. Before the night shift came in, I had filled over two dozen more rooms. For a small hotel of only forty rooms, I didn't feel like that was too bad.

The trend continued over the next few days. But I was becoming antsy. I hadn't seen or heard from Chaille Donovan again. Nor did I meet the police chief or Officer Kerr.

***

I went to bed late on Monday night only to be awakened when my night employee—the young woman I had met for the first time the previous week—called me a short while later. She was very agitated and apologized profusely for interrupting my sleep. "It's okay, Paige," I said calmly. "Whatever the problem is, I'm sure we can handle it."

Paige Everest, a member of my mother's LDS ward, was just nineteen and had been hired about three months ago. She seemed like a very nice girl, vivacious and bubbly. She was small, slender, and very pretty. She'd told me when we met how much she appreciated the job. She didn't appear to be appreciating it now. "Please hurry, Mr. Tempest. I don't know what to do."

I rested the phone against my shoulder as I began to pull my jeans on. "What's going on, Paige?" I asked.

Before she could answer, I heard an angry voice in the background. "Tell that little brother of mine that he better have a room for me in five minutes." Despite the slurred words, there was no mistaking my brother's voice. It was at that moment that I remembered something: I had failed to tell Paige that when we were down to one room, we were to light up the No Vacancy sign on the off chance Sean should show up and want a room. "It's your brother, and he's been drinking," Paige whispered, her voice indicating that she was near tears.

"Don't worry about it, Paige. I'll deal with Sean," I told her calmly as my stomach began to roll. It would be on the one night we filled up that Sean would show up wanting a room.

"Keene!" Sean shouted the moment I entered the lobby. He'd been more than just drinking; he was drunk. Even when he was sober, Sean was short-tempered and ornery, but when he was drinking, he was totally out of control. "I made myself clear! There is always to be an empty room when I need one. This little floozy tells me they're all full."

I saw Paige go white when he referred to her so crassly. The rolling in my stomach settled instantly as anger filled me. "You will not refer to Paige in that manner," I said, fighting to keep from saying something I might regret. "She's a good girl and a right fine employee."

"That may be," Sean retorted, approaching me with clenched fists. "You're the one who messed up. You have fifteen minutes to clear and clean a room for me. I'm going over to the café next door to get a cup of coffee. When I get back, my room better be ready."

I took a deep breath in an attempt to keep my temper from boiling over. Then I said, "Every room is filled with paying customers. I forgot to tell Paige about you, but it's too late now. I have an extra bedroom in my apartment. I'll help you carry your bags there." That seemed silly to me the moment I said it. After all, he was a great deal larger than me. He could carry his own bags just fine, drunk or sober.

"I'm not sleeping in the same apartment with you, you little religious freak," he said, referring, I was quite sure, to the fact that I had joined the Mormon Church a couple of years ago, shortly after our mother had. He was far from a religious man, even when he hadn't been drinking.

"It's the best I can offer," I said. "The bed is made up and the sheets are clean. It seems reasonable to me."

"You have your orders, Keene," Sean said darkly as he moved one step closer and forced my temperature a few degrees higher.

"This hotel is as much mine as it is yours," I reminded him, my own voice raised higher than I should have allowed. "And I'm the manager."

"You little wimp," he said. "I'm the oldest, and I'm in charge. You'll do as I say."

"No, I'll just quit!" I shouted. "I'm here as a favor if you'll remember."

"You're not quitting, and you're doing no one a favor. You're doing what your mother wanted you to do—and what *I* want you to do."

I glanced at Paige. She was standing behind the counter, her mouth hanging open, running a trembling hand through her long brown hair. Her blue eyes met mine, and I could see fear in them. I didn't know if the fear was for her or for me. She needn't have worried because I wouldn't let Sean do anything to hurt her or me.

"Why don't you go get your cup of coffee and sober up a little bit. When you get calmed down, you can come back and I'll see that you have a place to sleep," I said as I found my temper cooling. I attributed that to the fear in Paige's pretty blue eyes. Losing my temper was not going to help either of us. "The room in my quarters is available when you come to your senses."

"You little . . ." Sean began as he took one more step and swiftly threw a hard punch at my face.

The punch never landed; my instincts and training kicked in. In an instant, Sean was on the floor, dazed and silent after I had given him a couple of lightning-fast karate chops. I suppose he was wondering what had just happened. He shook his head and rubbed his jaw. After a few moments he looked up, his eyes unfocused. I watched as they cleared, and he seemed to recognize me standing over him.

"What . . . what . . ." he mumbled.

I scowled down at him. "Let that be a lesson, brother. I'm not a kid anymore. Don't you ever try to hit me again." Then I reached a hand down to him. "Let me help you up."

He got to his knees, swaying slightly, ignoring my offer. After a minute or so, he managed to get to his feet. Sean was always a slow learner when he'd been drinking. He'd picked a poor time to demonstrate that fact now. He had no more than established his balance when he said, "Ten minutes, scum. Have that room ready in ten minutes."

I glanced over at Paige, who was slowly shaking her head, a tentative grin on her face. Then I turned back to my brother. "Sorry, Sean. It's not going to happen."

In my police training, I'd learned that the first part of the brain to be affected by alcohol was the part that controlled a person's judgment. Sean's judgment was definitely impaired. He foolishly attempted to throw another punch. This time it took him a lot longer to get to his feet. I didn't offer to help him this time. I just stood and watched him struggle. But once he managed and was on his feet, I grabbed his right arm, twisted it behind his back, and shoved him toward the door. Paige, who hadn't budged from her place of security behind the counter, hurried out now, grabbed the door, and pulled it open for me while I propelled my brother outside. "Next time you need a room, make a normal reservation like anyone else," I said.

He looked back at me and growled, "You shouldn't have done that, Keene."

"You threw the first punch," I reminded him, knowing I was wasting my breath. I stepped back inside.

When the door closed, I locked it. For a couple of minutes, Paige and I stood there and watched as my older brother staggered to where his car was parked and opened the door without looking back. His small red Corvette, when he finally managed to fold himself into it, sped onto the street. I prayed he wouldn't cause a wreck and hurt anyone. He was way too drunk to be driving.

"I hope he doesn't come back," Paige commented after the Corvette disappeared from view.

"That makes two of us," I said blandly.

"I thought he was going to kill you. He's a big man. But apparently you have some skills he didn't know about."

"He does now," I said as I thought glumly about the next time he and I might have a confrontation.

"Mr. Tempest, I'm afraid to stay here alone. What if he comes back?"

"Call me Keene," I told her. "Mr. Tempest makes me sound old." I smiled at her. "I'm not that much older than you."

She blushed slightly and nodded. "Thanks, but I'm still afraid. I'm sorry."

"The door is locked."

"It's glass."

I knew what she was implying—glass breaks. "There's a recliner in my apartment," I told her. "If you'll help me bring it up, I'll doze here while you keep an eye on things."

She smiled with relief—a very pretty smile, I noticed. "Thank you," she said.

Sean did not come back that night, but he did telephone—from the county jail. I had finally managed to fall asleep in the recliner when Paige gently shook my arm. "I'm sorry, Keene. There's a phone call for you," she said with a tremble in her voice. "I think it's your brother."

She handed me the receiver, and I said hello, hoping Paige was wrong.

She wasn't. "Keene, thanks to you I'm in jail. You need to come right now and get me out." He was shouting.

I didn't even know where the jail was, but I knew it wasn't in Hardy. It was probably quite some distance away. "Sorry, Sean, but you're on your own. You can make your own bond, or you can stay there," I responded unsympathetically. "You had no business driving in your condition."

Sean uttered a few choice words that I was glad Paige didn't have to listen to, and then he concluded with, "You have no appreciation for what I've done for you, little brother."

I had no clue what he was talking about. I wasn't aware of him having done anything for me, so I simply ended the call. Then I made one of my own. From a corrections officer at the county jail, I learned that my suspicions were correct: Sean had been arrested for driving under the influence. He'd also been charged with resisting arrest—no surprise there either.

When I asked who had arrested him, I was told that it was Officer Payton Kerr, the third member of the Hardy Police Department. When I asked if the officer was injured, I learned that for the second time tonight, Sean had more than met his match. Officer Kerr, it turned out, was six-foot-six and weighed 290 pounds. He had handled my intoxicated brother all by himself. I was also told that no one could bail him out until he'd sobered up—and that wouldn't be for at least ten hours. I assured the officer that I had no intention of helping Sean anyway. I hung up the phone and turned to Paige. "He'll be there at least until late morning."

"Oh, good," she replied. "He scares me a lot." I settled back into the recliner only to hear, "You don't have to stay here now, Keene. I'll be fine."

That was good news because I was really tired. "Call me if you have any more problems." I yawned. "But I'm sure you won't."

The phone rang before I'd even gotten back into bed. It was my *other* brother, Grady. He was the biggest of us all. I had Paige transfer the call to my apartment. "I just talked to Sean," Grady said as soon as I spoke. I knew what was coming. "I think it would be in your best interest to bail him out, Keene. He's already angry and—"

I cut him off. "I can't. The jail has a policy of sobriety before release."

"Liar. You're making that up."

"No, I'm not," I countered, instantly angered at being called a liar. "I called the jail after I talked to Sean. The officer in charge told me I couldn't bail him out until he was sober."

"So you *were* going to get him out," Grady erroneously concluded. "Sean thought you weren't." I didn't bother to correct him. In fact, I said nothing and let Grady go on. "You really should give him a room next time. He told me what happened."

"All of it?" I asked.

"Yep, all of it," Grady said. "He told me that you asked him to leave when he asked for a room and that he did. He said he didn't want to create a scene in front of the pretty girl working the desk. But the more he thought about it, the angrier he got. It really is your fault, Keene."

"Whatever." I kept my voice steady. I didn't want another argument. I just wanted sleep. I was too tired to even tell Grady that Sean hadn't left nicely. "I'm tired. I need to get to bed."

"Me too," Grady agreed. "Make sure you get Sean out in a little while. Talk to you later, little brother."

"Good-bye." I hated being called *little brother*. My siblings all knew that. My sister, Bree, never called me that, but both brothers did. I placed the phone back in the cradle.

I had finally gotten back to sleep when Paige called again. "I'm really, really sorry, Keene," she started. "Some woman named Bree says she has to talk to you."

I shook my foggy head. "You've got to be kidding," I said.

"I'm really sorry, Keene." Her voice was trembling. "Do you know this woman? Should I have not told you?"

"It's okay, Paige," I said. "It's not your fault. Bree is my sister. She's not as bad as my brothers."

"Oh." Her tone seemed to imply that my family was a bunch of strange people.

"Transfer the call," I said with resignation.

I thought about my family while I waited for Paige to send the call through. My Irish father had given us all Irish names even though my mother was of Danish decent. Bree was the one closest in age to me. She was thirty and married with two kids. She was the only one of the three I'd ever felt close to at all, and even that was a bit of a stretch. She came on the line. "Sorry to bother you, Keene," she began. That was something neither of my brothers would have ever said.

"It's okay." I sighed.

"What's going on with Sean?"

"He got himself—"

She cut me off. "I know he's in jail, Keene. He called me."

"Surprise, surprise," I said sarcastically.

"Wouldn't it be easier if you just bailed him out? After all, he is your brother. And it sounds like he only got arrested because you wouldn't give him a room."

That made me mad, but I didn't want to argue. Instead I told her the jail policy. She said she understood that Sean would have to be patient until I could get him out. That was something I didn't intend to do, but I let her think what she wanted. "You should have let him have the spare bedroom in your apartment," she chastised. "Why didn't you think of that?"

"I did; he wouldn't take it."

"Oh. He didn't tell me that," she said slowly.

"That's not all he didn't tell you," I said with a touch of anger and terminated the call before she tried to get me to go into more detail. I lay back on the pillow for a moment and then called Paige. "There should be no more calls tonight. I don't have any more siblings. I'll see you in a few hours."

"I'm sorry, Keene," she said.

"Not your fault," I reassured her. "I'm going to try to sleep now."

CHAPTER THREE

I WAS AWAKE AND UP long before I'd had enough rest, but I had work to do. When I walked to the desk, Paige, looking sleepy, smiled at me and said, "So did you finally get some sleep?"

"Not enough, but it will have to do." I smiled back at her. "I got more sleep than you did. These graveyard shifts are rough, aren't they?"

"Yeah, but at least I can go home and sleep a little while." She paused. "I'm sorry about last night."

"My family lives up to our name," I told her. "We have lots of tempests. My dad stirred a lot of them up, and my mother was always hurt by them. Life wasn't easy for her. I'm just glad she found the Church. It gave her a lot of comfort."

"So did you," Paige said, and then her face went just a little red. "She talked about you a lot. And it was all good."

I just shook my head. "I have a nasty temper. She was always telling me to calm down. I'm still working on that. She was a good mother. She didn't deserve the contention we had in the family."

"So, are you going to get your brother out of jail this morning?" Paige asked, nervously fingering the end of her long brown ponytail.

I shook my head, took a deep breath, and said, "I don't think so. He deserves to be where he's at, although I don't think he'll be there much longer. He'll find a buddy or coworker or someone who'll help him make bail."

Paige's eyes widened. "He'll come back here."

"I suppose so," I responded. "When he does, maybe he'll be sober. He's not quite as bad when he's sober. But either way, I'll just have to deal with it."

Paige left a few minutes later, and I took over duties at the front counter. My cleaning staff was busy, and a few guests wandered in and out as I worked. As I sat there, I thought about what Officer Chaille Donovan had told me. I couldn't imagine that she was right about someone hastening my mother's death. I hoped she was wrong. For now, since I didn't have much to do besides answer the phone and check guests in and out, I decided to look closer at the hotel's finances. My earlier cursory glance had told me that the Tempest Hotel was doing okay. But I'd only looked at the past couple of weeks. If I was going to manage the place, I wanted to be familiar with its long-term patterns.

My mother had used a small accounting firm in town to do her taxes and some of the bookwork, but she had also done a lot of it herself. I called the head of the firm, a CPA by the name of Fred Moser, and asked him if it would be possible to meet with him in the next day or two.

"Is something wrong, Mr. Tempest?" he asked, sounding quite concerned.

"Oh no, it's not that, but if I have to manage this place, I need to know everything I can about it, and that includes all aspects of accounting, taxes, and so on," I replied.

"Of course, that makes good business sense." He sounded like an older man, maybe sixty or so. "Your business is in the best of hands, Mr. Tempest. I employ two other accountants, and they both do excellent work. The past two years, my accountant Tess has been working with your mother. I'll have her give you a call and set up an appointment."

"That will be great," I assured him. "I appreciate it."

"Not a problem," he said, and then he chuckled. "You're single, I understand."

I couldn't see how my marital status was any of his business, but I didn't say so. I just grunted an affirmative answer.

"Then you'll get along well with Tess. She's both pretty and smart— and frankly, I think it's time she found a husband and settled down."

Now Mr. Moser was going too far. "I'm sure she'll take care of that aspect of her life." My tone was perhaps a little too sharp. "The sooner she can call the better. I really need to get myself up to speed on things. Thanks for your time."

"You're most welcome," Mr. Moser said. "By the way, I'm sorry about your troubles during the night. I hope you can keep your brother out of your business. It doesn't sound like he's a very good person, I'm afraid."

Fred Moser was apparently nosey. But how could he possibly have known about Sean and the scene he'd caused? Rather than provoke more questioning, I tried to brush off the whole episode. "Oh, it was nothing, really. I can handle Sean. I'll be awaiting a call from Tess. What did you say her last name was?"

He hadn't said, but I wanted to know just in case I had to ask for her directly before he got around to having her call me. "Tess Everest," he said. "Her little sister seemed pretty upset this morning. She stopped by here on her way home."

That explained a lot. Tess and Paige were sisters, and of course Paige would have mentioned the night's drama, poor girl. I was actually relieved. I had formed the impression that this little town was full of busybodies. I had jumped to an erroneous conclusion. "Paige was understandably upset, but I have the matter under control." I knew the statement was a stretch. Sean was still in jail, but when he got out, I'd have to deal with him.

"I'm sure you do, but could I give you one little piece of advice?" Fred asked.

I supposed that I would get the advice whether I wanted it or not, so I said, "Sure."

"Leave your brother in jail. That's where he deserves to be."

I couldn't have agreed more, although it irked me that the accountant would say what he did. I didn't consider it any of his business. "I have no plans on bailing him out," I said. "I need to run now. I'll be looking forward to hearing from Miss Everest."

I guess he got the message because he simply said, "I'll have her call you this morning as soon as she's free." Then he hung up.

I sat back and looked at the phone in my hand for a moment. Fred Moser had rubbed me wrong, and yet nothing he'd said was anything I should take offense to. I was just glad at that point that it would be Paige's sister I was working with, not him. I put the phone down and began to concentrate on what information I had. A few minutes later, my concentration was interrupted by the ringing of the phone.

"Tempest Hotel," I answered, picking the receiver back up. Surely Tess Everest wouldn't be calling already. It had only been a few minutes since I'd talked to her boss. "How can I help you?"

It was not a pleasant voice that answered and not even a female voice. "You can have a room ready for me this afternoon," my brother said. "I'm making that reservation just like you asked. I'll be getting out of jail in a little while, and I'll need that room tonight."

"It'll be ready. Thanks for the advance notice, Sean," I said as nicely as I could muster. Before he could say anything else, I put the receiver down.

Apparently, someone was coming to his rescue. Even though he'd made no threats, I'd heard them in his tone. And if he got to drinking again, I needed to be on guard. With that thought, I went back to my apartment, got my 9mm pistol, and carried it back to the front with me. I put it in a drawer where I could get to it if I needed it—I prayed that I wouldn't, but one never knew.

Fifteen minutes and two calls later, the phone rang again. "Keene Tempest?" a very sweet voice asked.

"This is Keene."

"I'm Tess Everest. Mr. Moser said you'd like to meet with me."

"Yes, that would be great," I responded. "Thanks for such a prompt callback."

"I'm here to serve," she said, a lilt in her voice. She sounded really sweet. "I just loved your mother. I'm so sorry about her death. I'll miss working with her. Not that you won't be good to work with too, I'm sure."

"I'm afraid you won't find me as nice as my mother, but I'll try." I found myself looking forward to meeting this girl.

"I'm sorry. That didn't come out right. I'm such a dork sometimes. Anyway, when would you like to meet?"

"As soon as you have time," I said.

"Today's very busy. How about tomorrow afternoon?" Tess asked. "Let's say one o'clock?"

"That would be great if you can come here. I'll be covering the front desk," I explained.

"That'll be fine. I'll be there at one o'clock."

"Sounds great."

"See you tomorrow then," she said. But before I could reply, she added, "Thanks for helping Paige out last night. She was scared, but she said you were great. I appreciate it."

"I hope it didn't upset her so badly that she quits. I really need her here."

"Oh, no, I don't think that even entered her mind. Anyway, I'll see you tomorrow. I really look forward to meeting you after all the good things your mother told me about you."

If nobody in Hardy liked me, it wouldn't be because of my late mother's lack of trying. It would be hard to live up to the expectations she had planted in the minds of the people.

The next conversation I had was not on the phone. Chief Damion Thompkins, the man in charge of the tiny Hardy police force, came through the front door. "Keene Tempest, I assume." He greeted me with a broad smile as I stood and started around the counter.

"That's right," I said. "And you must be Chief Thompkins."

"In person." A chuckle escaped as he held his hand out.

I made a quick assessment of the man as we shook hands. I was seeing a slightly pudgy man of about forty-five to fifty, a good four inches taller than me, in a spotless uniform. My first impression was that Chief Thompkins was a friendly man, good-natured, not as concerned with his own fitness as he was with his uniform, but whose dark green eyes shone with intelligence.

He was looking me over at the same time. He saw a small, stocky man with blue eyes and short, curly red hair with quite a collection of freckles. He spoke directly. "I take it you and your brother aren't on the best of terms."

"I guess you could say that," I responded as he drew his hand back.

"He's in a whole lot of trouble," the chief added.

"All very much deserved, I'm sure."

"It sounds like he was a bit upset with you."

"I suppose he was," I said. "But he'll get over it. He always does." *More or less*, I added to myself.

"He didn't impress Payton Kerr, one of my officers. In fact, I understand that from what your brother said in jail, he doesn't like cops in general."

"Yeah, that's what he says anyway. I honestly wouldn't know if he doesn't like them at all or just when he's drunk."

"Well, that's what he said to the releasing officer, and he was sober by then. Correct me if I'm wrong, but you're sort of a cop yourself," the chief ventured.

"I'm a certified officer in California. I've been working as a reserve officer with the LAPD while I'm finishing school, but I had to put that on hold when my mother died."

"You were working on a degree in criminal justice?"

"That's right." I nodded, wondering where he had gotten his information and where he was headed with all of this.

He rubbed his chin and looked thoughtful for a moment. Then he asked, "Are you giving all that up for this place?"

"Apparently that's what my siblings seem to think. Sean told me at the funeral that Mom wanted me to take the place over someday. 'Someday' came quicker than anyone anticipated. But anyway, I'm not here long-term," I continued. "I came here planning to stay the summer, but if I have more trouble with Sean, it might be even more temporary. I hope to make a career out of law enforcement."

"I could use a part-time officer while you're here," he said, surprising me. "I was hoping you'd stick around for a while and help us out from time to time before you head back. The pay's not great, but it's okay. And I think you'd find the three of us easy to work with."

"Gee, I'm flattered, Chief Thompkins. You don't know anything about me except that I have a brother who gets nasty when he drinks," I observed, leaning back against the counter.

He grinned. "Actually, I know a quite a bit about you. I've been doing some checking up on you ever since Officer Donovan told me about meeting you. She was quite impressed. And so is the LAPD. They hope to get you full-time. Your grades at school are outstanding. Your police certification in California, as you mentioned, is valid, and I can help you get certified here very easily, if you agree."

His offer suddenly made staying in Hardy a whole lot more attractive. I could hire more help here if I was picking up a few bucks from the city, I thought. And so far, even though I'd only met two of the three officers, I liked what I'd seen. "That might be something I'd consider," I said, trying not to sound too eager even though I was, quite frankly, very eager. The whole idea clicked with me in a most unexpected way.

"I'm serious. I have the funds in my budget to pay another officer for twenty to thirty hours per week. I've been looking, but it's hard to attract anyone for a part-time position. It was Chaille's suggestion that I talk to you. After checking your background, I agreed. What do you say? Would you be willing to give it a try?"

"Despite my brother giving Officer Kerr so much trouble last night?" I asked, even as I tried to find a way to say yes without appearing overly excited.

"A man can choose his friends, but he's born with family. Some of us just luck out better than others. You have a very good reputation, and that's all that matters to me," the chief said with a smile.

"May I think about it for a day or two?" I asked. I was ready to accept, but I didn't think it would look good to appear overly anxious.

"Sure thing, Mr. Tempest."

"Keene," I said.

"Sure thing, Keene. I'll check back with you in a couple of days. Now, about your brother—I think you need to be careful with him."

"He's always blustery," I said. "He only gets real mean when he's drinking."

"I just think you need to consider him a threat after the way he was acting last night when he was arrested."

"I'll do that," I agreed, thinking about the pistol in the drawer behind me while praying that I'd never need to use it on Sean.

"I have a spare service revolver in my car. I thought maybe you could start carrying it. I already know you're proficient with firearms. Like I said, I checked on you. You ought to carry it just in case, you know, your brother gets drunk and comes around again."

"I'm not licensed to carry a concealed weapon in Wyoming," I reminded the chief.

"You're still a peace officer in California. That makes it legal for you to carry here. You do still have your LAPD ID, I presume."

I did, and I fished it out of my wallet and showed it to him.

"That's all I need." He turned and started toward the door. "I'll go get that pistol for you."

"Actually, I've got one of my own that I could carry," I said, glancing toward the counter behind me.

"Carry mine. That way, maybe you'll be more likely to say yes to my job offer when I come back tomorrow."

My "day or two" had been interpreted as one day. Oh well, that was okay. I planned to accept the position. The chief turned toward the door but stopped when he reached it, and then he turned back to me. "Why don't you ride with one of my officers tonight for a few hours? It might help you make up your mind," he suggested.

I pictured the pretty red-haired officer, Chaille, and, suppressing a grin, said, "That would be great—on one condition."

"Name it," he said with a straight face.

"I need to swing by the hotel occasionally. Paige Everest is working for me again tonight, and she had a rather bad time with Sean last night."

I hadn't completed that last statement before the chief nodded with understanding. "You're afraid he might come by."

"I know he will. He already called and reserved a room," I told him without explaining Sean's demands regarding a room. "Paige will be tense if Sean is on the premises even *if* he happens to be sober."

"Okay, I see. That's fine. And she can call you any time during the shift. Will that be okay?" he asked.

"I guess it will have to be if I ride with your officer tonight." That was something I really wanted to do. It would give me a chance to talk with Chaille about her suspicions. And it would give me a chance to get to know a very pretty lady a little bit better.

CHAPTER FOUR

SEAN SHOWED UP AT FIVE, well before I was scheduled to ride with the officer. I could smell alcohol on Sean's breath, but he didn't appear to be more than slightly drunk. He made no threats, nor did he mention the previous night's trouble. Being as friendly as I could, I checked him into a room. With nothing but a nod of thanks, he headed for the room I'd assigned him—carrying his own bag.

At around seven, Sean left his room near the back door of the hotel. He passed the desk with only a grunt of acknowledgment and entered the café next door. I watched him go in and then checked in another patron. When Paige walked in a while later, she gave me a wan smile. I wasn't sure she'd slept very well that day. I smiled back at her. "It's good to see you, Paige. We're filling up fast."

She nodded an acknowledgement but then immediately asked, her face quite sober now, "Is Sean out of jail?"

"He's staying in room 133 tonight," I said. Her face paled. "Actually, he's over at the café right now. He seems to be in a better mood this evening." That was true, but knowing my brother, if he decided to drink heavily again, that could change rapidly. But I honestly didn't think that was going to happen. I passed my feelings on to Paige. "I don't expect any trouble from him tonight."

After Paige had taken over, I went to my room and attempted to take a short nap. The chief had told me to expect to be picked up around nine or ten. I needed sleep, but I was determined to spend a few enjoyable hours with Officer Chaille Donovan. I set the alarm on my iPhone for eight forty-five and stretched out on my bed. It seemed like only a couple of minutes before it went off.

I quickly changed into a pair of clean slacks, a shirt, tie, and sports coat. The chief's spare pistol was in a shoulder holster beneath my coat when I left the apartment and entered the lobby. Paige looked up at me and asked, with a slight look of concern on her face, "Are you going somewhere, Keene?"

Fear filled her eyes when I reported, "The police chief asked me to ride with an officer tonight, but he told me I could check on you as often as I needed. I'll keep an eye on you, Paige, I promise. If you need me, you only have to call my cell phone."

She nodded, obviously still uneasy. "But Sean is here."

"Yes, but I honestly don't expect trouble from him tonight. Anyway, it's me he dislikes, not you. Have you seen him since you came on duty?" I asked.

"He came in about ten minutes ago."

"Did he speak to you?"

"No, he just walked past. He looked at me, but that was all."

"Was he drunk?" I asked.

"Not like last night," she answered. "He didn't come close enough for me to smell anything on him, but he was carrying a bottle of what looked like some kind of whisky or something. He looked angry though. Of course I expected that," she finished with a failed attempt at a smile.

"I'm guessing we've seen the last of him for the night. I doubt he got much sleep last night at the jail, and he'll probably just drink himself to sleep," I said, trying to lift her spirits.

"How can you function tonight with as little sleep as you've had?" she asked, changing the subject. "I'll be worried about you."

"Don't do that, Paige. I'm used to it. In LA I'd go to school all day and then work a reserve shift at night. I've learned to make the most of what sleep I can get. I'll sleep tomorrow morning. I arranged for Byron Rowe to fill in for me tomorrow. He'll relieve you."

"That's good; I like Byron. He helped train me. He'd been working the night shift for a long time and was happy when I volunteered to do it for a while. What kind of reserve shift did you work?" She scrunched her eyebrows and tipped her head to the side.

"I worked for the Los Angeles Police Department. I plan to go into law enforcement as a career."

Her eyes grew wide. "You're a cop?"

"That's what I plan to do as a career," I repeated.

"No wonder you handled your brother so well last night," she said, shaking her head. "I had no idea. I thought you were going to run this place for a living."

"This is temporary," I said. "But Chief Thompkins knows that, and he wants me to work part-time for his department while I'm here."

"So you're actually working for the police tonight?" she asked.

"No, I haven't given him my answer yet. I'll see how I feel after spending a few hours with one of his officers. I think he wants an answer in the morning."

A patrol car pulled up out front. "Well, there's my ride," I said. "Remember, if you need me, call. And I'll check in every little while, regardless."

As I started toward the door, Paige asked, "Does Sean know you're a cop?"

I turned back to her and chuckled. "Oh yes, and he doesn't approve. He's not real big on police."

Just then the officer got out of the patrol car out front, and a pang of disappointment went through me. I don't know why I'd assumed that Chaille would be working tonight. I guess I'd just hoped. Anyway, it was a very large man who came around the front of his patrol car.

"You'll like Payton." Paige interrupted my thoughts. "Everybody likes him. He's a good guy. And he has a really sweet family."

"He's big," I observed. "I mean, really big."

The officer opened the door. "Hi, Paige," he called out in a deep bass voice. Then he looked me over for a minute. "You must be Keene Tempest, my partner tonight."

"You can call me Mutt," I said as I held out my hand.

His large fist swallowed mine, and he laughed heartily. "That makes me Jeff, I take it?"

"They told me you were a big guy," I said, chuckling inwardly that he caught the reference to the comic-strip duo. "My brother must be a bigger fool than I imagined."

"He is. Sorry, Keene, but I'm not a fan of your brother after last night."

I glanced at Paige and then said, "I guess that makes three of us."

"Where is he tonight?" Payton asked. "Please tell me he's left town."

"I'm afraid not," I replied as Paige involuntarily shivered. "He's here in the hotel."

"That's not good news," the officer said. But he smiled and added, "Especially not for him if he happens to decide to leave his room tonight and drive drunk again. He'd have to deal with both me and his brother."

"Hopefully he'll do his drinking in his room tonight," I commented wryly. "If he's smart we won't hear from him until sometime tomorrow."

As I got into Officer Kerr's patrol car, I was still feeling bad about not getting to spend the night working with the pretty redheaded officer, but Paige had been right: I had taken an instant liking to Payton. He seemed like a really nice guy. He appeared cheerful, talkative, and competent.

It began as a relatively uneventful night. Frequent checks at the hotel found Paige doing just fine. Each time I spoke with her, she indicated that she hadn't seen or heard from Sean.

Payton and I talked a lot. He was the one who brought up Chaille's concerns about the death of my mother. "She thinks there may have been some foul play involved. Chief Thompkins and I both tried to tell her she was worrying over nothing. She hasn't said anything about it for a while, but I've been thinking about it."

"She mentioned it to me," I ventured. "But she didn't explain why she felt like she did, and I haven't had another chance to talk to her."

"Chaille is a very smart lady, and she has good instincts," Payton said as we drove toward the south end of town on a back street. "You were probably disappointed when it was me that showed up tonight instead of her." He looked toward me in the gloomy interior of the car and grinned. "I don't blame you. She's a great gal."

I felt myself flush and was glad he couldn't see that. "But you think her instincts are wrong about my mother?" I probed, glancing over at his large profile as he again concentrated on the road ahead.

He looked back at me and said very seriously, "I did at first, but now I'm not so sure."

"Really? What changed your mind?" I asked, significantly worried about that change of mind.

"Like I said, I've been thinking about what Chaille said. She mentioned that your mother was worried about someone but that she never did say who. And then when Chaille told me that your mother seemed afraid and stressed, it got me to thinking."

"Did she even give Chaille a hint of who was worrying her, or did she tell Chaille that she was afraid of that person, whoever it was?"

"Not really. Your mother apparently mentioned it and then clammed up. That, in and of itself, is something else that got me thinking. Chaille and your mother were very good friends. For her to suddenly decide not to confide in Chaille was most unusual."

"I wonder if Mom said anything to anyone else," I mused.

"That's what I've been wondering about. She's LDS—as I suppose you know—so is Chaille. I was wondering if Chaille should talk to some of the other members of her church in town."

"Or I could," I suggested as Payton turned left onto the last street in town.

"Are you LDS too?"

"I am," I said. "Maybe I could get with Chaille and find out who else my mother was close to in the ward."

"That's a good idea. But I can tell you a couple of people right now. I've heard that your mother was particularly fond of Paige, Tess, and their widowed mother. Do you know Tess?"

"I've talked to her on the phone, and I have an appointment with her to go over the hotel's finances. Maybe I should ask her what Mom might have said and see if she has any ideas."

"That would be a good beginning point," Payton agreed. "I'll stay out of it for now and give you and Chaille a chance to see what you can learn. But I'll let Chaille know that I support her in her concerns now. That might help."

"That would be great," I said, trying not to show my own concern.

***

Things were fairly quiet that night. We checked out the complaint of a barking dog, but when we got to the address, the dog was in his pen and being quite still. Traffic on the highway that went through town was light. A couple of cars came through town too fast, and Payton stopped them and had a talk with the drivers. A black-paneled van passed down Main Street shortly after we had pulled in and parked among other cars at the hotel. It was going quite slow. The windows were dark, so the occupants couldn't be seen. "This is profiling, I know, but vehicles like that always make me suspicious," Payton said as he strained to get a better look.

"We have lots of such vans in LA, and you're right: a large percentage of them spell trouble," I agreed.

"Did you notice the plates?" he asked. "It looks like one of yours found its way out of California."

I chuckled. "Looks like it. It did have California plates."

We watched until the van was out of sight, then we went into the hotel and visited with Paige for a few minutes. As we were leaving, the barking dog complaint came in again. "I guess we better have a talk with the owner," Payton said with a sigh. He drove across the highway and headed for the western edge of town again. There wasn't another car in sight.

The owner of the dog apologized and took the dog inside. She explained that she usually let the dog sleep indoors but had neglected to bring him in that night. After that, it was very quiet, and we drifted around the outer edges of town.

Payton indicated that if things stayed quiet, he'd take me back to the hotel at five o'clock. "The chief will come on at around eight. Chaille is taking time off, so there are some hours that we simply don't have anyone on duty. That's one of the reasons Chief Thompkins would like you to work with us. You will, won't you?" he asked, looking sideways at me in the near darkness of the car.

"I'll decide and let him know today sometime," I told him. I still planned to say yes, but I wanted to tell the chief himself, not have him get word secondhand.

The latest check we made with Paige was by phone at four o'clock. She sounded sleepy but again reported that everything was fine. It was about ten minutes later when the peace of that night's shift was shattered. The county dispatcher informed Payton that the alarm at the local grocery store was going off.

Even as Payton jammed the accelerator to the floor, he said, "Probably nothing. An early morning employee most likely forgot to turn off the alarm or something. But you never know."

Upon our arrival, it was clear that this was not an employee error. The front door was shattered, and two figures dressed in black were emerging through the broken glass, their arms full of boxes. When they spotted the patrol car, the culprits dropped the boxes and ran for a black-paneled van parked just a few feet away.

Officer Kerr brought the patrol car to a stop at the edge of the parking lot, telling the dispatcher what was going on and to send backup if possible. "That's probably the same van we saw when we were at the hotel. Hang on," he warned me and accelerated toward the van. The two figures leapt in, and the van began to move. At that moment, another black-clad figure ran from the store, sprinting toward the van and shouting.

Payton tried to cut off the van's retreat, but at the last minute he swerved when it became obvious that the burglars were going to hit us.

He slammed on the brakes and shouted, "Secure the store, Keene. I'll go after the van."

I bailed out and ran, hunched over, toward the third burglar. I had barely tackled the burglar when I heard gunfire up the street. The man I'd captured struck out at me with his right arm. I struck him in the face with a hard karate chop, and he flopped onto the pavement. I'd hit him hard enough that he appeared to have lost consciousness. I rapidly checked him for weapons, pulling a small revolver from inside his belt. I shoved it in my own waistband and looked toward the door of the store. A fourth suspect ducked back inside at that moment.

Sirens sounded in the distance. I left the now-unconscious man where he lay and darted toward the store. Very much aware that these burglars were armed, I didn't want to let whoever was still in the store get a chance to take a shot at me. I was also praying that Payton was okay. Chief Thompkins was the first backup officer to arrive. He joined me at the store, where I was keeping myself tight against the wall near the broken door.

"There were shots on the street," I began.

"Payton's fine," he said. "I've been on the radio with him. He was fired at, but when he returned fire, he put their van out of commission. It was one man and one woman. They gave up after that. How many are left in the store, and what's the story on the one in the parking lot?"

"I knocked him out," I reported, "and then disarmed him. I know there's at least one more in there. That may not be all."

"Chaille will be here in a moment, and so will some county and state officers," the chief informed me.

Just then the young female officer roared up from behind us and slid to a stop, jumping out with a pistol in her hand. Like the chief, she was not in uniform, having apparently thrown on the first thing she could get her hands on—a red blouse and white slacks. She looked stunning.

"Cover the back door," the chief told her, and she jumped back in her car and sped around the store.

"There's someone back here," she radioed a moment later. "He's at the loading dock." As she was speaking, there was the unmistakable *bang* of a gunshot. It was followed by another.

"Chaille, are you okay?" the chief asked urgently on his radio as he signaled for me to stay put, and then he roared around the store in his patrol car.

I hadn't heard a response, and I felt bile rise in my throat. Other officers arrived, and one of them joined me. "I don't have a radio," I said. "Do you know if Officer Donovan is okay?"

"She's fine, but apparently the burglar isn't. I heard the chief say that Officer Donovan's car was hit with a bullet. He requested an ambulance, but it clearly wasn't for her," the middle-aged officer answered. "You and I are to stay here while other officers come. By the way, I don't know you. Are you new with Chief Thompkins's department?"

"I am," I said. I thought it best to not let on that I hadn't actually been sworn in yet. I intended to tell the chief that I accepted his offer as soon as I had a minute. "I'm Keene Tempest."

"Roger White, deputy sheriff," he reciprocated without looking at me. His eyes were on the guy I'd put down in the parking lot. "That guy's moving," he noted. "Is he armed?"

"I've got his gun."

"Is he cuffed?"

"I don't have any with me," I responded lamely.

"Cover me," the deputy said. He was a lanky man with short brown shaggy hair and no hat. He moved quickly to the man I'd put down. The burglar was getting to his feet, but Roger put him down again, slapped cuffs on him, and told him to stay put. The tone of the deputy's voice left the burglar cowering, and he simply slumped on the pavement. The deputy ran back to where I was waiting beside the door.

The next hour was a busy one—the injured burglar was taken by ambulance to a hospital, the other thugs arrested and taken to the county jail, and the store searched for other suspects. Finding none, officials finally allowed the owner and several employees inside to get an estimate of the damage. A couple of cases of beer were recovered from the van, and some cases of cigarettes were gathered from near the front door where they'd been dropped. Thanks to the alarm, we'd intercepted them before they'd gotten much merchandise loaded.

I called Paige, making sure everything was okay at the hotel. She seemed fine, for which I was grateful since I would've had a hard time leaving under the present circumstances. She was anxious to know what all the sirens were about and why she'd seen police cars speeding past the hotel with their blue-and-red lights flashing. I gave her a quick explanation and made sure she understood that everything was under control.

It was eight o'clock by the time we were all back at the small police station. "Keene," the chief said, "you're a good hand. I hope you'll accept my proposal."

"Hey, I didn't expect so much excitement in such a sleepy little town. You betcha, Chief. I'll work for you."

"I hoped you'd say that. I'm going to swear you in right now, but officially I'm going to put you on the payroll as of yesterday. So if anyone asks, you were an officer last night. And frankly, I appreciate your help." The chief thought for a moment. "Before you go home, we'll go to the city office to get the paperwork done. You'll have to work plainclothes until we can get you some uniforms. But that won't take long. Also, I took the liberty of clearing things with the state on your certification." He chuckled. "I was pretty sure you'd accept."

An hour later I had a badge, a pistol, a shotgun, a laminated ID card, and I'd been officially sworn in as a city police officer. It felt good— really good. I was in my realm again, right where I wanted to be.

CHAPTER FIVE

By the time I got back to the hotel at around nine thirty, Paige had been relieved by Byron Rowe. He reported that well over half of the guests had already checked out and that the cleaning staff was busy getting rooms ready for the afternoon check-in time. I already knew that Sean hadn't checked out: his red Corvette was still parked outside.

"I see my brother's still here," I commented.

"Haven't heard from him," Byron said. He smiled mirthlessly. "I was hoping he'd be gone before I relieved Paige."

I didn't blame him. "I'm exhausted. I need to get some sleep. I'm expecting Tess Everest at one. Would you make sure I'm out here before then, just in case my phone doesn't wake me up? I'm sure it will, but I don't want to miss that appointment."

"Sure thing, Keene. You do look drained."

I was asleep almost before I hit the pillow. The hotel phone awoke me at eleven thirty. I didn't feel like I'd gotten any sleep. Byron's voice came through the phone, his voice filled with annoyance. "Keene, sorry to wake you, but you need to come up here right away."

I struggled to my feet, put on some fresh clothes, and stumbled into the office. "What's up, Byron?" I asked as I noticed Sheri Johnson, one of the cleaning ladies, sitting near him. Sheri had an attractive face, was short and a bit on the heavy side, and had given me no reason to believe she wasn't a good worker. Right now she looked very unhappy.

He pointed to her and said, "Sheri needs you."

"What's the problem, Sheri?" I tried to keep my voice even, remembering that she was a young mother who was just trying to pay the bills by working for the hotel.

Her slightly chubby face was long, and her eyes avoided mine as she spoke. "It's your, ah . . . your brother," she said and then drew silent.

"What about my brother?" I was losing my patience. I was very tired, and whatever Sean had done or said, I wanted her to come right to the point.

"I walked into his room, but he was still lying on his bed," she began. "I didn't know it was his room or I wouldn't have gone in. He hadn't put out the Do Not Disturb sign, and it was after checkout time, so when no one answered my knock, I called out 'housekeeping' like your mother told me to. Then I went in."

"And he shouted at you," I guessed as a surge of anger flowed through me. I could only guess what Sean had said to her. "Maybe he even threatened you."

"No, he didn't say anything," she said. "He didn't move at all. There is a bottle on the floor by the bed. I think it might be a whisky bottle. And I think he's passed out. I couldn't tell for sure because it was fairly dark in there. The curtains were closed and the lights were off. I just backed out of the room and came up here and told Byron."

"You did the right thing," I told her as I tried to control my anger. I didn't want her thinking I was upset with her. "I detest alcohol," I said. "It usually brings out the worst in people. Come let me in, and I'll see if I can get him awake and sobered up. Let's not worry about the room for now."

We headed quickly down the hallway, past the stairs, and then around the corner to room 133. I nodded toward the door, and Sheri unlocked it for me. I pushed it open. The smell of alcohol hit me instantly. I flipped on the light in the entrance and approached the bed where Sean was still lying on his back, his face toward the far side of the room. I looked at the bottle angrily. Both Paige and Sheri had been right. It was a liquor bottle, but the lid was on and it looked almost full. I kicked it out of the way and glanced back at the door. Sheri was standing there holding it open.

I turned back to the figure on the bed and said sharply, "Sean, get up!"

Sean didn't stir. I reached down and shook him roughly then let go and stared. He was cold and stiff. I turned on the lamp next to the bed as my stomach began to roil, then I looked again at my brother. As a reserve officer in Los Angeles for the past two years, I'd seen my share of dead bodies. I knew I was seeing one now. Sean was dead.

I stepped back, shaken. My police training kicked in. I knew I shouldn't touch another thing until I had some officers here. Oh yes—I was an officer now, but I needed someone else to call the shots. I backed clear to the door and spoke to Sheri. "Sheri, I need for you to go up to the office and write down everything you observed and did from the time you first approached this room right up to what you saw just now."

The poor lady was shaking. "Is . . . is he . . . is he dead?" she stammered, frozen in place.

"He is," I said as I pulled my cell phone from my pocket and opened my contact list. I had entered the dispatch center's number that morning. I called it now.

"This is Officer Keene Tempest with the Hardy City Police. There's a dead man in one of the rooms at the Tempest Hotel in Hardy," I said, stepping into the hallway and closing the door behind me. "Send Chief Thompkins right away."

The chief showed up in less than five minutes. I stayed at the door to room 133 while Sheri went to the front to meet the chief and escort him there. "What's going on, Keene?" he asked as he came around the corner and approached me. "You look like you could collapse."

"It's my brother," I said without commenting on my condition. "He's in there." I pointed to the room's door. "He's dead." I was embarrassed that I couldn't keep my voice from shaking.

"I'm sorry, Keene." His face paled. "Let's go in."

I again had Sheri unlock the door and let the chief lead the way. "You can go up front and write your statement now, Sheri," I instructed.

The door shut behind me as I followed Chief Thompkins into the room. He stopped as soon as he was out of the entry, then his eyes scanned the room. "Whisky bottle," he noted, pointing to where it lay near the head of the bed.

"It was right there," I said, pointing to where it had been when I came in, just a couple of feet in front of where we were now standing. "I slid it out of the way with my foot when I came in. It's almost full though. He didn't drink much of it."

The chief nodded. "Do you have a camera on your phone?" he asked.

"Yes," I said as I pulled my iPhone from my pocket.

"Would you take a few snapshots before we go in any farther? If you're sure he's dead, that is."

"Oh, I'm sure," I answered as I began to take pictures. A minute later, I followed the chief toward the bed. I snapped a couple more pictures before he said, "We need more light in here. Would you open the drapes?"

I stepped carefully around the bed and toward the window. I opened the drapes, and the afternoon sunlight flooded in. I turned back, took a couple of steps back toward the bed, and drew up short. "Chief, there's blood on the carpet—a lot of blood."

I took a couple of pictures of the large pool of blood soaking the floor as Chief Thompkins stepped to the bottom of the bed and looked for himself. The blood trailed up to the bed, and there was quite a large pool right beside the bed. "It looks like he was killed there," I observed, pointing to the main pool of blood. "And then was dragged onto the bed."

The chief shook his head. "What happened to my quiet town?" he muttered. "Step around that, and let's take a look at the body. I suppose this blood could be his—or not."

But before he pulled the covers down, he paused. "I'm not thinking straight, Keene. This is your brother. You don't need to help. I'll see if I can get ahold of Chaille and, if necessary, Payton."

"I'm fine," I said. I wasn't really, but I could function and wanted to help.

"Suit yourself." As he pulled the covers down, my worst fears were realized. There was a deep, bloody wound or, I should say, several wounds in the center of my brother's chest. He'd been repeatedly and violently stabbed. Someone had dragged him onto the bed and thrown the covers over him. Someone strong. Or someone who'd had help.

I took some pictures while fighting the churning of my stomach. In the meantime, Chief Thompkins began to make calls on his cell phone. I heard, "This is Chief Thompkins. I'm at the Tempest Hotel. We have a homicide case here. See if the sheriff will send a crime-scene crew down. This body will need to go to the state lab for autopsy."

Next he said, "Chaille, I'm sorry to bother you again on your day off, but I need your help." He was silent for a moment as he listened, then he continued, "Keene and I are at the hotel. His brother's been murdered." He listened again for a moment and glanced at me before responding. "He's hanging in there." I assumed that Chaille had asked about me.

He talked with her for only a brief moment longer, and then he dialed again. I'd taken all the pictures I could think of, and anyway, I knew that many more would be taken with more appropriate equipment. I stepped back and listened again as the chief spoke. "Sorry, Payton. I know you haven't had much sleep, but we have a murder here. I need all the help I can get." Another pause, then, "It's at the hotel. Somebody stabbed Keene's brother, Sean—somebody with some real anger issues, I'm afraid."

Suddenly, I could no longer fully control my calm facade. I slipped out of my dead brother's room and stumbled out the back door of the hotel just in time for the contents of my stomach to empty into the shrubs outside. I broke out in a cold sweat, and I felt my face pale.

After a few minutes, I regained control, and that familiar feeling of anger started to replace my now-empty gut. Someone had been murdered in my hotel, and that someone was my brother. Whether I liked him or not was no longer an issue. I turned with new resolve and went to rejoin the other officers.

Between my brother's murder, the investigation that was underway, and my extreme fatigue, I forgot about my appointment with Tess Everest, the hotel's accountant. I was reminded when Byron called my cell phone. "Tess is here, Keene," he said. "She's here for the meeting you told me about."

"Oh heck. I forgot," I confessed. "Tell her I'll be right there."

I had been speaking to an investigator with the sheriff's department in his parked car when the call came. He acted like he knew nothing about me except for my role as manager and part owner of the hotel and my relationship with Sean. I'd been getting bad vibes from him for the past ten minutes. Detective Vernon Bentley had heard about the tension between me and Sean, and I got the feeling that he thought I might somehow be involved. The chief, he informed me, had asked him to head up the investigation since the Hardy PD was so small. That made sense, but I wasn't sure this man was the right one for the job.

After ending the call with Byron, I told Detective Bentley that I would need to go up front.

"Not until I get through with you here," he snapped, an ugly tone in his voice.

"Whoa, there," I said, staring at him with angry eyes. "I've got a meeting with my accountant, and I intend to keep it. If you need to talk to me later, I'll make myself available, but right now I've got a business to run."

I opened the car door, and he grabbed my arm. "Not so fast, mister!" he snarled. "You've got some explaining to do."

I shook my arm loose and said in a low voice as threatening as I could make it, "Don't you *ever* grab me like that again."

He looked startled, but before he had a chance to say or do anything else, I was out of the car. I slammed the door emphatically and entered the back door of the hotel. Chaille was just coming out of the room where my brother had died.

"Hey, Keene," she said as I started to pass her in the hallway. "Where have you been? The chief wants to talk to you."

"Tell him to ask Detective Bentley where I've been, and while you're at it, tell him to keep that creep out of my face," I responded, unable to keep my anger in check. I was still marching up the long hallway. "I don't have time to meet with him right now."

"So you've met Bentley," she said, matching me step for step. "I'm sorry if he's been bothering you."

"Apparently Chief Thompkins asked him to head up the investigation. That's a mistake."

Chaille chuckled, and the sound served to take the edge off my anger. I slowed down and she said, "All he did was ask him to help where he could. The chief himself is heading up this investigation. By the way, congratulations on getting the job, Keene. I look forward to working with you."

I came to a stop. "And I with you," I said, finally managing a weak smile. "I just hope we can find whoever did this to Sean. He was a hard guy at times, but he was still my brother."

"We'll do that, Keene. I believe we will, especially since you'll be helping."

"I will be, but someone needs to keep Bentley at bay. I think he wants to take me down for it," I cautioned.

She shook her head, and a smile creased her face again. "He'll be surprised when he finds out that you were with Payton all night. I don't know why the sheriff keeps him on. He seems to think he's real bright, and I guess he does handle some cases okay, but I personally don't have any respect for the guy. Like you, I've tangled with him before. He doesn't like the idea of women cops, although there are a lot of us around. Besides that, he's lied to me before. I don't trust him at all."

"It's too bad he's such a jerk. Hey, let's talk later. Right now I've got to meet with my accountant." I started walking again.

"Would that be Tess Everest?" Chaille asked as she kept walking down the long hallway with me.

"Yes."

"She's a good person, Keene."

"That's what I've heard. I'm hoping she can shed a little light on what was going on with my mother." I stopped again and faced Chaille. "I talked to Payton last night. Please keep this to yourself for now, but he mentioned that he was beginning to think you might be right about my mother's death being suspicious."

Chaille's eyes lit up. "If that's the case, we need to talk about it—you and me and Payton," she said earnestly.

"Yes, we do. But please don't say anything to him until I give you the go-ahead," I replied. "Now I've got to get up front. I'm keeping Tess waiting. Tell the chief I'll try to get back with him soon."

***

"She's in your office," Byron said with a nod of his gray head in that direction as I approached the front desk.

"Thanks," I called and stepped in. "Sorry I kept you waiting," I told Tess as she rose to her feet. "It's been a hard day." She was an attractive girl like her younger sister. And she had an intelligent look to her.

As I looked at her, she looked closely at me. She looked concerned. "You look really tired, Keene. I can come back another time if you need me to."

"No, that's okay. I need to know everything I can about what's happening with the hotel's finances."

She looked like she was going to argue, but instead she said, "I understand." She picked up her briefcase. "Are you sure you have time? I saw some cop cars out back."

"Yeah, we've had a problem. But I want to meet with you now. You can spread stuff out on the desk if you need to," I said as I sat down. Meeting with her was certainly preferable to meeting with Detective Bentley.

"I only have a few papers," she stated. "But I have a small laptop in here." She pulled it out, opened it, and while it booted up, put several sheets of papers on the desk. "I did print statements from the past four months." She looked at me, a slight frown on her face, and began. "Aside from the past few weeks, the profits have been slipping quite a bit each month. I compared it with last year's statements for the same months. This is the time of year when things pick up. Last year it did a little. This year it didn't. That's not what I would expect to see."

"Nor would I." I stifled a yawn. I didn't ever remember being so tired. I closed my eyes for a moment while she began looking for something on the computer.

"Keene, are you okay?" Tess asked.

I jumped. I had dozed in that few seconds. I quickly reoriented myself and then said, "I haven't had much sleep for the past couple of days. I'm sorry. Where were we at?"

"The profits have dipped the past few months," she said. "And that's not all. I did a comparison of the past couple of months with the same period a year ago. The profits of your hotel are down quite a bit. I have a feeling that if I did the same for each month of the past year and then compared them to the year before, we'd see a constant drop."

Her depressing statement woke me up. Something was wrong with the business, and I needed to know what. I asked, "Is it just the general state of the economy that is causing the downward trend? Maybe people aren't staying in hotels as much?"

She slowly shook her head, her brow furrowed. For a moment, our eyes met, and then she looked down at her laptop and began to tap the keys. I waited. In a minute or two, she looked up, turned the computer toward me, and said, "Take a look."

As I studied the comparisons she had brought up, I felt my gut tighten. "I thought you said there'd been a dip," I said still looking at the screen. "I'd call this more of a depression."

"I'm afraid so," Tess admitted. "I'm sorry. But on the positive side, I looked at the numbers from the week before your mother passed away until yesterday." She hesitated, flipping her long brown hair away from her face. I waited for her to go on. She finally continued, "I don't know if you knew this or not, but I'm able to pull up the hotel's records each morning. Your mother set up a direct link to your computer for me." She hesitated again, looking quite troubled.

"And . . ." I prompted.

"It's way up now, more like it should be this time of year."

"From a week before Mom's death?" I said as much to myself as to the accountant. I knew the place had been busy; I just didn't know it hadn't been that way the past year or so.

"That's right," she confirmed.

My police experience was somewhat limited, but my suspicious mind wasn't. An idea began to form—a dark, troubling idea. I decided to keep it to myself for the moment, and instead I asked, "Do you have any idea why that might be?"

"Your mother was well aware of the negative trend, but she seemed to not want to talk about it. I finally sat down with her and told her I was worried that unless something changed she wouldn't be able to keep the hotel afloat. I even suggested she might want to sell it." Her eyes were locked on the computer screen. "She didn't like that idea at all. In fact, she told me that Hugo Starling, the owner of the café next door, had been trying to get her to sell to him. She made it clear to me that selling to him or anyone else wasn't an option. All she told me was that she'd see what she could do to turn things around."

"She must have done something; although, I can't imagine what she could have done to make things improve so much so quickly." I watched Tess as I spoke. Her dark brown eyes met mine. I would swear I saw fear in them. "Tess, what aren't you telling me?" I asked, leaning across the desk toward her. "Something's bothering you. I need to know what it is."

She took a deep breath, smoothed her hair, and bit her lip until I thought it would bleed. Her eyes filled with moisture as she answered, "Your mother was scared about something. She wouldn't tell me what it was—didn't really admit it, I guess. I'm an accountant, Keene, not a detective, but if I had to guess, I'd say that someone was threatening her in some way."

My suspicions sharpened, and the twisting of my gut increased. I needed to talk to Chaille and Payton. Their feelings and Tess's suspicions were too much to ignore. But I didn't want to so much as hint to my accountant that my mother's death might not have been due to a heart attack. "Can you forward these computer files to me so I can study them more closely?" I asked as I pointed to the back of her laptop.

"I'll do it right now," she said. "And you can keep these." She indicated the sheets she'd copied and brought with her.

"Please send them to my personal e-mail instead of to the hotel's," I added.

"Of course," she responded. I gave her my e-mail address, and she worked the keyboard for a few moments then said, "They're on the way."

"Is there anything else I should know right now?" I asked as Byron poked his head in the door.

"Just one thing," she began.

Byron cleared his throat. "Mr. Tempest?"

"What is it?" I asked, hoping there wasn't still more bad news on a day already filled with way too much.

"Your sister's on the phone. She says she wants to talk to you right now. She sounds quite agitated," he said.

"She must have heard about Sean," I replied. "Give me a moment here, and then I'll take her call."

"There was one more thing," I prompted Tess as Byron backed out.

"I can wait if you want to talk to your sister first," she said. "And speaking of Sean, is something wrong?"

"My sister can wait," I said. "And yes, there is a problem."

"Does it have to do with the police cars in the back?" she asked.

"I'm afraid so," I answered. "But I don't have time to talk about it now—maybe later."

She again took a deep breath. "There was one more thing. I went over your mother's personal accounts a few days ago. I had complete access to them as well as those of the hotel," she explained. "She had been sending money to a security firm in Los Angeles."

CHAPTER SIX

TESS EXCUSED HERSELF WITH THE promise to meet again soon. I picked up the phone, my head spinning with the latest bit of news from Tess—my mother had retained an LA security firm. That was just plain bizarre.

"Hello, Bree." I spoke into the receiver, not wanting to talk to my sister but knowing I had to. I braced myself as she began.

"What is happening up there?" she asked. Before I could form any kind of response, she fired another question. "What happened to Sean? I got a call telling me he was dead. Surely that can't be true."

"I'm afraid—" I began, but she cut me off.

"Why didn't *you* call me, Keene?" she demanded. "If he's dead you should have told me."

I waited for her to ask another question, but when she was finally silent for a few moments, I explained, "Yes, Sean is dead, but honestly, Bree, I haven't had time to call anyone. I was up all night, and I am so tired I can hardly think straight."

"Why were you up?" she asked suspiciously.

"I was working with a cop. I'm going to be doing that part-time for as long as I'm here. Last night was my first shift."

"So you weren't at the hotel when Sean died?"

"No, I'm afraid I wasn't."

Bree's voice softened ever so slightly. "Do you have any idea what happened? Could it have been a heart attack—like Mom?"

I wasn't prepared to tell Bree my thoughts: our mother might not have had a heart attack. After this with Sean, I felt certain that Mom's death was not what it looked like.

"Keene, I asked you a question," she pressed, the anger back in her voice. Whoever had called my sister apparently didn't have any details. I knew the chief was trying to keep things contained for as long as he could. I hadn't told Tess what was happening, but I decided to give Bree a little bit of information.

"Bree, I'm afraid it's not that at all. The police chief has been trying to keep the lid on things until we figure something out, so what I'm going to tell you needs to stay with you until I tell you otherwise."

A bit of hardness entered her voice again. "Keene, Sean's my big brother. I deserve to know what's going on."

I may not have had extensive law enforcement experience, but I certainly had enough to know that you had to keep an open mind when it came to murder—anyone and everyone could be considered a suspect. That included family, as Detective Bentley had so recently demonstrated when he'd all but accused me. As I thought about how much to tell Bree, I felt just a touch of my anger at the detective slip away. Could my own sister be behind it? With that disturbing thought, I decided to exercise caution and not tell Bree as much as I'd intended a moment before.

"Bree, we don't know much yet. The chief is being cautious by calling his death suspicious. I'm sorry, but that's all I can tell you right now," I said.

Apparently that was enough to silence my usually very talkative sister, for there was nothing but breathing on the line now. I waited for a moment or two, and then I attempted to shift the focus of our conversation. "Bree, I've been meeting with our accountant. The hotel has been doing very poorly for the past year. There doesn't seem to be any visible explanation for it."

Bree finally spoke. "Keene," she said, a catch in her voice, "I knew that. We all did. We should have told you."

I felt a touch of anger. "So why didn't you?" I demanded.

"Keene, I know you think none of us like you, and I admit we've always picked on you, but all three of us know you're a very honest kid."

I ignored the *kid* bit, but I asked, "I assume Mom told you."

Bree hesitated again. "She did. She told Sean, and he told me and Grady. Later, all of us talked. She begged us not to tell you, so we didn't."

"Why would she do that?" I asked, puzzled. "Mom and I talked on the phone at least once a week."

"I guess she didn't want to worry you. Keene, I guess I better get up there. I'll call Grady." Bree changed the subject a little too quickly. I was almost certain there was something she wasn't telling me.

I wasn't particularly fond of the idea of my surviving siblings coming here, but they certainly had every right. After all, they were a whole lot closer to Sean than I'd ever been. "That would be great," I said lamely.

"It'll take me a few hours. I think I'll fly up and rent a car at whatever airport is closest. Then I'll drive from there."

I was glad that she and Grady lived far enough away that they couldn't get here before at least a few questions could be answered about Sean's murder.

Another thought entered my sleep-deprived brain. She knew about the declining financial health of the hotel. Maybe she also knew about the bolt from the blue Tess Everest had dropped on me just before she left. "Bree, before you go, maybe you could help clear up something that our accountant told me. She said Mom's been sending money from her personal account to a security firm in Los Angeles. Do you know what that would be about? It makes no sense to me at all."

Again, my forward, talkative sister hesitated—very uncharacteristic. Finally, she said, "I have no idea. When I get there, we can call the company she was paying and ask them."

I had no intention of waiting that long to call, but I didn't tell her that. Instead, I said, "I better let you get ready to head up here. I'll make sure there are rooms ready for you and Grady."

After hanging up, I entered the main-floor hallway again and worked my way back to Sean's room. Chaille met me in front of the door. "They've taken Sean's body away," she said soberly. "The chief wants to leave the room like it is for now though."

"That's not a problem," I told her. "We'll keep it locked until he says otherwise. It'll have to have new carpet, a new mattress, and a deep cleaning before I can rent it out again anyway."

"Thanks, Keene," she said.

"Is there anyone in there now?" I asked, pointing toward the door.

She nodded. "The chief and your favorite detective are still in there."

"I'm going in," I said as I pulled a master key from my pocket and turned toward the door. I'd grabbed the key from the front desk after meeting with Tess.

"I don't think that's such a good idea." Chaille stopped me with a shake of her head. "Detective Bentley doesn't seem to care too much for you. Chief Thompkins will take care of him, so you don't need to worry about him undercutting you. Anyway, you look like you're about ready to drop, Keene. Why don't you go rest for a while?"

There was nothing I wanted to do more, but I wanted a word with my new boss first. So despite her continued protests, I unlocked the door, nodded my head at Chaille, and said, "Would you like to come in too?"

She shook her head. "I'm supposed to be keeping people out."

"I guess I'm not people," I said, and I shoved the door open and walked in.

"What do you think you are doing in here?" Detective Bentley demanded from his position near the soiled carpet on the far side of the bed. "Chief, you need to do something about your officer out there." He pointed beyond me. "She was told to keep people out while I talked to you and looked the place over again."

"It's okay, Bentley," Chief Thompkins said.

"No, it's not," the detective countered. "This man is a suspect in this case. He needs to be kept out, and your little officer should know that."

The chief's face darkened, but before he could say anything, Detective Bentley spoke to me. "You need to leave right now, Tempest. Be where I can find you in a few minutes. We haven't finished our interview yet."

"Maybe you aren't finished, but I am," I returned sharply. "Now, why don't you leave? I need to speak to the chief."

The chief's face was growing darker, but he let me carry the ball for the moment.

"Leave," the detective commanded again, pointing to the door.

"Not going to happen," I said. "This is my place. And I work for the police department. You don't. So *you* leave while I speak with Chief Thompkins."

Bentley began to shake his fist and started around the bed toward me. The chief, however, stepped in front of him. "He's right, Detective. He works for me."

"That's stupid of you," the angry officer spat. "He probably killed his brother."

"That's not possible," the chief said as he shook his head, his face purple with rage. "He was working last night. He spent the entire night with Payton. So you see, he couldn't have done it."

Detective Bentley gave the chief a blank stare. "But he's the—"

"He's not a suspect. He's helping me on this case, Detective. I don't think I'll need your help any longer. You may go now." The chief was working hard to keep his anger in check. I admired him for it.

Bentley started to speak again, but the chief's look cut him off, and the angry officer finally left.

"Sorry about that, Keene," Chief Thompkins said. "He has a habit of trying to take over whenever he's invited to assist. Now, you needed to talk to me?"

"Yes," I said, and I spent the next couple of minutes bringing him up to date on what I'd learned about the financial state of the hotel. I didn't mention my suspicions about my mother's death, but they were very real. I wanted to talk that over with Payton and Chaille before we approached the chief with it.

When I had finished, he said, "That is strange. This place always seems to be busy. We'll have to look into that. But for now, why don't you go get some sleep, Keene? You must be awfully tired."

"I am."

"Then go. Call me when you wake up," he said. "Oh, and let's keep this room empty for a while if that's okay."

"Of course," I said. "I'll make sure the housekeeping staff leaves it alone. Maybe as a precaution we could put a note on the door, something that won't frighten other patrons."

"That's a good idea. I'll have Chaille do that."

When we stepped into the hallway a moment later, I took one look at Chaille and knew she was boiling mad about something. I had an idea what it was. I caught her eye and asked, "Bentley give you a hard time too?"

"He's such a jerk. He shouldn't even be a cop," she responded hotly.

"He's off the case," the chief said.

"That's good. He has it in his head that Keene killed his own brother, and it doesn't matter what we say; he's not going to change his mind."

"That's okay," I said. "I'm going to go sleep for a while. I'll talk to you guys later."

I left Chaille and Chief Thompkins talking in the hallway, and I headed for the front. But I didn't go directly to my apartment. Instead, I went to the laundry room. My housekeeping staff was there, working hard. They all looked up at me when I walked in, fear in their eyes. I tried to calm them, but then I explained the reason for my visit.

Five minutes later, I let myself into my apartment, puzzled but not surprised by what I'd learned. Every one of them agreed that they had not been aware of any downturn in the number of rooms that were used each night. They assured me that the hotel had stayed busy year-round and that it had been filled almost every night since midspring.

That could only mean one thing: someone had taken the money, and my mother—my dear, honest mother—had not been truthful with our accountant. I knew her well enough to know that she would never have done that unless someone was forcing her hand. The week before she died, the women had told me, hadn't been any busier than the week before that or even three weeks before. All those weeks had seen the hotel filled nearly to capacity every night. The staff members were under the impression that business was very good.

I had to talk to Chaille and Payton and then to the chief. I fell asleep thinking that my mother must have finally stood up to whoever was causing her to falsify the records and that a week later she'd died for doing so.

I awoke in a little while, having slept soundly. I got up, showered, fixed myself a sandwich, and left my apartment. It was nearly five o'clock in the evening when I went up to the registration desk. Paige was already on duty. She was pale and quiet. It appeared the tragedy that had struck the hotel was no longer much of a secret.

"I didn't like Sean, but why would anyone do such a horrible thing?" she asked.

"I don't know, but I intend to find out," I assured her.

"You will be here tonight, won't you?"

"I'll either be here or not far away. I'm working for the police department part-time now. Do you have any idea who I might hire to help out here?"

"I might," she said, "if anyone dares to."

"Hey, it's okay. Sean's dead, and I can't think that whoever killed him will be hanging around here. It's safe," I assured her.

I stood beside her behind the counter and pulled out my iPhone. Chaille was the only one at the station. "The chief and Payton went home to get some sleep. I'm the only one working now," she reported.

"Are you busy?" I asked. "There's something I need to talk over with you. Would you mind coming to the hotel?"

"Can you give me fifteen minutes?" she asked.

I assured her I could and put my phone away.

"Thanks for having Chaille come here instead of you going to the police station," Paige said. "I feel better when you're close by."

I smiled at her. "I hope I don't have to leave," I told her. "But if I do, there really isn't anything to worry about. Are there a lot of empty rooms tonight?" I figured that if word of the murder had gotten out, it might somehow affect my business.

I was wrong. "Every room is full except the one Sean was in and the two reserved for your brother and sister."

"Good. I'll be in my office if you need me."

CHAPTER SEVEN

WHEN PAIGE SHOWED CHAILLE TO my office a few minutes later, I was busy studying the material Tess had e-mailed me.

"Are you okay?" Chaille asked, concern etched on her lightly freckled face.

"I'm okay," I said and waved her to a seat. "I'm pretty sure you're right about my mother being murdered."

Her eyes grew wide and her face paled. "I didn't say she was; I just thought it was a possibility," she said. "How do you know?"

"I don't," I said, "but I think it is a very strong possibility. Let me tell you why." By the time I finished telling her what I'd learned from Tess and then from my housekeeping staff, she was as convinced as I was that we had not one but two murders on our hands as well as some major theft. Someone had it in for my family.

Chaille said what I was thinking. "Keene, I hope we don't have to exhume your mother's body to do an autopsy."

"That's just something we'll have to wait on. I would hate to do that, and I'm not at all sure that Bree and Grady would agree to it. For now, I'm not even going to consider that."

"Keene, you've got to be really careful. Your life could also be in danger."

"I'll be okay," I said, trying to reassure myself as much as her—if not more than her. "But I'm not going to stop until I find whoever is behind all of this—the theft and the murders."

"Okay, then let's decide where to begin," she said resolutely.

"There is one thing I didn't mention when I was telling you about Tess Everest's report," I said as I leaned back in my chair and stared at the wall beyond Chaille. She leaned forward, resting her elbows on my desk, looking at me expectantly. I met her eyes and continued, "My mother had been sending money to a security agency in Los Angeles."

She sat back and drew her eyebrows together. "That's odd."

"Very," I agreed.

We were both thoughtful for a moment, and then, as before, she vocalized what I was thinking. "You lived in Los Angeles. It has to have something to do with you."

I nodded. "But I can't imagine what. I suppose there is a way to find out though. I need to get the name of the company and give them a call."

"Better yet," Chaille said, "maybe I should do that. They might refuse to tell you what they were doing since you're her son. Of course, if you call as a police officer, that might help." She was thoughtful for a moment, and then she continued, "Let me call. I'll tell them I'm investigating your mother's death, and they'll probably tell me. If not, we'll get a court order and get the information anyway."

"It's too late tonight," I pointed out, "but maybe you could see Tess first thing in the morning."

"I'll see her now," Chaille said with a firm set of her jaw. "There's no time to waste. I'll call you later." With that, she tossed her long red hair with a flip of her head, stood up, and moved quickly from my office.

I followed her to the door, watching as she walked past the reservations desk and out the front door. She maybe wasn't the most beautiful girl in the world, but there was something about her that was very attractive to me. I liked the way she moved, the way she smiled, the color of her hair, and even the freckles scattered across her face.

"Pretty, isn't she?"

My face reddened as I realized that Paige had caught me staring.

She grinned broadly when I looked at her. "She's okay," I said. "So are you and Tess."

That brought a flush to her face, and she said, "Thanks." Then her face grew very serious. "Keene, what's going on?"

"I don't know, Paige, but like I already told you, I intend to find out." I looked through the glass at the front of the hotel and watched as Chaille got into her patrol car; then I amended what I'd just said. "*We* will find out."

"What time do you expect your brother and sister to get here?" she asked.

"I don't know. Maybe I'll call Bree and ask her. I'll let you know," I promised then went back into my office and shut the door.

As I sat down at my desk, a shudder ran through me. The horror of what had happened was sinking in. My life could be in danger, and so could that of my brother and sister—and maybe even their families. I took out my iPhone and called my sister's number. It rang several times and then went to voice mail. "Hi, Bree," I said when the tone had sounded. "It's Keene. I was just wondering what time you expect to get here and if you have any idea when Grady is coming. I have rooms saved for both of you. Just give me a call when you get this."

After putting my phone back in my pocket, I sat back in my chair, my hands behind my head, and looked around the room. It was not a large office, but it was neat. My mother's touch could be seen everywhere. Nothing had been moved in the bookcase to my right. Her pictures were still on the wall opposite it. They were of the entire family at various ages. In most of them, we were smiling. We looked like a happy family. *But that's not true*, I thought.

A vase of colorful plastic flowers stood on the filing cabinet in one corner. An assortment of feminine knickknacks were scattered throughout the room as they were in the apartment I was now calling home. Some of them were from various countries where we had lived during the military years. I got up, stepped around the desk, and opened the top drawer of the four-drawer filing cabinet. I'd looked in it before, had pulled various records out of it to study, but I hadn't worked my way through all the drawers. That could wait, I decided. I shut the drawer and went back to the desk.

It was a large desk, and as with the cabinet I'd only looked far enough to find things I needed—pens, pencils, paper. I opened the top drawer to my left and studied the contents for a moment. It held simple things like a stapler, a ruler, pencils, pens, erasers, a letter opener, and a few other items. I closed it and opened the one below. It held the envelopes, stamps, and writing pads. The top right drawer, the only drawer—I'd noticed before—that was not neatly organized, seemed to beckon to me. I pulled it open. It held an assortment of papers, ones I supposed she either hadn't gotten around to filing yet or had simply put there as if she wasn't sure if they were worth keeping. Perhaps they were things that didn't seem important yet she hadn't quite felt like throwing away. More than anything in the room, this mishmash of papers intrigued me.

I decided I'd go through them now—perhaps throw most of them away—at least to satisfy my curiosity. I thumbed my way down through the papers and pulled one out about halfway down the stack. It was a standard-sized paper folded in thirds like it had at one time been in an envelope. I opened it. It was a handwritten note. It was addressed to my mother but not dated. I skipped to the bottom where it was signed simply *Jim*. I knew a lot of Jims, but I was sure I didn't know whoever this one was—probably a friend of Mom's.

More than a friend, I concluded as I read through it. It was short, but I could tell that the author was someone who had more than a passing interest in my mother. It talked about how wonderful he thought she was and that it would be nice if she would consider going to dinner with him again when he was back in town. It didn't say when that would be. The writer mentioned how impressed he was with the hotel and that he'd never stayed in a place that was more inviting and clean.

A guest, I concluded—perhaps a frequent guest. *Perhaps a greedy guest*, I thought as suspicion crossed my mind. I let go of the paper, thinking that maybe I should check it for fingerprints. What if this was someone who was at first just a friendly guest, then a friend, then someone who had found a way to steal? I shook my head, thinking that perhaps I was being a bit paranoid. But I quickly put that feeling aside. My mother was dead, as was my brother. Paranoia was not only okay, it was essential.

I left the note lying on my desk and went in search of some latex gloves. The curiosity I'd felt about the drawer had now taken a sinister turn. I didn't want my fingerprints messing up others that might be of value to the investigation. I went directly to the housekeeping supplies and found what I needed.

As I returned to my office, Paige stepped from behind the registration desk and called to me down the hallway. "Have you heard from your sister yet?"

"I left her a voice mail," I said. "I'm hoping she'll call back soon."

She nodded, and I went back into my office, where I shut the door. Then, on an impulse, I dropped the latex gloves on the desk, stepped back out, and walked to the registration desk. "Paige, do you happen to know a man by the name of Jim who might have stayed here fairly often?"

She smiled at my inquiry. "Jim McLaren, maybe. He comes every month or so. I think your mother kind of liked him. I know they went out to dinner a few times."

He had to be the one. "What kind of guy is he?" I asked.

"Nice. He's very polite. He smiles a lot and speaks with a bit of a drawl," she said. "Why? Had your mother mentioned him to you?"

"Not that I recall. What does he looks like?" I asked.

"He was probably in his late sixties or early seventies. He had gray—no, I'd say more like silver hair. It was very thick and always neatly combed. He was what I would call very distinguished."

"How big?" I asked.

"All of six feet but well built. He had a cleft chin. It looked good on him. His eyes were light blue, almost gray." She was thoughtful for a moment. "He was always dressed nice. I never saw him come in without a sports coat and tie on."

"What kind of work does he do, or was he retired?"

"Your mom spoke of him a few times. Apparently he's a salesman of some kind. That's all she ever said. I don't know where he lives."

"Thanks, Paige. That's helpful."

"Why?" she asked as her face suddenly took on a worried look.

"Just is," I said. "I'll let you know if and when I hear from Bree."

Back in the office with the door shut, I pulled on the gloves and resumed my search of Mom's miscellaneous drawer. I pulled everything out and began to sort through it on my desk. As I suspected I would, I found more notes from Jim, six in all. None of them had a date or return address. All the envelopes, if there had ever been any, were gone. With just a cursory glance, they looked about the same as the first one. I decided to read them later. After I'd stacked them in a separate pile, I again went to speak with Paige.

"Did this Jim McLaren guy ever leave notes with you to give to my mother?" I asked.

"Yes. A few times, when she wasn't in, he'd give me a sealed envelope with her name on the front and ask me to make sure she got it," she replied. The look of worry on her face deepened. "Was he a bad guy?" she asked, uneasiness sounding in her voice.

"I don't know, but I need to find out. If you think of anything else about him, let me know," I instructed.

"I will," she promised.

I returned to the office and sat down at the desk again, ready to look through the rest of the papers when my cell phone began playing the ringtone. I answered quickly when I saw that it was Bree. "Hello, Bree," I said. "Thanks for calling back. I was just wondering when you and Grady would be here."

"I'll be there before too long. I'll be driving a rental car from the airport," she said.

"Do you have any idea when Grady will get here?" I asked.

Bree hesitated, and then she said, "Keene, we don't know where Grady is."

That was alarming. *Not another member of the family gone,* I thought. "What do you mean *we?*"

"His wife and me," was her reply. "When I called Jean right after talking to you, she said she hadn't seen him for a couple of days. I asked her if she knew where he was. She said she didn't, that they'd had an argument and he'd stormed out. He hasn't called or texted her or anything."

"He hasn't been here," I said for lack of anything more intelligent to say.

"I wouldn't expect him to be. I've called Jean twice since then; she still hasn't heard from him. His cell phone just goes to voice mail. She's left several messages. I've done the same. She told me that she even called his boss, but Grady hasn't been to work. In fact, his boss is quite angry. He told Jean that if he doesn't get to work pretty soon, they might give his position to someone else."

"Do he and Jean fight often?" Keene asked.

"She says that they have a lot of disagreements, but this was the worst it had ever gotten. She wouldn't say what it was about." Bree paused. "Keene, I'm scared. What if something has happened to him too?"

"He's probably okay, Bree." I tried to sound reassuring despite the fact that I was far from sure he was all right. "Maybe he's just gone on a binge."

"Maybe, but she says he hasn't been drinking all that much."

"Well, I guess there isn't much we can do until we hear from him. If he calls you before you get here, call me," I told her. I hesitated and then decided it was time to level with my sister. "Bree, I don't mean to upset you worse, but there's more you need to know."

"You mean about Sean's death?"

"Yes. He was murdered, Bree." I heard a sharp intake of breath; then, at her urging, I gave her some of the details and waited as she digested the information.

"Now I'm really worried about Grady," she finally responded with a sob.

"Me too," I agreed. "I'll tell you more when you get here."

"Thanks. This is just horrible. I'll see you in a while. And Keene . . ." she began, a catch in her voice.

"Yes?"

"I, ah, I know I haven't said this before, but I . . . ah . . . I love you, Keene."

I was shocked almost speechless. It took me a moment to respond, and when I did, all I could say was, "I'm glad. I feel the same about you."

I truly did care about her, about all of them for that matter. But I was surprised she felt that way. Maybe it was just that there might now only be the two of us left and she felt like I was all she had. I'd never felt like I was anything but a lower form of life to any of them before. Her admission squeezed tears from my eyes, and I looked forward to seeing her, not a feeling I'd felt much of before. I had to wipe my eyes dry before I left the office to tell Paige that Bree would be here before too long. I didn't tell her I was afraid Grady wasn't coming, just that I didn't know when he'd get there.

"Keene," she said when I'd finished delivering my message, "are you okay?"

"I've been better," I replied with a wan smile. "And I'll be okay again."

"You said you would need another person to help out here," she said hesitantly.

"Yes, that's for sure. Have you thought of someone?"

"I have, and I talked to Tess about it. Our mother has been talking about looking for a job. She says she's bored at home since we are all grown. Dad passed away a couple of years ago, and I'm the only one who lives with her now."

"Why don't you have her call me if she's interested?"

"Okay, but I know she is. I talked to her right after I talked to Tess," she admitted.

I glanced at my watch. *If she was anything like her daughters,* I thought, *I might give her a try.* "So you think she'd be willing to talk to me now?" I asked.

"I think so. Should I have her call you?"

"Please do, Paige. I'll be in my office."

"Keene," she said again. I waited. "Why are you wearing gloves? Is your office dirty? I'd be glad to clean it for you if you'd like."

"Thanks, Paige, that's sweet. And sometime, I'll probably take you up on it, but right now it's in pretty good shape," I said.

Her eyes drifted to my hands. I hadn't answered her question. I debated for a moment, and then I said, "I'm going through some of my mother's papers. It's probably not necessary, but I don't want to get my fingerprints on anything. That's the law enforcement training coming out in me." I smiled at her, and she smiled back. She still looked puzzled, but I made no further attempt to erase her confusion, and I went back into the office.

I had only looked at a few other loose pages when the phone on my desk rang. "Mr. Tempest, this is Joy Everest, Paige's mother. She said it would be okay to call now."

"Yes, thanks. I understand you might be interested in a job." I leaned back in my chair.

"I would, very much," she replied. "If it's okay, I could come over to the hotel now. Or if it's a bad time, you just tell me when."

"Now would be great," I said. The sooner I could get someone to help out, the more time I could devote to my new part-time job and to finding the killer—or killers—of my mother and brother.

"I'll be right over," she said.

I tackled the stack of papers, wanting them off my desk before Joy Everest arrived. I found a number of miscellaneous receipts, some notes Mom had written to herself, reminders of appointments, a couple of personal invoices—nothing to do with the hotel—and so on. She'd apparently stuffed things in the drawer when she was clearing her desk of clutter. Apart from the notes from the mysterious Jim, the items from the drawer certainly looked like clutter. I stuffed them back where I'd found them and turned my attention to the notes. When I heard the bell on the front door jingle, I opened the drawer below the junk drawer, intending to put the notes in there until I could read them, but that drawer was almost full. So instead, I got an envelope out, carefully folded the notes, put them inside, and laid them on a corner of the desk. Finished with the papers, I pulled my gloves off, put them in the top junk drawer, and stood up just as there was a knock on the door.

I walked over and opened it.

"Keene, this is my mother, Joy Everest," Paige introduced formally.

"It's nice to meet you, Mrs. Everest," I said as I stepped back and signaled to a chair in front of the desk. "You certainly have nice daughters," I added with a wink in Paige's direction.

Paige's face flushed, and she ducked her eyes and turned away. If this tiny woman moving toward the chair was as sweet as her daughters, she would be nice to have on the payroll.

Paige closed the door as she left, and I moved around my desk, sat down, and looked at Mrs. Everest for a moment. She was indeed petite like her daughters, and her smile was as infectious as theirs. She was a very attractive woman. Her brown eyes were lit with intelligence. "Thanks for coming in," I said.

"Thanks for allowing me to," she replied politely. "Your mother was a wonderful woman. She was such a comfort when my husband had his heart attack. We've been very close friends. I'm so sorry about your loss."

"Thank you," I said.

"I understand you've had a second tragedy in the family. I'm sorry about your brother too," she added.

I nodded in acknowledgement, and then I got down to business. Ten minutes later, satisfied that she would be great for the job, I offered it to her.

"When do I begin?" she asked.

"As soon as possible. I suppose there's some paperwork that needs to be filled out, but I'll have to find it. It's probably in that filing cabinet," I said as there was another knock on the door.

"Come in," I said.

"Are we intruding?" Chaille's head appeared in the doorway.

"Not at all," I said, wondering who the rest of *we* was. "I just hired Mrs. Everest to help out here so I can spend more time doing police work."

"She'll be great," Chaille said. "Joy, I'm sorry to interrupt, but Tess and I need to speak with Keene for a moment. It's quite important."

I thanked Joy and told her she could come in the next morning and work with Byron if she'd like to.

"If you don't mind, I'd like to stay and see what I can learn from Paige for a few hours. I won't expect pay for it."

"That would be fine, but I will pay you," I said. "I'll see about the paperwork in the morning."

"I can help with that," Tess said as she slipped into the office. "I know where your mother keeps things. I helped her when she hired Paige and one of the housekeepers."

"That would be great, Tess. Thanks. Now, what have you ladies got on your minds?"

CHAPTER EIGHT

"It took some work to get this information," Chaille said. "I ended up talking to three different people at Offerman Security and Investigations, but not until I told them I'd get a court order did the head of the firm agree to talk to me. They were just being cautious. I'm pretty sure they'll be cooperative from here on out."

"Mr. Offerman was at home at the time, but Chaille convinced him to go to his office," Tess said. She smiled at Chaille. "She sounded pretty professional to me. I'd have promised to cooperate too."

Chaille smiled in return. "It might have taken a couple of days to get a court order, and I don't feel like we have time to waste. Anyway, Mr. Offerman did admit that your mother was paying him to do a couple of things. His is not only a security firm, but as you can tell from their name, they do investigations as well. First, she asked them to look into the background of a man by the name of Jim McLaren."

"Wow," I said before I could stop myself. "Why doesn't that surprise me?"

Both of my visitors looked alarmed. "What?" Chaille said, leaning forward as she spoke.

I touched the envelope that was sitting on the corner of the desk. "This is what," I said. "This envelope is full of notes to my mother from a man by the name of Jim, a man who stays here about once a month. Paige knows him. He sometimes left notes with her to give to Mom. I have a bad feeling about the guy."

"For good cause," Tess said. "But before we get into that, Chaille will tell you what else the Offerman Agency was doing."

The two women exchanged glances, and then Chaille said, "They'd been keeping an eye on you. Mr. Offerman said that your mother was worried about your safety, so they were checking on you regularly."

"That's weird. I never felt threatened," I said, but even as I spoke, I recalled an incident I had put off as something that was unrelated to me, something I thought was aimed at a neighbor. Suddenly, I wondered.

"What's that look?" Chaille asked, pointing a slender finger in my direction. "Did you just think of something?"

I slowly nodded. "There was an incident. It happened after I got off of a swing shift at the police department just a few days before Mom died." I stopped while I tried to remember more of the details.

"What kind of incident?" Tess asked.

"It wasn't a big deal. I lived in an apartment complex," I began. "I hadn't been home long; it was around one in the morning. My apartment was on the second level, and there's a full-length balcony along the front of the apartment building. Someone threw a brick with a note tied to it onto the balcony. It bounced off the wall between my front door and my neighbor's front door. He was a big Tongan fellow, very tough and quite loudmouthed. We both ran out when we heard the brick hit."

"You say there was a note attached?" Chaille asked. "Was it addressed to you?"

"I didn't think so. This neighbor, he got to it first, picked it up, read the note, and began to swear," I said. "He got really angry. I tried to look at the note, but he tore it off the brick and tossed the brick into the street out front. He nearly hit a passing car."

"So did you even get to read the note?" Tess asked.

"No, but he read it to me. I don't recall exactly what he said, but it was something like, 'Your family will pay dearly for not cooperating.' That might not be exact, but he and I both assumed it was for him. I recall the guy saying something about nobody better mess with his family, and then he went back inside, slamming the door behind him," I explained. "He kept the note, and I didn't let it bother me. I put it out of my mind—until now."

"Could there have been more to the note than he told you?" Chaille asked.

I thought about that for a moment. I remembered thinking at the time that he probably hadn't read it all, but I guessed it didn't matter because it was directed at him, not me. "There could have been. But since there was nothing going on with my family that I knew about, I didn't think anything of it. I assumed he knew what it was about, so I left it at that," I said. "But now, with what's happened, I can't help but wonder."

Before I even finished, Chaille was making a call. "Sorry to bother you again, Mr. Offerman," she said when her call was answered. "This is Officer Chaille Donovan in Hardy, Wyoming. We spoke earlier about Keene Tempest."

She listened for a moment and then continued. "There was an incident at Mr. Tempest's apartment about a week before his mother died. He doesn't know if it has anything to do with him, but let me explain what happened, and maybe you can tell me if your agent saw it or knows anything about it."

She was silent for a moment, listening, and then she told Offerman what had happened. She talked briefly with him after that and then said, "That'll be fine. Thanks for your help."

After disconnecting, she reported, "He'll see what he can find out and call me back. It might not be until tomorrow unless his employee happens to be on duty."

"It's probably not anything relating to us," I said, but I was having a hard time convincing myself.

"Probably not, but we need to find out for sure," she agreed.

I couldn't argue with that. "Okay, so tell me what else you learned. I'm assuming they found out something about this Jim McLaren fellow."

"Yes, they did," Chaille told me. "He's a life insurance salesman with clients all over the western United States."

"That sounds pretty harmless," I observed.

"It's his personal life that's curious," she went on. "Apparently he's been married at least a half dozen times. That's how many they know about. There could be more, probably are, according to Offerman. At least one time he was actually married to two women at the same time. He did a few days in jail and some probation for that up in Oregon. That was a number of years ago. I guess since then he's been more careful about ending one marriage before beginning another."

"I'm assuming he skimmed his wives for their money," I said as I thought about the hotel's finances. "It sounds like he would have done the same thing to Mom if she'd married him."

Tess must have read the rest of what had just crossed my mind. "Maybe he did anyway," she commented with a frown. "We know the hotel lost a lot of money, but we don't know for sure if he took it. We also don't know how he might have done it, or rather, how he may have gotten your mother to agree to do whatever she must have done. Does the guy have something on her? If so, what could that be? How could he have forced her to do something that was so against her principles?"

"I guess that's the million-dollar question," Chaille commented. "I asked Mr. Offerman if they knew where McLaren was now. He didn't know, but he said he'd try to find out."

All three of us thought about things for a moment. Finally, it was Tess who voiced what we all must have been thinking. "Could McLaren have somehow threatened to do something to you if your mother didn't cooperate?" she asked.

"Why wouldn't she have warned me directly?"

Both ladies shook their heads, but Chaille smiled. "Would you have taken heed of her warning if she had?"

She had me there. I probably wouldn't have. "I'm not sure what I would have done," I admitted lamely.

We all agreed that we had a viable suspect in Jim McLaren, at least as far as my mother was concerned. But it didn't seem likely that he could have had anything to do with my brother's death. Whoever killed Sean had to have been a lot younger than McLaren. At least that seemed logical when I thought about how large my brother was. "We'll need to find out if there was any kind of connection between Sean and this Jim guy," I said. "But it doesn't seem likely. Is it possible that Sean's death and my mother's are totally unrelated?"

"Keene, there's more," Chaille said with a very sober face. "At least three of McLaren's former wives are deceased. Offerman said there could be more former wives we don't know about, but when your mom didn't send her last check, they decided she didn't require their services anymore, and they quit looking for others."

I processed the information for a minute and then spoke. "Okay, Chaille, the first thing we need to do is find out what caused the deaths of those three women."

"And then you'll probably want to find out if there were other wives or girlfriends and if anything has happened to them," Tess added.

"So how do we go about this?" I mused. "These women could be from anywhere; although, I think they would most likely be in the states where he did business. And I'd bet in many cases they were clients."

"Maybe I should call Offerman again," Chaille suggested. She looked at me, scrunching her eyebrows. "I don't know what he charges or if you can even afford his fees, but maybe he would at least tell us exactly what he knows and how he found it—a report of some kind."

"Find out what he charges and I'll consider asking him to do some looking for us," I said, not excited about having to shell out money for something I should be able to do myself but simply didn't have the time for. I had a hotel to run and work to do in helping solve the murder of my brother.

Chaille made another call to Offerman, but after talking to him for a moment, she handed the phone to me.

"Mr. Offerman," I began. "I'm Keene Tempest."

"Yes, Mr. Tempest. So I was told. What exactly can I do for you?" he asked.

"It depends on what it's going to cost me," I said. "But I'm interested in a couple of things. First, I need to know more about why you were protecting me and from whom—if you even know that. And second, I need to know more about Jim McLaren."

"Well, since your mother has passed away, I suppose I can give you a complete report of everything we did for her," he volunteered.

"That would be great."

"I'll send you a full written report in the next couple of days," he promised. "But in order to help you decide what, if anything, you want us to do for you right now, I'll give you a verbal report."

Tess and Chaille stood a few feet away, chatting with each other, as I listened to the security chief's report.

He discussed the surveillance they had done, even telling me about the night the brick was thrown. "I think that note your neighbor took might have been meant for you," he noted when I told him what the big Tongan fellow had said.

I was afraid he was right. I wished I'd known. "Did your agent see anything else, or were there other incidents that might have been threatening to me?" I asked.

"No, but you need to understand, your mother was mainly concerned about when you were by yourself. She couldn't afford the money it would have taken to watch you all day when you were attending classes or on the shifts you were working with the LAPD. She figured, and I'm sure she was right, that you were as safe as you could be with other police officers. It just didn't seem likely that anyone would try anything while you were on duty."

A sudden realization hit me like a blow to the head. *Sergeant Tom Brolin may have taken a bullet that was meant for me.* I knew I couldn't prove it, but deep in my gut, I was certain it was true. My mother had been wrong about when I was safe and when I wasn't. I made a mental note to follow up on the shooting.

Offerman recited pretty much what I already knew about Jim McLaren's dead ex-wives.

"Is there any reason to suspect foul play with any of those deaths?" I asked.

"Yes, I would say there is. The simple mathematics of it is too much to be ignored. Three women are dead, each dying within months after being married to him. Those three lived in three different states, and all three deaths were ruled either accidental or from natural causes."

I felt a burning in my gut. "I don't think my mother died of natural causes," I bit out. "And she wasn't even married to him."

We talked some more, and finally, after discussing costs, I told him to see if he could find out anything more about other wives or *any* women who may have been involved with McLaren in any way. I promised to send a check for the first week and then we'd see what happened.

I told the two women what I'd learned and then placed a call to my friend Sergeant Tom Brolin of the LAPD.

He was at home, he told me, going stark raving mad from sitting around. "They say they might clear me to return to work within a couple of weeks. I'm ready to go back now."

"Tom, has there been any progress on identifying the shooter?"

"No, and they've worked hard at it. They've checked out over two dozen people who might hate me bad enough, but all of them have been ruled out. You know, they had alibis that were rock solid."

"I'm not surprised." I paused and then said, "I have a feeling you weren't the target."

"Are you suggesting yourself?" Tom asked, sounding incredulous. "You haven't worked with the department long enough to have made those kind of enemies. No, it was me they were after, whoever *they* are."

"I *was* the target, and let me tell you why I believe that," I said with as much firmness as I could project over the telephone. "Two members of my family have died recently."

"I heard about your mother." His voice softened. "And I'm sorry for your loss. However, hadn't she been ill? That's what you told the lieutenant when you told him you would have to leave for a while. At least that's the way he made it sound to me."

"I have reason to believe she was murdered," I told him. "I didn't know that then."

"Oh, Keene, do you really think so?"

I told him that I did, and then I continued. "Last night one of my brothers was killed—stabbed to death."

"Keene!" he said with shock in his voice. "You better be watching your backside, young man."

"Believe me, I know," I agreed. "Let me tell you about something else." I then spent a couple of minutes explaining about the brick-and-note incident. "I dismissed it as having nothing to do with me—"

"But now you think you were wrong," he injected.

"I'd almost be willing to bet on it." I paused as a thought came to me. Then I said, "I wish I was close by. I'd go see my neighbor and ask him if he still has the note, or at least if there was any part of it that he didn't read to me."

"By golly, Keene," the sergeant said with sudden eagerness in his voice. "That's something I could do on my own even though I'm not back on duty yet. I'll head over there right now if you give me the address."

I looked at my watch before I said, "Are you sure you're up to it?"

"I'm fit to go back to work full-time, Keene. They just won't let me. But I can sure give you a hand with this if you'd like."

"I would really appreciate it," I told him. "I was just trying to remember what kind of work schedule my neighbor has. And unless I'm mistaken, he *would* be off work now."

"Give me the address, and I'll be on my way," Sergeant Brolin said. "Boy, it sure will feel good to be doing something productive. I've been going stir-crazy the past few days. I'm sure I'm driving my wife right up the wall."

I recited the information he needed. Then, just before I was ready to hang up, I had another idea. "Sergeant, there's something else I'd like to talk to you about."

"What is it?" he asked eagerly. "If there's something more I can do, you have but to ask."

"Do you know anything about a company called Offerman Security and Investigations?"

"I sure do," was his quick reply. "It's one of the better private detective agencies in the area. In fact, I'd probably say it's the best, the most reputable. They work with us from time to time and are very cooperative. Offerman is a retired LAPD captain. Why do you ask?"

I spent the next several minutes filling him in on Jim McLaren, my mother's relationship with him, what the Offerman agency had been doing, and what they'd learned. When I finished, Sergeant Brolin let out a whistle. "Your mother spent some money, Keene. Those guys are good, but they're also expensive."

I'd already learned that.

"Why don't you let me do a little looking too?" the sergeant asked.

"I appreciate the offer, Tom, but I can't afford to pay you too," I said, wishing I'd had his offer before I'd agreed to spend a ton of money on the agency.

"I may have a few expenses that I'd need covered, but other than that I'd work for free, Keene. It's like I said, I need something to do. I'll call Offerman and coordinate with him. He's a great guy. I actually worked under him at one time."

I couldn't turn Tom down. So I thanked him. He promised to get back to me as soon as he'd met with my neighbor.

I filled Tess and Chaille in on the details, and they both expressed relief then excused themselves. Suddenly I was alone again in my office, still trying to work out what all these new developments meant. I hoped I could figure it out soon—before anyone else got hurt.

CHAPTER NINE

MY BIG SISTER WASN'T NEARLY as down on me as my brothers had always been. In fact, she didn't even hesitate, an hour or so later, to agree to let me put her suitcase in my spare bedroom even though she knew I'd saved a hotel room for her if she wanted it. She was glad to have access to the kitchen and even said she would like being near me so we could visit some. And she felt a little safer there. She was tired when she arrived, and she had red eyes. I guessed she'd shed a few tears on the way to Hardy.

She embraced me, and then I helped her put her things in the apartment. That done, she got right down to business. "What have you learned, Keene?" she asked. "What else can you tell me?"

We sat in my small living room as I filled her in on everything, including my latest conversations with the Offerman agency and Sergeant Tom Brolin. She was as shocked as I had been about the apparent theft of funds. She was also surprised that our mother had even been dating; although, she admitted that she didn't blame her. The conversation finally turned to our other brother, Grady. "Have you heard from him yet?" she asked me.

"No, I was hoping you had."

She shook her head. "Neither has his wife. Jean sounds like she's getting quite worried."

That's not a good thing, I thought. And I could tell by the look on Bree's face that she felt the same way. She was the first to voice her worries. "Keene, what if something's happened to Grady too?"

Even though I'd had a rocky relationship with my siblings, it didn't mean I didn't love them. I was genuinely worried about Grady, and I admitted as much to Bree. She nodded her head, worry creasing her brow.

"Keene, I know I haven't always been very nice to you, but you are my little brother. I admire you. In fact, I, ah, I . . ." She hesitated. I held her eye. Finally, she finished. "I know I haven't always acted like it, but I meant what I said on the phone. I do love you, Keene." She hesitated, and her eyes got moist. I waited, watching her. Finally she spoke again, her voice catching. "You and I are in this together. I hope we can figure out what's going on."

"So do I," I responded, feeling a touch of warmth in my chest. This was new ground for me, but it felt good.

A moment later my phone went off. "This is my friend, Sergeant Brolin," I said as I prepared to take the call. "Tom," I answered my phone, "what have you learned?"

"Believe it or not, your neighbor must be some kind of collector. He still had the note," he reported cheerfully. "I have it now."

"Did he seem to think it wasn't for him after all?" I asked.

"He did. Nothing has happened, and he's had no further threats. When I told him what was happening with you and your family, he gave me the note."

"That's great. So what does it say? Is there more than what he read to me? Can you learn anything else from it?" I peppered him with questions.

"No. It's just a short, typewritten note, and it says just what you told me." Tom chuckled and then added, "If it had been intended for your neighbor, I would have pitied the person who wrote it. He's big, he's strong, and I think he's capable of doing whatever's necessary to protect his family. He even offered to help if he could. He seems to like you."

***

Even though it was late, Bree called our sister-in-law, Jean, and asked if she'd heard from Grady yet. She spoke briefly before putting the phone on speaker so that I could hear. "I have no idea where he's at," she said, and I was quite sure I detected more than just worry in her voice. She sounded angry.

"Hi, Jean," I said. "This is Keene. Has Grady done this before? I mean, has he left for a while without letting you know what he's doing or where he is?"

"He didn't used to, but lately we've been having trouble, and whenever we fight he storms off. But I usually hear from him within a day at the most."

"Jean," Bree broke in, "how bad was your fight?"

"It was a big one," our sister-in-law admitted. "He was really angry when he left."

"Can you tell us what it was about?" I asked.

"What's with all the questions?" Jean suddenly demanded, sounding annoyed.

Bree looked at me and then said, "Jean, we don't mean to be nosy, but Sean didn't die of natural causes like I led you to believe. Someone murdered him, and someone also threatened Keene. In fact, the whole family was threatened."

It was silent for a moment, and when Jean didn't speak and Bree offered nothing more, I said, "We also have reason to believe that our mother may have been murdered."

That got her attention. "Are you suggesting that Grady might be in danger?" she asked, much meeker now.

"That's exactly what we're trying to say," Bree said. "We're very worried about Grady."

"Did he know that the family had been threatened?" Jean asked. "Maybe that's why he's been so hard to get along with lately. Maybe he was worried."

"I doubt he knew unless he'd received something like I did," I told her. I explained about the note and the rifle shot that hit my partner. "Did he ever receive any threats?" I asked when I'd finished.

"If he did, he didn't tell me," she said. "But he could have. He hasn't been himself lately. Maybe he's worried. I'll bet that's it. Maybe it's not all about me. Maybe he's just taking his worries out on me."

Bree nodded at me as Jean was speaking. I guessed that she was thinking what I was—that it sounded very plausible. We talked for another couple of minutes, and then Bree said, "I'm sorry to worry you. But please, Jean, if you hear from him, call right away. I don't care if you have to wake me up."

Jean promised to do so, and the call ended. Bree took a deep breath and sat back on her chair, her head tilted back. For a minute or more, she just stared at the ceiling. Neither of us said anything. Finally, she sat forward and looked at me. "What is going on, Keene? I know we weren't the closest family in the world, but we never hurt anyone so badly they would want to wipe us out, did we?"

I just shrugged.

***

My phone rang. It was Chief Damion Thompkins. "Would you be willing to give us a hand tonight, Keene?" he asked. "If you've had any rest, that is."

I was exhausted, but I also wanted to do whatever I could to help find my brother's killer. "What would you like me to do?" I asked.

"I'd like you to go with Chaille and visit the bars, both here in Hardy and in neighboring towns. I want to know if anyone—patrons or employees—saw Sean the past few days and if they did, what he might have said. Also, I'd be interested in knowing if he was seen with anyone."

"I'd be glad to do it," I said. "What time should I meet Chaille? I know she left here a short while ago."

"You can ride with her," the chief said. "She'll pick you up in about five minutes."

After we hung up, I explained to Bree what was going on.

"I'll help around here if I'm needed," she said. "But first I need to call my husband. Ron's probably beside himself by now. He's a worrier at best, and I need to let him know exactly what's going on."

I smiled at her. "And then maybe he won't worry?"

She nodded. "Yeah, I know. Then he'll go crazy, but he needs to know, and I want him to be careful too."

Chaille picked me up a few minutes later, and we began the tedious job of interviewing everyone we could in both the bars in Hardy and those in the closest neighboring towns. We showed around a photo of Sean, and several people recalled seeing him, but he always entered alone, and only one person we interviewed had spoken with him at any length. That man had spent a couple of hours with him, and Sean had sort of opened his heart. Sean had told him he'd just gotten out of jail and that he was ashamed about it. I suspected the fellow might have been drunk when he talked to Sean, but he did seem to have a pretty clear recollection of what had taken place.

The man identified himself as Ollie Brown. He appeared to be in his seventies, but when I asked him his age, he told me he was sixty. It seemed pretty clear that a lifetime of alcohol abuse had aged him terribly. He was a small man with thinning gray hair, watery gray eyes, and far more wrinkles than a man his age should have. The yellow of his few remaining teeth hinted at the heavy use of tobacco. However, he was in reasonably good shape when Chaille and I sat down to speak with him at an isolated table in a deep corner of the room.

His breath was strong enough to sink a battleship. Chaille's face went pale, and she looked like she was going to gag when he shook her hand, leaned close, and said, "Hello, pretty lady. It's a pleasure to meet you."

Chivalrous man that I am, I sat exactly opposite of Ollie, Chaille beside me so as to give the "pretty lady" room to breathe. My actions brought a quick grin and a soft, "Thanks," from her.

"What did you mean when you said Sean opened his heart to you?" I asked as Chaille began taking notes.

"Well, he just sort of looked sad, and I asked him what was bothering him besides having just gotten out of jail. He said that his mother had recently passed away and that they'd never been very close," Ollie said, his bad breath suffocating me and a fine mist of spittle spraying my face. His voice was gravely and surprisingly deep for a man of his size.

I sat up straighter and tried to lean back. "You say he told you he and his mother hadn't been very close?" I asked.

"No, I didn't mean that. He said he and his little brother hadn't been close," Ollie clarified. "He told me that he and his other brother and sister had always been mean to the kid." Ollie looked at me thoughtfully for a long moment. Finally, he continued, "The guy was twice your size, but he sure looks a lot like you. If I didn't know better I'd think you two were related."

I glanced at my partner. She nodded at what she must have guessed I was thinking, so I decided to level with the guy. I wanted to learn all I could from him, and being honest with him was probably going to help. So I told Ollie, "I'm his younger brother, Keene Tempest."

The man's wrinkled face lit up, and he said with a grin, "So you're the kid he talked about."

"I suspect I am," I admitted.

"Was he mean to you?" Ollie asked.

I nodded. "Yes, I'd say he was at times. But I still loved the guy. What else did he say?"

"Funny you should say that," Ollie began. My head was as far back as I could get it without spraining my neck. "He told me he loved the kid . . . ah, you, I guess he meant. He said you have a sister and that she thought you were okay too. Let's see, he mentioned another brother. He said he was sure he liked you as well. He said he wished they'd been nicer to you. Anyway, he told me that he and his mother—your mother too, I guess—thought you were in danger, so they hired somebody to protect you." Ollie paused as he cleared his throat and pulled out a cigarette. I was having a hard time digesting the news that Sean was part of the hiring of Offerman Security and Investigations. "Do you mind if I smoke?" Ollie asked, shaking the cigarette in my direction.

"I'd rather you waited until we're finished here," I said, glancing at Chaille again. She nodded her agreement.

Ollie put the cigarette down on the table. "Bad habit, I know, but I can't break it. I'm too old now to even try again. Okay, so where was I?"

"You had mentioned me being in danger," I prompted.

"Oh yeah, that's right. He and your mom hired somebody to keep an eye on you. I think he said you were in Los Angeles. Were you a cop there too?"

"I was," I said, not wanting to get into the long story of what I did there.

"Yeah, well, after his mom died, he said he convinced the rest of your family to pressure you into moving here and running the hotel. He said he wanted to get you closer so he could keep an eye on you."

As farfetched as this all sounded, I knew the drunk across the table couldn't possibly be making this up.

"Did he say why he thought Keene was in danger?" Chaille asked. It was the first time she'd spoken since we'd sat down.

The watery gray eyes shifted to the pretty officer sitting beside me. "He said something about some danger to the family but especially to young Mr. Tempest here. Ah, sorry, I mean Officer Tempest. Didn't mean no disrespect." He gave me a quick smile and turned back to Chaille. "Didn't say why he thought it or nothing like that."

He turned his wrinkled face back to me when I began, "Did he say anything about my mother being in—"

The old drunk cut me off. "God rest your mother's soul. Your brother said he thought someone had murdered her. He cried when he said that. He was sitting right across from me, just like you are, only he was holding a beer in his hand."

Now that really set me back. I wasn't sure how to respond. Sean, in our short, rather violent encounter had certainly never said anything like that to me. Chaille apparently picked up on my shock, for she continued smoothly, "Did Sean say who he thought might have killed Mrs. Tempest and why?"

Ollie nodded his head, and my heart quickened.

"Can you tell us?" Chaille pressed when he didn't say anything for a long, dramatic moment.

This time Ollie shook his head, brushed at his greasy, thin gray hair, and said, "He didn't tell me, but he said he knew who it was."

"He knew who killed her?" I asked, trying to hide the shock I was feeling.

"That's what he claimed. He said he was going to take care of it and soon. He said he wasn't going to bother you none with it. He said you probably wouldn't have believed him anyway."

I certainly wished that Sean would have given me the opportunity. Maybe he'd still be alive if he'd confided in me instead of treating me the way he'd always treated me.

Despite the terrible odor of Ollie's breath, Chaille leaned in a bit, her eyes shining in anticipation, and asked, "Surely he said something about who it was, Mr. Brown. Did he say if it was a man or a woman?"

Ollie shook his head. "He didn't say."

"Did he say why someone killed Mrs. Tempest?"

Ollie hesitated for a moment, and then he rubbed his watery eyes. He seemed deep in thought, so Chaille and I simply waited. Finally, Ollie looked first at Chaille and then at me. "I think it was about money," he said. "Someone had been stealing from your mother. I think that's what he told me."

Once again my partner and I exchanged meaningful glances. It was Chaille who finally asked, "Does the name Jim McLaren mean anything to you, Mr. Brown?"

He thought again for a minute. "No, should it?"

"Just wondered," she said. Her eyes, as she looked over at me, mirrored the disappointment I was feeling. It would've been nice to be able to tie McLaren to the crime—or crimes—but we'd still learned a lot from Ollie Brown. We both hoped we could learn more, but that seemed to be all he could tell us that was of any help.

I finally said, "We'll need your address and phone number. I'm sure we'll be needing to talk to you again."

Chaille wrote down the information and then handed him a card with her name and number on it. "Call me if you think of anything more, even if you don't think it's important. You have been a great help to us tonight."

Chaille and I both stood up and stepped away from the table. Ollie just sat there, staring at his tobacco-stained fingers on the table in front of him.

"Thanks again, Mr. Brown," I said.

He looked up then. "Can I ask a question now, Officer?" he asked.

"Of course," I replied.

"Did you really whip that big strapping brother of yours in a fair fight?"

I shook my head. "No, it wasn't a fair fight, but I did whip him. I hated to, but he didn't give me much choice."

Ollie grinned, exposing the disaster that was the inside of his mouth. "He said he provoked you and took a swing at you. Said he was drunk and mad and that he got what he deserved. He said you whipped him so fast he didn't really know how you did it."

Chaille spoke up then. "Officer Tempest is a trained fighter," she said with what sounded like a little bit of pride in her voice. "His brother didn't know that. I suspect that's why Keene said it wasn't a fair fight. But it was as far as I'm concerned."

"Sean thought so too," Ollie said. "But he did admit he had no idea that you could fight like you did."

"I suppose I learned karate largely because of the way my brothers used to beat on me," I admitted. "But I honestly didn't ever want to have to use it in fighting either of them." My eyes were looking over at Chaille as I said that. I didn't care what Ollie Brown thought about my relationship with my brothers, but I did care about what Chaille thought.

I turned back to Ollie, who was again rubbing at his watery eyes. "I sure hope you catch the guy that killed him—and the one that killed your mother."

Outside the bar a minute later, Chaille and I both hungrily sucked in deep breaths of the clear air, trying to purge our lungs of the tobacco smoke that had filled the bar and clearing our sinuses of the wretched smell of Ollie Brown's breath. Back in the car, we discussed what we had learned.

"Do you believe him?" I asked Chaille.

She favored me with one of her pretty smiles, one that displayed a near perfect set of white teeth, the exact opposite of Ollie's. Then she answered, "I did. He couldn't have made that all up."

"I agree, but I've got to admit I was surprised when he said that Sean loved me. I never felt that from him," I said.

"I think it must have been true."

I nodded my head. "I think we need to see what it's going to take to step up the search for one Jim McLaren. He's involved in the murders, or I miss my guess."

"Involved, yes," Chaille said. "But honestly, Keene, I think he had help. I just hope he can be found and that he'll tell us who that help was."

We still had more people to search out, but we both doubted that we'd find anyone who could tell us more than Ollie. But I could still hope. It would be nice to find someone who had talked to Sean who might be able to give us some names. "I wonder if Bree's heard from Grady," I wondered aloud as we pulled away from the curb and headed for the next bar.

CHAPTER TEN

I CALLED BREE WHILE CHAILLE drove the patrol car. I prayed that Grady had finally contacted his wife. In the back of my mind, I could see him in the same horrible situation as Sean. The thought made my stomach roll. It made me nervous for both my sister and me, and I told her exactly that when she reported that Jean had still not heard from Grady.

"I'm nervous too, Keene," she said, sounding depressed and worried. "Have you and Officer Donovan learned anything?"

"A little," I said, and I spent the next several minutes giving her a brief overview of our interview with Ollie Brown. "Don't mention this to anyone," I cautioned her when I'd finished. "I'll fill you in more later. Did you talk to your husband?"

"I did, and he's worried sick." She paused for a moment, and then she continued, "Actually, I think he's scared."

"We all have plenty of reason to be," I commented, although I was more angry than afraid.

"He's going to see if he can get some personal leave from work so he can come up here," Bree went on. "He thinks we'll all be safer if we stay together until the killer is caught."

I didn't know if I agreed with that, but I didn't relay my thoughts to her. Instead, I asked, "What about your kids?"

"He'll probably bring them too," she said with a quiver in her voice. Bree and her husband had two daughters, ages four and six. I barely knew them, but I was concerned about their safety.

"Did you talk to Jean too? What does she want to do?" I asked.

"She just wants Grady to come home. She's worried about him and hopes if she can talk to him that maybe they can work out the problems in their marriage. She's really having a hard time. It probably doesn't help that she's pregnant. She's been quite sick."

"Gee, I didn't know she was expecting," I said. "When's the baby due?"

"Not for about seven months. She just found out for sure. I guess that's part of their problems. She says Grady didn't want children and is angry with her. That's what the fight was about when he took off the other night."

"I didn't know Grady didn't want kids." I was bewildered by the news. "But I really don't know him that well. I didn't know that Sean didn't hate me either. I guess there's a lot I don't know. I just hope he calls soon. I'm sure he'd want to know about Sean."

"I would think so," Bree said with a bite to her voice. "I'm really disappointed in him, treating Jean the way he is."

"He's probably scared about the baby and isn't sure how to handle it. Grady is a proud man, but I do believe he cares for Sean. He made quite a fuss when I didn't bail Sean out of jail." The car slowed. "I've got to go now. We just got to another bar that we need to check out," I told Bree as Chaille found a parking spot. "I'll talk to you later."

We entered the dark, smoky bar a moment later. No one there, including the bartender, remembered ever having seen Sean in the establishment. The same proved true everywhere else we went. That left us with Ollie Brown as the only person who could shed any light on Sean's activities or state of mind in the days prior to his death, and that was on the very afternoon before he died.

Later, back at the police station, Chief Thompkins—who looked as tired as the two of us felt—reminded us that we'd need to make repeat visits the next day and on another evening. "There could easily be others who weren't there tonight who might have talked to Sean."

"So that means more bar hopping tomorrow?" Chaille asked with a tired grin.

"I'm afraid so," he said. "But let's be grateful for what your Mr. Brown told you. We're making progress."

"Has anyone else learned anything?" I asked Chief Thompkins.

"Not really. Detective Bentley still insists that you are the most likely suspect."

"He's a jerk," Chaille interjected angrily.

"And he's incompetent," the chief agreed.

"Then why is he even allowed to work on the case?" Chaille asked. "I thought you'd taken him off it."

"I'd intended to, but I changed my mind. I need the assistance of the sheriff and his department, and he doesn't realize what Bentley's really like. I don't really think he'd deny us any help if I told him I didn't want Bentley, but I'd rather not rock the boat. We may not like it, but we'll have to put up with Bentley until we get this thing solved."

There was nothing to say to that. So I steered the discussion in another direction. "Chief, based on what we've learned so far, do you agree that my mother could be a victim of homicide?"

He leaned back in his chair with a sigh. He ran his fingers through his hair, stared for a moment at the ceiling of his office, then finally said, "Chaille, begin an investigation. As unlikely as it seems, I'm afraid we better treat her death as suspicious."

Chaille and I exchanged a glance, and then she said, "Thank you, Chief. I'll get on it."

"In the morning," the chief instructed. "Right now, you two both need to get some serious sleep. Payton is covering the rest of the night. I'm going to go home as well. Can the two of you meet me here in the morning at nine?"

We agreed, and ten minutes later, I was back at the hotel. Bree was sitting in the small living room of my apartment when I walked in. She looked like she'd been dozing. But she came right to her feet and asked if there was anything new to report. After sharing a few more details of the interview with Ollie Brown, I asked her the same question I'd asked before. The answer was the same: there was still no word from our brother. Discouraged and heavyhearted, we went to our respective bedrooms.

***

Before my alarm could wake me up at seven, my ringtone awoke me instead. I groggily picked up the phone from the stand beside my bed and answered it without looking at the screen. I came fully awake when I heard the voice on the other end.

"Keene, it's Grady. What's going on? Jean says you and Bree have been trying to get ahold of me. I asked her why, and all she'd say is that she wanted you to tell me. So tell me."

"Grady, it's good to hear from you. I'm glad you're okay," I said.

"Why wouldn't I be?" he asked. "So what do you want to talk to me about?"

"Jean didn't say anything at all, Grady?" I asked, thinking that she surely must have given him some kind of hint.

"Only that it was about Sean, nothing more. We aren't seeing eye to eye right now."

"You've got a good wife, Grady," I said, unable to resist an attempt to get him to reconcile his differences with her.

"That's your opinion," he snapped. "Anyway, it's none of your business. Just tell me what's going on."

"Sean is dead," I said abruptly.

"What?" he asked with anger in his voice. "Did a cop kill him? That would be your fault, you know. You left him to the mercy of the cops by leaving him in jail for so long."

I bristled, but shoving the barb aside, I continued, "We don't know who killed him. What we do know is that it was murder. Someone stabbed him in his room, right here in the hotel."

There was silence for a prolonged moment. Finally, as if in denial, Grady spoke, "Are you sure he's dead?"

"Yes, I'm sure. And whoever killed him probably killed Mom as well," I responded.

"So what's being done about it?"

"We're investigating."

"What do you mean when you say *we*? You stay out of it, Keene. I mean it. You're not a cop anymore. You left LA, remember? You're just a hotel manager now, and *that's* probably more than you can handle."

"I'm actually working for the Hardy Police Department part-time."

"You are a cop again?" Grady asked angrily. "You haven't got what it takes for that."

"I think I do. And, Grady, we are going to get to the bottom of this," I vowed. "And did you hear what I said about Mom?"

"Yeah, I heard you, little brother. But you are, as is quite normal for you, wrong. She was sick and she died. It's that simple. You need to face that fact. As for Sean, if what you say is true, I'm sure the other cops can handle it better than you can."

I took a deep breath. "Grady, Bree and I were trying to reach you so you would know you might be in danger. You need to watch your back. Someone also tried to kill me. Bree and I are both being very careful. You need to be as well. Someone has it in for our family."

My brother was silent for a moment and then whispered hoarsely, "Do you really think that?"

"Yes, I do, Grady. So please, just be careful."

Another pause. "Thank you, kid." His tone was again haughty. "Now you've told me, and believe me, I'll take care of myself. You don't need to worry about me. Anyway, I can't really believe that I'm in danger, but if I am, I can take care of myself."

I was almost chewing my tongue to a pulp to keep myself from exploding. He really didn't realize how serious this all was. I took a couple of deep breaths before I felt in control. Then I said, "Why don't you come here. Bree and I would like you to."

"I can't right now. But I'll keep what you've told me in mind. And tell Bree that too. I'll let you know when I can come." The connection was terminated.

For a couple of minutes, I stared at the phone in my hand without seeing it. Grady could be next. I silently prayed that he would come to his senses and take what I'd told him more seriously.

I looked at the time on my phone. It was almost seven o'clock. It was time to get back to the task of finding a killer. I shut the alarm off, showered, dressed, and thought about fixing myself a little breakfast, but then I decided to go next door to the café and let someone else cook. I hadn't heard a sound from the spare bedroom and assumed Bree must still be asleep. I started through my small living room, but just as I opened the door, my sister spoke from behind me.

"Where are you going, Keene?"

"I thought I'd go over and get a little breakfast," I said, motioning north toward the café as I watched her emerge from her room, wrapped in a long pink bathrobe.

"If you give me a few minutes, I'll go with you."

Even though I felt like there was a lot that I needed to do, I wasn't sure just where I was going to start this morning, so I relented. "Sure. We need to talk anyway. Grady called."

"Oh, Keene, thank goodness. So he's okay?" she asked.

"Pretty much, I guess. I'll tell you about it over breakfast."

"Give me ten minutes, and I'll be ready," she said. I sat down with my scriptures to wait.

***

After arriving at the café, we found a private table near the back of the room. When the waitress came to bring our menus, Bree said, "Two coffees, please." Before I could protest, she went a light shade of red. "Sorry, Keene. I forgot you and Mom swore off coffee." She looked back up at the waitress and corrected, "One coffee for me. Keene?"

"Just bring me a large glass of orange juice."

After we'd perused the menus and made our decisions, Bree began, "So when will Grady be here?"

"It didn't sound like he was coming anytime soon, but he said he'd let me know. He also didn't give me the impression that he was going home anytime soon."

"Did you tell him he was in danger?" she asked, her eyes misting up slightly.

"Yes, and he said he'd take care of himself. It didn't sound like he took me very seriously." After giving her the details of the call, I continued, "I was wondering if he'd listen to you. Maybe he'd take you more seriously than he took me."

"I'll try," she said. "He's got to understand. Do you have his number?"

I pulled out my iPhone and read the number he'd called from. She punched it into her phone as I said, "I guess that will reach him. I didn't think to ask for any other numbers."

Before she'd hit the Call button, our waitress came back and asked us for our orders. When she walked away, Bree said, "Maybe I'll try to call him right now before I get my mouth full of eggs and toast."

But at that moment, a short, pudgy man with a neatly trimmed goatee and mustache walked up to our table. "You must be the Tempests. I'm Hugo Starling. I own this place," he said, sweeping a flabby arm around.

"Yes, we are. I've been in here several times," I told him, "but I haven't had the pleasure of meeting you. I'm Keene, and this is my sister, Bree."

He nodded his head and stared at me for a moment, making me feel quite awkward. I didn't know whether to concentrate on his green eye or his brown one. It wasn't just the color, but there was an odd look about them. He finally spoke, "So your brother got killed, I hear."

I nodded, and Bree stared at the guy. Hugo finally said, "Your brother wasn't the nicest man I've ever met, but it's still too bad he got killed. Of course, I don't suppose you care too much. I heard how you beat him up pretty badly."

Bree came to my defense before I could get a word out. "Sean had a temper, especially when he was drunk, Mr. Starling. But Keene didn't dislike him. The fight meant nothing. We are both heartbroken."

I nodded my agreement, and the café's proprietor said, "I suppose if your mother would have taken me up on my offer, your brother would still be alive."

"What offer was that?" Bree asked, puzzled.

"He wanted to buy the hotel from Mom," I informed my sister. "She wouldn't sell. I suppose he means that Sean would still be alive if he'd owned it instead of us."

"That's right, but your mother was a stubborn old woman," Hugo said with a scowl. "I made her an offer that was more than fair. I've been meaning to come over and see you, Keene. But since both of you are here, I'll talk to you both. I'd like to buy the place. I know you have lives elsewhere; your mother told me that. I'd like to make an appointment to visit with you soon."

"Thanks, Mr. Starling," I said, "but now isn't a good time."

"Call me Hugo. And I'll be in touch. You have a decent business there, but I have the skills to make it even better," he bragged with a cocky look on his pudgy face.

"Thanks, Hugo," Bree said. "We'll talk about it. It's nice to meet you."

He finally left, and Bree scowled. "I don't think I like that man. I'm glad Mom didn't sell to him."

I didn't like him either, but my mind was off in a different direction. I was suspicious and made a mental note to investigate the man's background. Could he be someone who would stoop to murder if he didn't get his way? He clearly didn't think much of our mother, and that was not normal. He was the first person I'd met who didn't think very highly of her.

"What do you think you're doing?" the café owner's voice thundered from across the room, jolting me out of my reverie.

I looked over at the man. Hugo was standing in front of the waitress, shaking a fat finger in her face, his face a mottled red color. She was shaking and fighting back tears. For a full minute, he berated her for not cleaning one of the tables to his specifications. I tried not to stare, so I looked instead across the table at my sister, but her eyes were glued to the unhappy situation across the room. The waitress, a pretty girl who looked like she must be about sixteen, simply stood there and took the full brunt of his anger.

When Hugo finally finished his rant, he stormed into the back, muttering and cursing. She looked over at us and then at another table with customers waiting for her to bring their breakfast. The look on her face nearly broke my heart, and for a moment I felt the impulse to jump to my feet and confront Hugo. But I calmed myself and watched to see what the girl would do.

I wondered if she'd just bolt out the front door, quitting her job on the spot. I certainly wouldn't have blamed her. But she didn't. She just rubbed at her eyes for a moment, sniffled, and bustled about her work again.

"Keene," Bree said, and I looked across the booth at her. She was vigorously opening and closing her fists. "I'd like to thump that guy."

"I thought about it for a moment myself," I confessed.

"If the girl needed to be corrected, he could have done it quietly, back in the kitchen," she snapped, her eyes flashing.

"That guy really disturbs me. He could be dangerous."

Her eyes suddenly grew wide. "Are you thinking maybe he's a . . ." She looked around and then leaned toward me. "Are you thinking he might have hated Mom bad enough to do something to her?"

My sister had just scored some points with me. Perhaps she and I were more alike than I imagined. "That's exactly what I was thinking," I told her. "Mom ate here quite a bit, and it would certainly have been easy for him to slip something into her food, something that worked slowly but was fatal. I'm going to see what I can find out about the guy."

"Oh, Keene, that's too horrible." She paused. "But he's not big enough or athletic enough to, you know, do what was done to Sean."

"You wouldn't think I was either," I reminded her.

"Oh yeah, I see what you're thinking. Maybe he's not the fat weakling he looks like. Or maybe he caught Sean off guard," she said.

"It's possible."

"Yeah, maybe he was meeting with Sean about buying the hotel and maybe Sean was looking at those strange eyes, and Hugo just, you know, stabbed him."

"I wouldn't put it past him," I said as the young waitress hustled into the kitchen. "You could be right. He may have approached Sean about buying the hotel."

We were both thoughtful for a moment, and then Bree broke the silence. "Maybe if we sold out to him, we'd be out of danger. I'm really thinking this Hugo Starling character could be the one who . . ." She trailed off as we both caught sight of the young waitress bringing our breakfast, but I knew exactly what Bree had been about to say, and I was in complete agreement. Hugo Starling warranted some serious checking out.

Bree didn't try to call Grady until we had finished eating and were walking up the sidewalk to the hotel. But she didn't get an answer. She left a message and then looked at me with sad eyes. "He can be stubborn. I'm worried about him."

I was worried abut Grady as well. Our family had an enemy, or enemies. We needed to be extremely cautious. I wondered if Hugo had been in touch with Grady about buying the hotel.

For some reason the guy wanted our hotel very badly. There had to be a reason. I just wished I knew what it was.

CHAPTER ELEVEN

BACK AT THE HOTEL, BREE and I went into the office, where I booted up the computer, connected to the Internet, and Googled Hugo Starling's name. There were several hits. One of them was in connection with the Hardy Café. That one was to be expected, but what I learned from the next site was extremely disturbing. Hugo had spent time in prison for armed robbery. It had occurred before my birth, when Hugo was only about eighteen. He'd spent five years in prison and then been paroled. I calculated his age now at fifty-two.

"I can't believe he only spent five years in prison," Bree said. She'd been looking over my shoulder at the computer screen.

"He was just a kid," I noted. "I suppose the parole board took that into consideration. That happens. What I'd like to know is how he ended up with that café and what makes him think he could afford to buy the hotel."

But I found nothing more of interest. I shut down the computer as Bree moved around the desk and sat down across from me. "So what now?" she asked.

"Rather than spend a lot of time trying to find out more about Hugo on the Internet, I think I'll just ask Chief Thompkins. He's only a few years younger than Hugo, and I suspect he knows a lot about the guy. I'll be meeting with him in a little while. In the meantime, why don't you try calling Grady again?"

She tried, but once again the phone went to voice mail. She left Grady a message saying, "Grady, this is Bree. Please, please call me. I really need to talk to you."

I stood up to leave, but Bree said, "Before you go, Keene, there's something I need to say to you."

"What's that?" I asked.

"I'm so terribly sorry for the way I've treated you all your life. I just always followed our brothers' lead. You're a great guy, and I admire you. I wouldn't have blamed you if you'd told me to just get lost when I got here," she said. Then she added a compliment that struck a deep chord in me. "You are just like Mom was. I guess the rest of us were more like Dad."

"Thanks, Bree. You have no idea how much that means to me."

We hugged. It was the first really genuine hug I remember ever having received from my big sister. This wasn't just a quick embrace like when she'd arrived the day before. This was a hug filled with family affection. When she let go, I headed for the door so she wouldn't see the moisture building in my eyes. But a sudden thought stopped me in my tracks. "Bree," I said as I turned and faced her, "be really, really careful. If Hugo tries to contact you, tell him to get an offer ready and that we'll look at it. Don't just turn him down flat."

She looked shocked. "But, Keene, you can't really mean we might sell to him."

"Not in a million years," I said. "But it might be safer if he thinks we will. In the meantime, maybe we can build a case against him and put him behind bars—if he's our man."

"I think he is," she said. "Now you go and do whatever it is you cops do to prove it. I'll keep an eye on the hotel . . . and keep trying to call Grady."

***

When I mentioned Hugo Starling's offer to buy the hotel, Chief Damion Thompkins's eyebrows shot up. He spoke immediately after I'd finished. "That opens up a whole new direction in this investigation, and it even makes sense that both your mother and your brother are victims."

"Keene," Chaille interrupted. I turned toward her as she spoke, worry in her eyes. "You're in danger too. You've got to be very, very careful. I wouldn't want anything—I mean, it would be terrible if something happened to you." A bit of a flush crept into her cheeks.

I looked at Chaille with a different perspective. I detected something in her voice and her entire demeanor that hinted at something deeper than just one cop's concern for another. Even in these difficult circumstances, her concern for me lifted my spirits. I caught myself gazing at her face, lost for words at the moment. She returned the gaze, and my pulse quickened.

Chief Thompkins broke the spell. "Keene, let me tell you a little bit more about our astute businessman, Mr. Starling." He didn't seem to have noticed the magnetism that had drawn his officers toward each other. We both, with effort, tore our eyes from each other's and listened to our boss.

"Hugo has an ugly past," he began.

I nodded. "Yes, I did some Internet research on him a little while ago."

"So you know he went to prison as a young man for an armed robbery?"

"Yes, but I didn't find all the details. I know he was eighteen at the time and that he did five years in prison for it."

Chaille moaned. "I didn't know that."

"It was a long time ago." Damion shrugged. "I am six years younger than Hugo, but I remember it all very well. Nobody around here ever cared much for the guy. He was always a bit aloof. Even though he's not a big guy—pudgy but not big—he acted like he was more important than everyone else."

"What did his parents do for a living?" Chaille asked. But before Damion could respond, she said to me, "I'm not from here. I came here specifically for this job with Chief Thompkins."

"I didn't realize that," I said.

She nodded and smiled in a way that made my heart skip a beat. "Just like you, in a way," she said with an even bigger smile.

I was touched that she found something besides our Irish roots and red hair that was common to both of us. *I could get to like her a lot*, I thought, *even if she is as tall as I am.*

The chief was still back on the question about Hugo's parents, still oblivious, it seemed, to the attraction building between me and Chaille. "They owned the café and the hotel. It wasn't nice then, like it is now, although they were in the middle of some renovations. Anyway, they were forced to mortgage the hotel for bail, and later they sold it to help pay for Hugo's defense. They did everything they could to keep him out of prison. Thinking about my own kids, I guess I understand how they must have felt."

"Did they think he was innocent?" Chaille asked.

"No, I'm sure they knew better, but they felt like he'd been forced into what he did by some older guy," the chief replied.

"What older guy?" I asked.

"There were two of them that committed the robbery. It was in Casper, and the officers there were alerted by an alarm that one of the cashiers had managed to set off. There were several shots fired. Hugo wasn't actually part of the shootout. His folks always maintained it was because he knew it was wrong to shoot at cops, so when they showed up, he threw his gun down. But a witness said that Hugo tripped coming out of the bank and that his gun was knocked loose and landed several feet away when he hit the sidewalk. The other robber, however, did shoot at the cops. They returned fire, but he got away in a car that was parked by the curb."

"Was Hugo hurt at all?" Chaille interjected.

"Not seriously. His knees were scraped and one wrist was sprained from when he tried to break his fall. Hugo was always overweight and quite clumsy. However, his partner was shot. He took a bullet to the leg, but like I said, he managed to get in his car and get away. They never did find him."

"How much was taken in the robbery?" I asked.

"It was over a half million dollars. I guess to Hugo's partner it was enough to attempt to kill a cop over."

"And I suppose that since they didn't catch him, they never recovered the money," I suggested.

"That's right. There were rumors that while he was awaiting trial, Hugo made contact with the guy. So he might have gotten some of the money, but he would never admit to that."

Chaille looked thoughtful. "Could he have used the money to buy the café from his parents?"

"No, he didn't need to. When he got out of prison, his father's health was failing. Hugo came back and went to work at the café. When his father died of a heart attack, his mother gave him the café with the stipulation that he take care of her."

Chaille cocked an eyebrow and asked skeptically, "Did he take care of her?"

"To his credit, he did. In fact, he seemed to dote on her."

"What about his siblings?" I asked.

"He was an only child," the chief responded. "The way he took care of his mother caused the people of the community to look at him with some respect despite what he'd done. To my knowledge, he hasn't committed a crime since then."

"Would you say he's been a model citizen?" I asked. "The way he treated his waitress this morning certainly made him look like a lot less than a model citizen."

"Hugo has a thing against women. He's never married. The only woman he ever really showed any respect to was his mother. I don't mean he doesn't treat his female customers with respect, but he does have a reputation, especially the past year or so, of being tough on his female help."

I steered the conversation back to the investigation. "What kind of shape is his café in financially? Would he have the means to buy our hotel?"

"I can't imagine he would. I don't think he could even make a decent down payment," Damion responded.

Chaille put her hand over her chin and was thoughtful for a moment. "What if he does have the loot from the robbery or at least his share of it?"

It was the police chief's turn to nod, and Damion did so vigorously. "If he's had it in a bank, earning interest for the past nearly thirty years, it could be quite a bit of money by now. That would make sense."

"Wouldn't the cops have checked that out?" Chaille shook her head. But before either of us could respond, she reasoned, "Of course, I suppose he could have it under a different name. Or he could have put it in several different banks under aliases."

"Or . . ." I said as a thought occurred to me, "maybe he put it somewhere that it wouldn't earn interest but where it would be safe until he could retrieve it. Chief, didn't you say that renovations were being made on the hotel at the time he went to prison?"

"Yes, that's right, but shortly after he was sent up, his parents sold the place and the work was completed under the direction of the new owners, the couple that sold it to your parents, Keene."

"Did Hugo know they were going to sell the place?" Chaille knew where I was going with this, her thoughts flowing quite smoothly with mine.

"That I don't know, but I suppose he might not have. He was, after all, a spoiled and selfish kid," Damion responded thoughtfully. "But I do know it was sold after he went to prison."

"So the money—"

"Might be somewhere in your hotel," Chaille finished for me.

We looked at each other, and once again I felt a pleasant chill run through me. Unless I was mistaken, I thought she was feeling the same thing. Finally, the chief noticed and said, "You two certainly think alike." He grinned mischievously. "My wife and I were like that when we first . . . ah, noticed each other. Still are sometimes."

I felt myself redden slightly and could see Chaille doing the same. My, but she did look good when she was embarrassed. Of course, I was becoming more aware of how good she looked anytime I happened to see her.

The chief chuckled. "Okay, so we've established a possible motive for the murder of your mother by Hugo. She wouldn't sell, so he killed her thinking that her kids would."

"I agree, Chief, and I also wonder if he might have sought out Sean, the oldest of her children, and made an offer to him," I said.

Following my reasoning, Chaille took up the narrative. "And maybe he either refused, like your mother did, or else he wanted a larger share."

"I see where you two are going here, but I have a hard time picturing a chubby little Hugo Starling stabbing big strong Sean Tempest to death," the chief said.

Chaille answered with more or less what I had said to my sister earlier that morning. "Sean's a lot bigger than Keene, but Keene didn't have any trouble handling him."

"She's right, Chief," I said. "He may have taken Sean totally by surprise."

"Or he might have learned some skills in prison," Chaille added. "Who knows, even though he's short and flabby, he might be very skilled with a knife."

Then I had another thought. "Or he might not have been alone. Maybe there were two guys in that room with Sean that night."

"But who do you think the other person might have been?" Damion sat back in his chair and folded his arms.

"Maybe it was his old bank robbery partner," Chaille said, again voicing my own thoughts.

Then another thought struck me, and I was curious to see if Chaille could again finish my thought. So I said, "The man, the accomplice, was shot in the leg, right?"

The chief nodded, and Chaille did not disappoint me. "So his partner might walk with a limp. Keene, call Paige Everest and ask her if the guy who was seeing your mother, the one we think might have been stealing from her, walks with a limp."

Wow, was I beginning to think that this girl and I could make a whale of a team.

"I agree with Chaille, Keene. Call Paige. Maybe there's a reason, other than old-fashioned romance, that Jim McLaren was trying to get close to your mother," Chief Thompkins said.

"Maybe Hugo hid all the money," Chaille and I both said in striking unison. The three of us began to laugh.

"And it might be somewhere in your hotel, someplace where it could not easily be removed unless you were the owner of the establishment," the chief said. "I suppose it could be in the walls or under the floor or someplace even more creative."

I nodded in grim agreement as I pulled out my cell phone, looked up Paige's home phone number in my contact list, and called it. She was groggy when she answered, but she perked right up when she realized who was calling.

"Paige, I'm sorry to wake you up. This will only take a minute, but it's important."

"That's okay," she said. "What do you need me to do?"

I was lucky to have an employee who was as loyal and willing to help as Paige was. "I need for you to think about Jim McLaren for a minute. You've described him to me before, but aside from his physical description, is there anything about him that might be unusual?"

"Hmm." She paused for a moment, thinking. "Do you mean something like his limp?"

CHAPTER TWELVE

THE FIRST THING I DID after receiving that rather significant bit of information from Paige was to call Tom Brolin. He was more than encouraging, telling me that it sounded like we were on the right track and that he was working hard to find Jim McLaren. He felt that this new bit of information would aid him in the search. He even said, "I wonder if he's the man who took a shot at you and hit me." Then he added, "Would you like to call Offerman Security, or would you like me to?"

"I'll call," I said. Once more the information was received with enthusiasm. After ending that second call, I looked over at Chaille and then at Chief Thompkins. "Where do we go from here?"

As we discussed what we felt would be most productive, a call came in for the chief. He spoke briefly on the phone. "Yes, I know where Keene is. He and Officer Donovan are seated right here in my office." He listened and then said, "How soon can you be here?"

Chaille and I looked at each other. She was looking hopeful, and I was feeling that way. *Perhaps*, I thought, *we're about to get another break in the case.* We waited until the chief was finished, and then Chaille asked, "Who was that, Chief?"

With a frown he answered, "It was our favorite detective from the sheriff's office. He says he has some evidence he wants me to see."

"Did he say what it is?" I asked hopefully.

"Nope, just that he wants to meet with me right away. He's on his way now."

"Then, if it's okay with you, Keene and I can wait and see what he's learned," Chaille suggested. "If it's any good—which would surprise me—maybe we can reassess our day's plans."

"I'd love to have you two stay, but Detective Bentley specifically asked about you, Keene. Then he told me that what he had was for my eyes and ears only," Chief Thompkins said with a scowl. "I'm like you, Chaille. I can't imagine that he's discovered anything that will help us, but I can't refuse to meet with him on the outside chance that it might."

"Why doesn't he want me here?" I asked, feeling a slow anger beginning to build.

"He said he doesn't trust you," the chief replied. "And as for you," he added, turning to Chaille, "he thinks you shouldn't be a cop. I think he's against women in law enforcement in general."

Chaille rolled her eyes. "He's told me that to my face. The guy is incompetent. And frankly, I'd prefer to not be here when he comes anyway."

"I'll talk to the guy," Damion said without enthusiasm. "You two go ahead and see if you can learn about what Hugo was doing when Sean was killed, and try to see what else you can discover about when he might have been seen with your mother. We need witnesses."

An hour later, Chaille and I, having learned nothing of value, were summoned back to the chief's office. He seemed quite uncomfortable when we walked in, and he waved us to the chairs we'd occupied earlier. "What did Detective Bentley have?" Chaille asked before the chief had spoken a word.

"He claims a witness approached him," Damion began. He paused, rubbing his hand over his eyes. Chaille and I waited for him to continue. "This is difficult, Keene," he finally resumed. "He says the witness was drinking with you in a bar the night before you took over the management of the hotel."

"Whoa right there," I exploded. "That's a lie. I can prove it. Who's the witness? I'd like to confront him face-to-face."

"You'll do no such thing," Damion said sternly. "I'll deal with the witness, and I'll do it this morning. But first, answer a question for me."

I got up and began to pace the room. It was not the unnamed witness that had my temper near the breaking point. It was Detective Vernon Bentley. I knew he'd made the whole thing up and that if there was a witness, he was put up to whatever he was claiming by the detective. I said nothing of my thoughts. I just let them churn in my mind.

"Keene, your mother, as I recall, was a Mormon like Officer Donovan here," he said. "You don't have to answer this, but I need to ask. Are you a Mormon too?"

"Yes, I am," I said angrily. "And no to your next question, Chief; I do not drink any kind of alcoholic beverage. And it's not just because of my religion. I've not tasted so much as a drop of the stuff in my entire life. My sister's at the hotel. She can tell you that. Furthermore, I never even go into bars except in the capacity of a police officer."

"I believe you," Damion said.

"So do I," Chaille said, touching my hand softly with her own. It sent a thrill through me.

To my regret, she removed her hand as I looked over at her. "Thanks," I said. I turned back to the chief. "And thanks to you too. What did Bentley say the so-called witness claimed?"

Damion's face darkened. "The witness, Bentley reported, says he had a conversation with you about Sean."

"Oh, that's interesting." My infamous temper began to build again.

"Yes, it is. But listen, Keene. It gets worse. He says the witness told him that you threatened to kill Sean."

I felt like steam could be escaping the top of my head. I needed something to break. Thankfully, there was nothing. I fought my temper and gradually began to get it under control. The chief and Chaille were watching me as I stormed back and forth across the back of the office. When I was finally enough in control to stop pacing, the chief spoke again.

"He says you were angry Sean made you come and take over the hotel."

"Now that much is true," I admitted. "But I did it for my mother, not for Sean or for Grady or for Bree." I sat down beside Chaille again. "Now I'm glad I came. Maybe I can get justice for my mother."

"Is there any more?" Chaille asked Damion.

"That's pretty much it. I'll find the guy and get it straight from him," he answered, his mouth tight with what appeared to be growing anger.

"He's lying. Either he is or Bentley is," Chaille said. "Or they both are."

"I'm sure you're right. Okay, so I guess while you guys go back to investigating Hugo Starling, I'll see if I can locate Detective Bentley's *witness*," he said, clearly upset as he got to his feet, shoving his chair back from the desk.

Chaille and I exited the office ahead of him. But he was right behind us, mumbling under his breath. He brushed past as we approached the outside door. He appeared almost as angry as I'd been just moments before. "Good luck, guys," he said with a tight voice. He blew through the front door, letting it swing shut. Chaille and I watched through the glass in silent surprise as he headed toward his vehicle.

***

Back in Chaille's patrol car, my anger melted away, and I began to chuckle.

"What's so funny, Keene?" Chaille asked, looking at me with raised eyebrows.

"You'd think that even an incompetent cop like Bentley would at least take the time to learn a *little* about me before saying what he did." I smiled at her. "It is funny, Chaille. Anyone who knows me knows that such an accusation is laughable."

She smiled back, and it made my skin tingle. She was a wonderful, supportive woman, and I felt lucky to get to work with her.

"I think we should go talk to Tess Everest. Maybe she knows something about Hugo and what kind of offer he made to my mother," I suggested.

"She might even be involved in doing Hugo's accounting," she pointed out. "She does work for the only accounting firm in Hardy."

As it turned out, Chaille was spot on. Tess handled the Hardy Café's accounts, but she was not about to divulge private information about the café's finances. I respected that. We could subpoena the information later if we felt we needed it. However, she did have some personal knowledge of an offer Hugo had made my mother.

"Do you know how much he offered?" I asked.

"No, only that he said it was very generous," Tess replied. "Why are you asking me this? Is he trying to buy it from you now, Keene?"

"As a matter of fact, he is. How much do you know about Hugo's past?"

"I know he spent time in prison," she said. "But as far as I know, he's done fine since he was released. Of course, all that was before my time, so I don't have any firsthand knowledge of his past."

"If you were in my shoes, would you sell to Hugo?"

Her face clouded. She slowly shook her head even as she said, "I can't tell you about his finances, but no, I probably wouldn't."

"Why not?" I asked.

She shifted nervously on her chair. But finally she said, "I just wouldn't. Let's leave it at that."

I was okay with that, but I did have another question. "Did my mother ask you if she should sell to him?"

She shook her head. "No, but as I told you before, she did tell me about him pressing her to sell. She didn't want to, and frankly, I told her that I agreed with her. It was shortly after that that the hotel began to lose money."

"Do you see any connection between that and my mother's refusal to sell?"

She was quick to reply. "No, the connection I see is what we discussed earlier. It was also when she started seeing Mr. McLaren that the hotel started doing badly."

"Thanks, Tess. You've been a great help," I said as I rose to my feet. Chaille did the same.

"I'm sorry I can't tell you more about Mr. Starling's finances," Tess said. "Why don't you just ask him yourself?"

"No, it doesn't matter that much. I'm not looking into selling the hotel. I, or rather, we are investigating a couple of murders," I said.

Suddenly, Tess's eyes grew wide, and her hands began to tremble ever so slightly. "You don't think Hugo could have been involved, do you?" she asked.

I shrugged my shoulders, but before I could answer, Chaille spoke. "This is a murder investigation. We'll consider anyone who crosses our radar."

"I agree. Well, if there's anything more I can do to help, don't hesitate to call," Tess responded, a worried look crossing her face. Then she asked again, "Do you really think he could be involved?"

"Yes, it's possible," I said. "And so we have to look into it. Is there something you know that would make it unlikely?"

"Yes," she said, after a short hesitation. "His cousin is a deputy sheriff, and it just seems like a guy with a law enforcement relative right here in the county wouldn't be as likely to do something like that."

"I don't know that that would make a difference for some folks," Chaille commented wryly. "Who's his cousin?"

"He's a detective with the sheriff's department. His name is Vernon Bentley," she said, causing the hair on the back of my neck to stand up. "He's a few years younger than Hugo."

Chaille and I exchanged glances, and we both, uninvited, sat down again. I leaned forward, looking Tess right in the eye, and asked, "How well do you know Detective Bentley?"

"I can't really say I know him," she said. "I mean, I may have spoken to him a few times, and of course I'd recognize him if I saw him, but that's about it."

I sat back, glanced at Chaille, and when she gave me a slight nod, I forged ahead. "What would you say if Detective Bentley told you that he talked to someone in a local bar who said he'd talked to me the night before I took over the hotel?"

"I suppose you did talk to people," she said warily. She clasped her hands together, and some of the trembling I'd observed stopped. "But that's not all you were going to ask, is it?"

"That's right. So suppose Bentley says the guy reported that I was drinking with him and that I was quite drunk?"

Her eyes went wide. "But you don't drink, do you?"

"No, I don't, and I never have. But suppose that Bentley further told you that I, in my drunken state, told the witness that I wanted to kill by brother?"

"Then I'd know that someone was telling lies, someone who wanted to get you into trouble," she said indignantly.

"And why do you suppose someone would do that?" I asked.

Tess was thoughtful for a moment, and then she ventured, "Maybe he was bribed." She was thoughtful once again. "Or protecting someone else he believed might have done it?" I looked at her clasped hands. She was gripping them so tightly they were turning white.

"Exactly." I wondered what I could say to the chief to convince him to get Bentley off the case and to investigate him as a possible conspirator or, at the least as a cop who was involved in a cover-up.

"Hey, you guys, maybe knowing what I know now, I can tell you just a hint about Hugo's finances. But you've got to promise me you'll never tell anyone I told you. My boss would be furious," she said, unclenching her fists and running one hand nervously through her hair.

"I don't want to get you in trouble, Tess. So don't say anything that you think might cause you problems," I told her.

"I will say just this much. Hugo Starling has borrowed against the café. There's no way he has the money to buy the hotel. I think he would even have a hard time getting a loan unless he could make a large down payment, and I'm pretty sure he can't."

"Could he have any money that you don't know about?" Chaille asked.

"I suppose so, but I can't imagine where he would have gotten it unless he's been hiding money so he doesn't have to pay taxes on it," she answered. Then she forced a grin and, trying to lighten the mood, added, "Or maybe he robbed a bank or something . . ." She trailed off when she saw Chaille and I look at each other. Then, without any prompting, she said quite softly, "He did rob a bank, didn't he?"

We both nodded our heads, and she spoke again. "I'm scared, you guys. I wish that I had nothing to do with Hugo." Not only her hands were trembling now, but her whole body was shaking.

"You'll be okay, Tess," I tried to reassure her. "Just don't let on that you know anything about what we've discussed today. Don't do anything different around him. I mean, talk to him in the store if you see him if that's what you would normally do. Or call him to report on his accounting when you usually would. Even meet with him if you have to, but when you do meet, just try to make sure someone else is around without it being too obvious."

"Keene, I'm not only scared for me. I'm scared for you too. If Hugo did kill your mother and your brother, what's to keep him from coming after you as well?" she asked.

"We are very much aware of the danger to Keene and the rest of his family," Chaille said. "That's one of the reasons we've got to solve this case sooner rather than later."

We left a badly shaken Tess Everest a few minutes later. Back in the car, Chaille said, "Do you think that maybe Detective Bentley could be involved?"

"It seems like a stretch, but he *is* accusing me without any evidence at all. Without even knowing that he and Hugo are cousins, I was beginning to be suspicious of the guy. But then, maybe it's just because I don't like him. Which I definitely don't," I concluded.

My cell phone rang. I answered it quickly when I saw who was calling. "Hi, Bree, I hope you have good news."

"I'm afraid not," she said, and my gut twisted.

"What happened?"

"Jean just called me in tears," she reported. "She was just served with divorce papers. Can you believe Grady's being such a jerk over not wanting a baby? He's divorcing Jean over it. And the fool apparently still doesn't believe he's in danger. What's the matter with him?"

I didn't have an answer for that. I thought they'd had a solid marriage, but I now supposed that there were marriage problems that went beyond the pregnancy. My sister began to cry and finally had to hang up because she could no longer speak.

CHAPTER THIRTEEN

CHAILLE AND I MADE A couple more stops which produced no further leads. I was anxious to speak with Chief Thompkins about what we'd learned from Tess. We listened to radio traffic, hoping he'd soon be checking out of his car back at the office. He finally did, and we drove directly there.

When we entered his office, the chief's mood was not much improved.

I broached the subject. "So how was your interview with the man who thinks I'm a drunk and a killer?" I tried to sound lighthearted.

"The guy's sticking to his story," he snapped, the anger clear in his voice.

Before I got a chance to ask him another question, we were interrupted by the dispatcher, who announced there was a shoplifting suspect being detained at the local grocery store. "First a break-in and now a shoplifter," the chief said. He looked directly at Chaille. "I'll need you to take that. Despite all that we've got going, we still need to take care of our local businesses. Keene and I need to talk."

"I'll get right on it, Chief," she said and rose gracefully to her feet. "I'll catch you later, Keene." With that and a quick smile, she left. And I felt her absence. Being with Chaille Donovan was getting to be something I enjoyed—a lot.

The chief looked at me with a worried face. "Somehow we've got to break this guy down. He swears it was you, that you were drunk, and that you threatened to kill Sean. He says you referred to your brother by name."

"I have a question, Chief. Did he contact Bentley, did Bentley contact him, or do you know?"

"He claims he went to the detective when he heard about your brother's death," the chief responded.

"Okay, so we dismantle him," I said wearily. "I didn't even get into Hardy until the morning I took over the hotel. I met Sean there as soon as I got into town."

"Who can corroborate that?" he asked. "I know Sean could have . . ."

When he trailed off, I said, "I bought gas at about five that morning at some station two hundred miles from Hardy."

The chief brightened up. "Do you have a receipt?"

"Yes, I do. I paid with my Visa at the pump."

"Great, that's what we need."

"I have something for you too," I said. "Officer Donovan and I spoke with Tess Everest earlier. She's the accountant who keeps the books for the hotel."

"Yes, I knew that," he said, leaning forward slightly, apparently very interested in what I was about to say. His mood was enough improved that I seriously wondered if he'd been harboring doubts about me after interviewing the so-called witness. "What did she have to say?"

"Several things, but the most critical was about the relationship between Detective Bentley and Hugo Starling."

"What relationship is that?"

"They're cousins."

Damion's fist came down on his desk so hard it bounced. "That explains it," he said. "I knew that guy was worthless as a cop, but I don't think a lot of people around here know that he's related to the town's most notable ex-con." He scrunched his face for a moment and then asked, "How sure is Tess of this? Could she be wrong?"

"She seemed totally confident."

"Okay, but do the men actually have anything to do with one another?" he asked. "Maybe Bentley doesn't even claim him. If we could find someone or, better yet, several people who can verify that the men actually have an association with one another, it would be helpful."

"I'll go to work on that."

"If you can find anyone, anyone at all, who's seen the two of them together recently, then I'll bring in the witness and find out exactly why he came up with his story," Damion said.

"I'm betting that he was paid by our not-so-friendly detective to say what he said."

Since my chauffeur was at the grocery store dealing with a shoplifter, the chief had me take another patrol car—an old, mostly retired one. I first drove by the hotel to check on things there. Joy Everest, my newest employee, was on duty at the front desk when I came in. "Good morning, Mr. Tempest," she said with a friendly smile that reminded me a great deal of her two daughters.

"Good morning," I greeted her, although I noted that it was slightly after noon by now.

"Your sister said that if you came in, she'd like to talk to you," Joy said. "She said she'd be in your apartment."

"Thank you. I'll go see what she needs."

I found Bree talking on her cell phone. She gave me a *just a moment* signal with her fingers, so I went into my tiny kitchen and opened a can of tuna. I had nearly finished making my sandwich when Bree came in.

"I was talking to Jean," she said. Her eyes were red, and I could tell it hadn't been a happy talk.

"I still can't believe Grady is divorcing her and leaving her to raise the baby on her own," I said. "I can't think of anything much crueler than that. Would you like a tuna sandwich?"

"Yeah, I could use one," she said, rubbing her eyes. "I talked to Grady too."

That caught me by surprise. "You did?" I asked. "Did you call him or did he call you?"

"I tried the number he called you from for probably the twentieth time, and I was surprised when he finally answered."

"Were you able to talk any sense into him?" I asked.

Bree snorted. "Not hardly. I didn't realize he was so stubborn. I thought Sean was stubborn, but Grady is unbelievable. He says he really doesn't think he's in danger, but if he is, that he can take care of himself. And as for Jean, his exact words were, 'You haven't had to live with her.' He didn't expound on that, but I could tell he had no intention of trying to work things out. I tried to talk sense into him, but he wouldn't hear it. He did say he wouldn't leave her financially high and dry, that he'd pay alimony and child support. And apparently, he told Jean that too."

"Well, that's something at least. Did you ask him where he was?"

"I did, but he just said he was on a business trip. That, of course, isn't true. I asked Jean when I called her, and she said his boss had called all irate and told her to tell Grady, when she heard from him, that he was fired," she reported. "Of course, maybe he's looking for a new job somewhere."

"If he wasn't, he'll need to now," I said. My heart was breaking for Jean. I finished the sandwiches, got us each a glass of milk, and then sat down to eat lunch, such as it was. After a couple of bites, I broke the silence. "What's Jean going to do?"

Bree chewed her sandwich for a moment, took a sip of milk, then answered, "She says she's going to look for a job; that even if Grady pays alimony, it won't be enough; that she has to get some money coming in."

"How's she feeling? I mean, you know, does she have any morning sickness?"

"She says a little but not too bad. She's just really, really broken up. She says she thought they had a good marriage. She'd hoped that it was his worrying about a threat that had caused their marital stress, but he says he wasn't ever threatened. It looks like he is determined, so she'll just make the best of it, as hard as it is."

We both finished our sandwiches in silence. I was thinking about my sister-in-law when an idea came to me. "Bree," I started as we both carried our dishes to the dishwasher. "I wonder if Jean would consider coming here and taking care of the hotel. I'd really rather work in law enforcement. Of course, I could help her for a while; although, I can't exactly say I know a lot about running this place."

Bree looked at me for a moment, and then she began to smile. "Keene, I think that's a great idea."

"She could make a living here, and she'd have a home to raise her child in," I continued. "But will she feel uncomfortable knowing that Grady is part owner?"

"That won't matter if you and I stick together. Between us, we own the majority. Anyway, I suspect that he really won't care. In fact, he might even think it's a good idea." Her smile faded. "What are we going to do about Sean's share? I suppose there will have to be a probate of some kind on his property, and this would be part of that."

"We'll cross that bridge later," I said. "First we need to catch the killer or killers. And we can offer to let Jean come up here right away."

"I'll call her, Keene, if you're sure."

"I'm sure," I said as my iPhone began to ring. I noted it was Sergeant Brolin calling from Los Angeles. "Good afternoon, Tom. Have you learned anything about Mr. McLaren?"

"That's why I'm calling," he said. "I have been summoned back to work, a desk job of some kind while I continue recuperating. It makes me mad. I can work as good as the next guy. I'm feeling just fine."

I was reading between the lines. "So you aren't going to be able to keep looking for McLaren."

"I can spend a little time, but I can't afford to lose my job, and if I don't do what they ask and warm a desk for a while, they might just let me go."

"I appreciate what you've done," I said. "Maybe Offerman and his people have come up with something."

"I talked to them this morning. They've come up with the route that McLaren follows. He goes from city to city in a very organized pattern. The company he sells insurance for turned the information about his route over to the agency," he said. "But they also told me it's going to be expensive to have someone follow that route and see if they can catch up with him."

I knew what had to be done. "Tom," I said, "I'll talk to the agency. You just get back to work. We'll catch up with McLaren. And I'll keep you informed."

"I'll help when I can, Keene. I mean it. This thing is personal. I want the guy that put a bullet in me behind bars," he said.

So did I. And I was determined not to rest until it was done. When I'd finished my conversation, Bree had finished another call to Jean.

"What did she say?" I asked.

"She's grateful, and she accepts," Bree told me. "She knows you didn't want to come in the first place and that she would love to do it. She says she isn't worried about Grady's portion. She's got a meeting with a lawyer later this afternoon, and she's going to ask him to help her get his share of the hotel and let Grady have the equity in their house in exchange."

"That just might work." I nodded. "When can she come?"

"She says she'd like to come in the next couple of weeks if she can get some things worked out down there," Bree answered. "I'm glad you thought of having her come. She's a good person."

"What do you hear from your husband?" I asked in a brighter tone.

"He should be here in the morning, but if not, he'll be here the next day for sure. He's going to take the girls to his folks' place instead of bringing them here like we'd planned. He figured they'll be safer there. His folks live quite a ways away from us. The kids are all excited about going to their grandparents. Anyway, he persuaded his boss to give him a couple of weeks off. What was your call about?"

I told her, and she moaned. "Bree, if you and Ron can take care of things here, I'll talk to the police chief about letting me go after Jim

McLaren. The Offerman Agency has a copy of the route he follows. I'll go to LA, meet with Mr. Offerman, get with the insurance company McLaren works for, and then see if I can catch up with him somewhere along his sales route."

"Keene, that sounds dangerous," she said with worry in her eyes.

"Everything about our lives is dangerous right now. Just living next door to a business run by Hugo Starling is dangerous."

She nodded her agreement. "We'll take care of things here if you really feel you should go."

"Thanks, Bree," I said. "You're a great sister."

She cleared her throat and rubbed at her eyes. Finally, she managed a smile. "I'll bet that's something you never thought you'd say."

She was right, but I didn't say so. I just gave her a hug and left the apartment. As I passed the registration desk, I thought I'd begin with Joy in my attempt to find out if anyone had seen Hugo Starling and his cousin, Detective Bentley, together recently.

So I stopped and stepped over to the counter across from Joy and said, "I suppose you know Hugo Starling and Detective Vernon Bentley."

She frowned. "I don't like to speak ill of people, Mr. Tempest, but I frankly don't care for either of those men. Do you know about what Hugo did when he was a young man?"

"I do."

"Well, I don't know that he's changed a lot since then. I go in his café sometimes, but whenever I do, I hope he isn't there. He makes me nervous," she said.

"What about his cousin?"

"I know he's a cop and that you are too. I suppose it's only natural to look out for one another. I've heard it said that there is a brotherhood among the police," she hedged.

"There is, but sometimes there are bad cops among us. We as a brotherhood like to weed that kind out."

"Then you should weed Vernon Bentley out," she said sharply. She clapped her hand over her mouth. "I'm sorry, Mr. Tempest. I shouldn't say things like that."

"In this case, it's quite all right. And call me Keene if you'd like."

"No, you're my boss. It just wouldn't be right."

I let that go. "Besides being cousins and not necessarily nice guys, do you know if they actually do things together? I mean, where Vernon's a cop and Hugo's an ex-con, I would be surprised if the cop side of Vernon would let him associate with Hugo, cousin or not."

"Oh, they associate, all right," she muttered, shaking a finger in the direction of the café next door. "A couple of my friends and I went in the café for lunch not a week ago. Detective Bentley came in while we were there. Hugo came out from the back, and the two of them sat and drank coffee together. They were talking softly, but every once in a while they'd laugh. Detective Bentley left before we did, and when he did, he slapped Hugo on the back and said something about something working out just fine, that it was only a matter of time until he got it. I have no idea what he was referring to."

I thought maybe I did. "Thank you for telling me that, Joy," I said, elated. "Is there anything I can do for you here before I go back to the police station?"

"No, Mr. Tempest. Paige filled me in quite nicely on what I need to do, and that sweet sister of yours has been a help today too. You know, she reminds me a little of your mother."

That was something I'd never seen before, but since Bree and I had worked out our differences and I was seeing a different side of my sister, I could see what Joy meant. And for that I was grateful.

I left the hotel and drove back to the station, feeling grateful that I'd made peace with one of my siblings. Now if I could somehow find Grady and make peace with him as well, I'd feel like we were a family after all.

Chaille was back at the office when I walked in. She greeted me with a smile. Boy, did I like that smile. I sent her back one of my own. "Did you get your shoplifter arrested?" I asked.

"I did," she said with a disgusted shake of her head. "It was a woman of about thirty. She admitted the theft but made a terrible fuss that she was being arrested for something that only costs about five dollars. I pointed out that to the owners of the store, that theft of five dollars was just one of many. The owner added that they lose at least twenty-five thousand dollars a year to theft, most of it in small amounts like that. The lady didn't care. She just wanted me to think *she* was the victim, being arrested and all. But too bad, I don't feel sorry for her. I'd guess that she's stolen a lot of times and gotten away with it. Anyway, now you and I can get back to work on the murders," she finished.

It was interesting how we all now simply accepted my mother's death as a homicide although we had nothing to prove it. There had been no autopsy, and the idea of exhuming her body and having one done now had been ruminating in my mind. But it was not an idea that gave me any pleasure. In fact, I prayed that it wouldn't come to that.

"Is the chief still in?" I asked.

"He is, and he wants to talk to the two of us again."

When we walked into his office, the chief got right down to business. "Have you had a chance to talk to anyone about Hugo and Vernon?" he asked as Chaille and I were sitting down.

"As a matter of fact I have," I replied, feeling just a tiny bit smug.

After I told him what Joy said, he reared back in his chair. "I'll be bringing in Mr. Alvin Cramer for a little visit," he said. "And, Keene, I'd like you to be here when I do."

"Alvin Cramer!" Chaille said hotly. "Is he the so-called witness? He's just a drunk and not a very nice man, even on those rare occasions when he is sober."

"I take it you don't like him very well," Damion said with a grin.

"I don't like him at all," she returned. "Would you like me to go get him?"

"Do you know where he lives?" the chief asked.

"Oh yes, I know, all right."

"Great, then go get him."

"I'll check the bar first," Chaille grunted. "After all, it's after one now, so it's open. He'll likely be there already. Do you want to come too, Keene?" she asked.

I started to get up because I did want to go, but Chief Thompkins said, "No, you stay here. You and I need to plan our approach in dealing with Mr. Cramer. And then, Chaille, when you bring him in, you may sit in if you'd like."

"Thanks, Chief," she said, and she left, my eyes following her until she was out the door and out of sight.

"She's a great girl." Damion was watching me with a smug smile.

I felt myself go red in the face. "Yes, she is," I stammered.

"Hey, she likes you, Keene. If I were to give you one piece of personal advice, it would be this: don't let her get away." Before I could try to figure out a response, Damion went on. "I want you to come into the room here after Chaille brings Cramer in."

He then went on to explain what his plan was, and I couldn't help but smile. I quickly agreed with him. With a little luck, the "witness" would be causing Detective Bentley some serious heartburn before the afternoon was over.

"There's something else I need to talk to you about, Chief," I said. I told him about my phone conversation with Sergeant Brolin. "I know it's asking a lot, but I'd like to pursue the matter personally. I'll do it on my own time. I know it'll leave you shorthanded, but I feel like I can catch up with him. And I think it's important."

"What about the hotel?"

"My sister and her husband will take care of it while I'm gone."

"Then go. The department will at least cover some of your expenses. After all, even though it is your family who are the victims, the crimes occurred in my town," he said. "How soon do you want to leave?"

"As soon as we're through with Mr. Cramer."

"Miss Donovan might not be too happy," he said with a twinkle in his eyes.

"Honestly, I wish she could go too," I told him with a smile. "I enjoy working with her."

CHAPTER FOURTEEN

I WAITED IN A SMALL office that was there for the use of the officers—
Chaille, Payton, and, I guessed, for me too. When Chaille came in, she
said, "I just left Cramer in the office with the chief. He told me to come
here and wait. I thought he was going to let the two of us be there while
he questions Cramer. And why are you in your jeans? Where's your new
uniform?"

"I went back to the hotel and changed. How do I look?"

"You look very good," she said, blushing. "I like you in cowboy boots
and a western hat. But I don't get it."

"Then maybe I better explain what we're going to do." As I laid it out,
the chief's plan made her smile. "So, I'll see you in a moment." Our eyes
held for a moment, but then I pulled mine away. I swear I could feel her
gaze on my back as I walked up the hall toward Damion's office. I looked
forward to getting to know Chaille Donovan a lot better.

When I stepped through the chief's door, he said, "Oh, Mr. Cramer,
I'm sorry for the interruption. This fellow needed to speak to me for just
a moment. This is Kenton Jones. I don't suppose you know him, do you?"

"No, never seen him before. What do you want, Chief Thompkins?
I'm a busy man," Alvin Cramer whined.

I kept my smile to myself. I didn't even let it show when I looked up
at the camera that Damion and I had placed on the top of his bookcase
while Chaille was picking up our "witness."

"Ah, Mr. Jones, why don't you just sit down here for a moment? Mr.
Cramer might be interested in what we have to talk about," the chief
drawled.

"I don't know what kind of game you're playing at here, Chief
Thompkins, but I really need to go."

"Your beer will wait, Alvin," Damion said. Then he looked past Alvin and called, "Officer Donovan, come on in. I trust you know what's going on here."

I looked at Chaille. She was smiling but wiped her face clean when Alvin twisted in his seat and looked at her. He started to get up, but the chief said in a commanding voice, "Sit down, Cramer. I didn't tell you that you could leave."

"What's going on here?" Alvin asked. "I already told you all I know. You should be grateful. I helped you solve your case."

"You did help but not in quite the way you suppose. Are you quite sure you don't know Mr. Jones here?"

"Of course I'm sure. I've never seen this squirt of a cowboy in my life. I'm getting angry, Chief Thompkins. I thought you needed my help."

"Actually, what I'd like is for you to tell Officer Donovan and Mr. Jones what you told me."

"It ain't none of Mr. Jones's business," he protested.

"Mr. Jones might look like a cowboy to you," Damion said. "But he's actually a police officer. I've asked him to help us with the case of the murder of Sean Tempest. He comes to us highly recommended."

Cramer had no response to that, so the chief repeated, "Tell them about your meeting with a Mr. Keene Tempest at the bar the other night."

"There ain't much to tell. Mr. Tempest comes in and starts drinking. He was already pretty drunk when he came in. But he's putting the stuff away. Pretty soon, he comes over to my table and asks if he can sit there. I told him he could, and so he did."

"What did the two of you talk about?" I asked.

"Oh, lots of stuff, but eventually he started telling me about himself. He says he's in town to take over the Tempest Hotel. He says his name is Keene Tempest and that his brother wants the hotel for himself. The guy said that his mother left it to him and nobody was going to horn in on his deal."

"What did he say he'd do about it?" I asked.

"He said he'd kill his brother if he got in his way. He said there was no way his brother was going to get the hotel."

"Was that all?" I asked.

"Pretty much. The guy was really drunk, so a lot of the time he just sat there and poured beer down his throat," Alvin said.

I was seated to his right and slightly in front of him in a chair the chief had placed near the side of his desk. I leaned toward Alvin and said, "Would you describe Mr. Tempest to me? You know, tell me what he looked like, what he was wearing, how big he is, that kind of thing."

Alvin looked at me suspiciously, and then he began, "Well, he was a redhead like you and Officer Donovan here."

"Okay, what else?" I pressed.

"Well, he wasn't too big. Shorter than me, as I recall."

"What was he wearing?"

"I can't remember exactly."

"Well, just tell me as closely as you can."

"Seems like he had on a pair of slacks and a shirt," he finally said.

"That seems logical. Were the slacks tan?" I asked, remembering that I had been wearing tan slacks the morning we found Sean's body, the morning Detective Bentley had spoken with me.

"Yeah, that's right," he said, his watery green eyes lighting up a little.

"And the shirt, was it maybe brown?" I asked.

"Yeah, I think so."

A brown shirt was hanging in my closet at the hotel. "Did he have a hat?"

Alvin seemed to search his memory for a moment. Slowly, he shook his head. "I can't remember. He might have had one."

I looked at the chief, who then took over. "Alvin, did that man look anything like Mr. Jones?" he asked, pointing at me.

"Same color hair, maybe about the same size. But other than that, no."

I took off my hat. The chief pointed to me again. "How about without the hat?" he asked.

He was looking a bit uncomfortable, like he knew a hammer was about to fall but not quite knowing why. "Not really," he finally responded.

"If Keene Tempest were to walk in, would you know him?" the chief asked as he leaned forward on his desk, his eyes boring into Cramer's.

He hesitated, looking at me, at Chaille, and at the chief, and then back at me. "Of course I would," he snapped. "Now can I go? I've told you everything I know."

"No, you can't go, but Officer Jones may." The chief turned to me and said, "Thanks." I got up, and carrying my hat, I left the office. I waited a couple of minutes, then, leaving my hat in another room, I again entered the chief's office.

Damion stood up as I came in. "Alvin, there's someone I'd like you to meet."

Alvin looked back at me and frowned. Then he stood up, shaking his right hand angrily at the chief. "I don't know what kind of game you're playing here, but I've had enough. I'm leaving."

"Alvin, sit down," the chief thundered, his face dark. Alvin slowly sat back down. The chief looked at him with contempt and then said, "Alvin, please meet Keene Tempest."

The man's ruddy face went white, and his watery eyes filled with fear. He looked around as if searching for a hole to crawl into. Finding none, he again got to his feet and turned as if he were going to make a dash for the door. But Chaille grabbed his arm, shoved him back into his chair, and then stood resolutely behind him.

I sat down where I'd been when I was Mr. Jones and let my eyes bore into the man. He squirmed, but with Chaille standing where she was, there was no escape. The chief cleared his throat. "Now, Mr. Cramer, would you like to tell us why you said that you met *this man*, who you just claimed you'd never seen before, in a bar and had drinks with him?"

"I, ah, I . . ." he stammered.

"Mr. Cramer. I hope you understand the seriousness of what you've done. You accused an innocent man of murder and lied to the police—myself, these two, as well as Detective Bentley. Would you like to explain why you did that?"

For a full minute, the chief and I stared Alvin in the face. He began to tremble.

Finally, he said in a whimper, "You gotta promise to protect me."

"Protect you from whom?" the chief asked.

"From that other cop."

"What other cop?" the chief pressed. "Why would a cop want to hurt you?"

"'Cause he'll be mad," Alvin said, his eyes studying the floor in front of his chair.

"Who will be mad?" I asked.

"Detective Bentley. This was his idea."

The chief's fist came down on his desk with a resounding thump. Alvin jerked like the fist had hit him.

Then, "He told me I had to do it."

"Oh, he did, did he? How much did he pay you?"

"I can't say," Alvin said. He was shaking like a leaf in a windstorm and refused to look at any of us.

"Read him his rights, Officer Donovan. Then take him to the county jail. We'll charge him with obstruction of justice, with lying to the police, and whatever else the prosecutor can get to stick."

Chaille helped Alvin to his feet, but before any of us could even attempt to ask him any more questions, he blurted, "He gave me $500. You gotta protect me now. I swear Bentley will kill me."

"Lock him up, Chaille," Chief Thompkins ordered. "Then come back here."

Chaille began to put handcuffs on him. As she did so, the chief said to me, "I'm going to have the sheriff and the prosecutor meet me here as soon as I can get them to. Can you wait to leave for Los Angeles until after that? I'd like for you to be here when I talk to them and show them the video we just made."

I looked over at Chaille. She snapped the cuffs in place and then stared at me, shaking her head. "Why are you going to LA?" she asked.

"I'll be looking for a certain Mr. McLaren," I explained. "When I find him, I'll be back."

She continued to shake her head. "You need someone with you. It'll be dangerous."

"I'll be okay. I'd take you, but the chief needs you here."

For a long moment, she looked at me, then she turned away, grabbed Alvin by the arm, and jerked him toward the door.

"I'll still be here when you get back from the jail," I promised.

She glanced at me, forced a brief smile, and then pushed her prisoner out the door ahead of her. After she was out of sight, Chief Thompkins said, "I wish I could spare her, but I really can't."

I knew that, but it didn't make me feel any better. I couldn't imagine how someone I'd known for such a short time and who I really hadn't spent much time with could have such a powerful effect on me, but she did.

The chief called the prosecutor and the sheriff and told them both that something critical had come up on the Sean Tempest homicide and that he needed both of them to come to his office as soon as they could. He told them he had something he needed to show them. Forty-five minutes later, the chief was introducing me to the two men.

An hour later, the sheriff and prosecutor left. Chaille came back just a few minutes after they had driven away. "What did they say?" she asked when the three of us were once again seated in Chief Thompkins's office.

"The prosecutor's going to draw up charges against Detective Bentley, and the sheriff and one of his other men are going to arrest him. That man's in a lot of trouble," the chief said.

"Was the sheriff surprised?" she asked.

"Shocked would be more like it. But after viewing the video, he was convinced. He knew Bentley was related to Hugo Starling, but he had no idea the two of them had anything to do with each other," the chief explained. "Honestly, I feel sorry for the sheriff. But he's a good man, and Bentley will pay a steep price for his treachery."

"The question now is this," I began. "Could Bentley be guilty of more than just covering up for Hugo? Could he be part of a plot to kill my brother?"

As that question hung in the air like a black fog, the chief turned to me. "Keene, I know you need to be going, but before you do, may I make a suggestion?"

"Sure, Chief, go ahead."

"Take Officer Donovan someplace nice to eat," he said with a sly smile. "I'll cover things here. Anyway, Payton will be coming on soon."

"Maybe she doesn't want to go out with me," I said and received a pretty solid punch on the shoulder from the lovely officer.

"I'll go on one condition," she said. "It can't be at the Hardy Café. It would ruin my meal if I saw Hugo."

"It would ruin mine too," I agreed. "So I guess that means we have to go out of town. Is that okay, Chief?"

He pointed to the door. "Of course it's okay. And, Keene, keep me posted on everything that happens on your trip. And when you catch up with our friendly insurance salesman, talk to him about the murder of your mother. The prosecutor has agreed to draw up the charges if you can get anything on him. In the meantime, we'll see what else we can charge him with. I'm sure there's something. Now go, you two, and try to relax for an hour or so. You both deserve it."

Chaille drove her patrol car to the hotel before we went to dinner so we could head back there afterward, and the next hour, despite the dark clouds that were swirling about me, was one of the most pleasant hours of my life. Chaille and I learned more about each other's personal lives: our pasts, our hopes for the future, and even our shared faith. My mind was made up. I prayed that hers, if it wasn't now, would be after we got to know each other better.

When dinner was over, we drove to the hotel, where she waited and visited with Bree while I packed. I'd barely gotten my suitcase in the truck when Bree came running out. "Grady just called," she said. "I think he's coming to his senses at least a little bit."

"Oh, is the divorce off?" I asked hopefully.

"Oh no, he's adamant about that, but he says he'll be here for Sean's funeral or graveside or whatever we decide to do."

"Well, that's something at least," I said as Chaille squeezed my arm, the one she had been holding with both hands.

"He says he's in New York, that he's being interviewed tomorrow for a new job. He said he had to quit his old job, that his boss was a tyrant. I don't know about that, but anyway, he says if the interview goes okay, then he'll need to be there for a couple more days before he can come. He wondered if we could wait for the funeral until after that."

"We'll have to." I nodded. "I doubt I'll be back very soon."

"I told him where you were going, and he said to tell you to be careful and to let him know when you get back. He says he'll probably get here first," she reported.

"Did you tell him that we're hiring Jean to run the hotel?"

"No, I didn't think that would be wise. If he knew we'd reached out to her, he might not come even though he would be gone long before she got here."

I couldn't argue with that. Bree gave me a brief hug, said, "Be careful, Keene," and went back inside.

My good-bye to Chaille was a little longer, a little more intense, and incredibly sweet. As I stared into her eyes, I could no longer resist doing what I'd been thinking about all day. Putting my hand behind her head, I pulled her close and kissed her gently on the lips. She returned the kiss, and I knew this was something I wanted to do more. I ached at the very thought of leaving her. But I had to go. I finally got in my truck, leaving her standing beside her patrol car with tears in her eyes. I pulled out, intent on catching up with and arresting the man I believed killed my mother or was at least involved in some kind of conspiracy that led to her death—and possibly my brother's as well.

CHAPTER FIFTEEN

I DROVE THAT NIGHT UNTIL I couldn't do so safely anymore. Then I pulled off the road in a rest area, let the seat of my truck back, and fell asleep almost instantly. I awoke to someone pounding on my window. It was light outside, and the pounding was being administered by a kid who looked like he was maybe ten. I rolled the window down and asked him what he wanted.

He apparently didn't want anything because he ran when I spoke. I watched him go to a woman with a bright red blouse and blue jeans. He was laughing, but she put an end to that. I don't know what she said, but between the look on her face and his reaction, I decided he was in trouble with his mother.

I got out of my truck and stretched, a smile on my face. The kid had inadvertently created a bright beginning to the day. I headed for the restroom. The woman in red stopped me, apologizing for her son's behavior. I told her that it was okay, that I needed to get driving again anyway. I added that I thought he was a cute kid. "With a good mother like you, he'll be okay," I concluded. She beamed and thanked me.

After using the restroom, I bought some breakfast from the vending machines: a Baby Ruth candy bar, a minuscule bag of chips, and a small bottle of apple juice. I was on the road again shortly after eight. The five hours of sleep I'd managed in the discomfort of my truck seemed to be enough, for I felt reasonably refreshed as I drove onto the interstate and continued my trip west.

***

My phone rang a couple hours later. "Hi, Keene," said a voice I adored immensely. "Are you doing okay?"

I assured Chaille that I was doing fine and asked her how things were going there. "Well, I don't suppose this will surprise you, but Detective Bentley denies everything. He claims that Alvin Cramer looked him up and told the story just like he'd claimed he had from the beginning. He swears that Alvin must have been trying to set both you and him up."

"What does the sheriff say, or do you know?" I asked.

"The sheriff isn't having any of it. And he's angry. He interviewed Alvin at the jail and got a few more details. When he asked Alvin where the $500 was, Alvin told him it was in a drawer at home. The sheriff checked, and sure enough it was there. The sheriff fired Bentley this morning. Now he's in jail and threatening to sue the sheriff and Alvin and the prosecutor and even you. He says you're behind it and that it must have been you that gave Alvin the money."

"The guy is a hard case, isn't he?" I said.

"He's evil to the core, Keene. I was so glad when I heard he was in jail. That's where he belongs. I sure hope he doesn't make bail."

"What is the bail set at?"

"The chief told me it was $250,000. He thinks it should have been a million."

"I think it should have been ten times that. I sure hope no one helps him make it."

"Well, for what it's worth, Hugo's been to the jail already. From what Tess told us, I doubt if he can come up with the $25,000 it would take to get a professional bond, but you never know. Maybe he'll rob a bank or something," she teased. I could picture a smile on her face as she said it.

"That could be a real possibility," I chuckled. "You will let me know if Bentley gets out, won't you?"

"You know I will," she promised.

We talked a little longer, and then she said she had to go. My blue Ford F-150 felt very empty after her voice was gone. I drove on, thinking mostly of her. And they were all good, comforting thoughts.

An hour later, the candy bar and chips were wearing off, so I pulled off the freeway and ate at Wendy's. I was just finishing up my meal when I got another call. This time it was Tess Everest.

"Good morning, Keene," she said, sounding a little stressed. "Are you doing okay today?"

I assured her that I was and asked her what she needed.

"I'm afraid we must have missed one of your mother's credit cards when we canceled them. I didn't know about the one in question, but somebody does. It's being used quite regularly. I just got a call from a bank I didn't know your mother had ever dealt with."

I felt a chill. "If you didn't know about it, maybe it's because it didn't exist," I said.

Tess followed my thinking. "Are you suggesting that someone used her personal information to open the credit card account?"

That was exactly what I was suggesting. "Jim McLaren," I said angrily. "I'm looking for him now. I guess we just *thought* he'd stopped stealing."

"Keene, be careful," Tess cautioned with even more stress in her voice. "If he's the person who caused your mother's death, then he wouldn't hesitate to do the same to you."

"I'm well aware of that."

"I know you are. But I worry anyway. We all do."

I wasn't sure who *we all* meant, but I was grateful for the good friends I had made in such a short time in Hardy. "Don't worry, Tess; just pray. That's the best protection I can think of."

"I'm doing that," she said. "We all are. Besides that, is there anything else I can do?"

"Yes, as a matter of fact, there is," I replied as a thought occurred to me that just might make my search for Jim McLaren easier. "Could you possibly have the bank trace the records of this credit card and see when and where it was used?"

"Of course," she agreed. "I'll get right on it."

I knew she would, but something in her voice bothered me. I was beginning to worry about her. I hoped she was okay. "Good. If you run into any resistance and need a court order, just call Chaille . . . or one of the other officers."

"I know Chaille will help," she said. "She likes you a lot—in case you hadn't noticed."

I had noticed, and I was very happy about it. But I didn't comment on that to Tess, a very attractive and eligible woman herself. Of course, I didn't really know much about her. For all I knew she had a boyfriend somewhere. I said, "It would help if I could find out where McLaren's been, and I have a feeling that the credit card just might be a way to establish that."

Tess promised to call me as soon as she was able to learn anything. I headed back out to my truck, started the engine, and drove on, thinking about what she'd said, how she'd reacted, and her tone that had left me worrying and a little disturbed.

I hadn't been off the phone with her for more than a few minutes before I got yet another call. This time it was from Mr. Offerman. After exchanging pleasantries, he got down to business. "I'm afraid we haven't caught up with Jim McLaren, but we have learned a little more about a couple of his ex-wives. The cops in both jurisdictions considered him a person of interest in the women's deaths, but he had tight alibis in both cases. The cases are still active, but investigators aren't looking closely at McLaren anymore. I have a feeling we'll find the same on other wives or girlfriends we might come up with. It's an expensive proposition for you, so I thought I better make sure you wanted us to keep working on it."

I thought about that for a minute. "I think maybe we should back off for right now. I'm hoping to find the guy using the route that your people discovered from his insurance company."

"I thought as much," Offerman said. "Now, I also have the areas that he usually goes to and the order in which he does so. Are you on the road?"

"I am," I told him. "I was planning to come down to LA and meet with you."

"I can save you some time and a lot of miles," he said. "Do you have a smartphone or an iPad with you?"

"I have an iPhone."

"Perfect. If you'll give me your e-mail address, I'll send you the information we have."

I gave it to him, and then I told him about the credit card. "Between my route list and a credit card usage trail, you just might be able to catch up with him," he said. "Oh, and Keene, there is one more thing I found out for you. McLaren is driving a silver Lexus, and I have the license plate number. I'll e-mail that as well."

I thanked him and ended the call.

A few minutes later, I pulled off the interstate and opened the e-mail attachment from Offerman. I studied it for a moment and then changed my travel plans. It seemed that I might not have to drive nearly as far as I had expected. I decided to head for Boise, Idaho. If, after hearing back from Tess that there was someplace else I should go, I'd change my plans again. But for now, based on what the company had told Offerman's agents, it seemed likely that McLaren was somewhere between Portland, Oregon, and Boise about now.

***

It was Chief Damion Thompkins who called to tell me Detective Bentley had been released from jail on bond. "Apparently, Hugo Starling was able to come up with the money, and he obtained a professional bond for his cousin," he reported.

"This worries me," I told Damion. "Would you kind of keep a close eye on my sister and her husband? He'll be joining her at the hotel soon. I think their kids are going to stay with her husband's parents."

"I'll drive over to the hotel right now," he promised. "At least Bentley can't do any more damage from inside since the sheriff fired him."

"But on the downside," I said, "it gives him more time to create problems for me elsewhere."

"I guess you're right," he said. "So, where are you now?"

I told him and then explained where I was heading and why. I also told him about the credit card problem Tess was working on.

"I'll help her if she needs it," he said.

***

Tess called me early in the afternoon. "Someone's been very busy with that credit card," she said. "Using it to pay for gas, food, and lodging."

"Where and when?" I asked.

She told me, and I felt a small bit of satisfaction. "It matches up with McLaren's regular route," I told Tess. "It's got to be him. Have you done anything about canceling the card yet?" I asked her.

"No, but I can get on that right away."

"No, don't," I said. "Just keep track of every time he uses it until I catch him; then you can get the account closed."

I was grateful for Tess's help, but once again she didn't sound like the girl who'd been so helpful earlier. Something was bothering her, but I had no idea what it was. I thought about calling Chaille and mentioning my concerns, but I decided against it. I thought it might all be my imagination running wild.

I got another call about an hour later. This one came as a shock. "Keene, it's Grady," my older brother said.

"Hello, Grady," I responded, not only surprised by his call but wondering what he would have to say.

"I'm sorry for giving you such a hard time," Grady said. "My marriage breaking up has really messed up my mind. I don't want to go into all the details of why we are divorcing, but believe me, it's my only choice. Jean isn't the kind of woman we all thought she was. She's trouble with a capital *T*. I simply couldn't take it anymore."

"But, Grady," I said, "what about your baby?"

He snorted. "If it's even mine," he said. "Believe me, that girl has her own agenda."

Wow, I thought. *Maybe Bree and I had misjudged Grady*. But if we had, we'd also misjudged Jean. *And I've hired her to come run the hotel*. I felt a twinge of doubt. Now I had that to worry about. I decided I better call Bree and tell her about my misgivings as soon as I was off the phone with Grady.

Grady and I talked for two or three minutes. It was the most civil conversation I remember having with him for a very long time. He knew that too, for he said, "Bree told me that the two of you are committed to being friends. I want the same thing. If you'll be patient with me, I promise I'll be the brother you never expected."

I was stunned, but I hoped that this was truly the beginning of a positive relationship with my brother. Maybe he and Bree and I could be family despite all the things that had happened in the past. My mind even flashed to what Sean had told the man in the bar about not disliking me. Maybe our family relationships were not as bad as I'd always supposed. Perhaps my insecurities of being the youngest and smallest had clouded my judgment.

"Grady, this means more to me than you can imagine. I really appreciate your call."

"It was long overdue," he said. "So Bree tells me you're after the guy you think might be behind Mom's death. I just can't believe she might have been murdered, but if you and Bree are convinced, then I have to believe it. You're both good, reasonable people."

"I'm pretty sure of it," I confirmed. "I'm also concerned about the safety of the three of us. Please, be careful, Grady."

"You have my word, Keene. I'll take care of myself. I have to go now. I'm working on a new job, a really good one, in New York. I'll tell you and Bree more about it when I come to Hardy."

"That's great, Grady."

"So are you making progress?" he asked.

"I am. I have a pretty good idea where the man is who was stealing from the hotel—the man who may be behind Mom's death. I mean, I know where he's been recently, and I know where he's headed," I told him.

"Where are you now? Bree said you were headed for LA."

"I was but not now."

"Oh? Where are you going?"

"I think Jim McLaren, that's the man we're after, is on his way from Portland to Boise right now."

"And where are you?"

"I'm getting close—to Boise, that is."

"Well, be careful. If we pull together, we'll take care of our problems. It's good to talk to you, Keene. And I promise we won't be having arguments in the future. I've turned over a new leaf. I'm a different man."

After talking to Grady, I felt both good and bad. I felt good because a healing was finally taking place in our fractured family, at least what was left of our family. But I felt bad for Jean, and I felt bad about her. I wondered if I'd made a huge mistake in trusting her. It was with reluctance that I made the call to Bree.

Bree was feeling about like I was, excited about the change in Grady but worried about how to deal with Jean and wondering who was really telling the truth.

Finally, I said, "I think we need to not let on that we have a different perspective about their problems. We'll have to handle her with kid gloves, but we also need to find a way to give ourselves an out, a way to keep from handing the management of the hotel over the way we'd planned if it turns out that Grady is telling the truth. I'm still not entirely sure he is."

"I just wish that she and Grady could work out their problems, no matter whose baby she's carrying," Bree said, emotion in her voice.

"I agree, but that may be hoping for a bit too much."

"I know, but it would be nice," she responded. "Keene, you be careful. With the three of us becoming friends at last, we don't need another tragedy to ruin it all."

"I'll be careful. Jim McLaren doesn't know I'm after him. That gives me the advantage."

"Yes, unless he and Hugo and Detective Bentley are working together," she pointed out. "And I'm afraid that's entirely possible."

That thought was very disturbing, and I felt the cold fingers of dread creep up my spine, but I shook the feeling off. "I doubt they know where I'm going," I said.

"This is a small town, Keene," she reminded me. "They could very well have figured it out. Even though Bentley's been fired, that's not to say that he doesn't still have friends in the sheriff's department, and if he does, who knows what he might be told. Be careful, Keene."

***

Despite every effort, I couldn't shake the feeling of worry that my conversation with Bree had instilled in me. I was beginning to feel like I had a bright red target on my back. Chaille called me just as I reached the outskirts of Boise. She had talked to Bree, and she was shaken. "Keene, what if Jim McLaren knows you're coming after him?"

"I'll just have to keep a lookout," I said, trying to sound nonchalant.

"That might not be enough," she said. "I wish you weren't alone. I wish I was there with you. Two pairs of eyes would be better than one."

"That's true, but as much as I'd like to have you with me, things are as they are. I'm here now, and I think I'm close. I can't back down. I owe it to my family, both those who are dead and those who aren't."

"Keene," Chaille said, the worry in her voice undiminished, "Hugo and Vernon know what you're driving. So by now, McLaren could also know. He might be watching for you."

"I also know what he's driving," I countered, trying my best to sound reassuring to her. "Mr. Offerman got the information from the company McLaren sells for."

"Did he give you the license number?"

"Yes, he did."

"That's good." She paused. "But wouldn't it be better if you changed vehicles?"

"What, trade in my truck?" I tried to sound lighthearted. "I'm attached to this truck."

She gave what could have only been a forced chuckle. "I didn't mean get rid of the truck. Just park it somewhere and rent a car."

"Hey, that's not a bad idea. I think I'll do that," I said. "First thing tomorrow morning, I'll find a place to store my truck and rent something."

"Thanks, Keene," she said quietly. I really was developing a soft spot for that girl.

When I completed my call with Chaille, the icy fingers tormenting my spine hadn't diminished. In fact, if anything, they were worse.

I drove off the interstate at the second Boise exit, pulled into a gas station, and began to fill my truck. It was late, and I didn't want to deal with changing vehicles until morning. I also didn't want to run out of gas.

While the truck was filling, I got a call from Tess. "The chief and I have been working together," she told me without a lot of enthusiasm. "He helped me put a trace on the credit card so that we can get fairly recent information. Mr. McLaren is in Boise now. He just checked into a Comfort Inn a few minutes ago."

"Do you have the address?" I asked as my heart began to pound.

She did and gave it to me. "Keene, be careful," she said. "And good luck." Why didn't it seem like her heart was in what she said?

I paid for my gas, put the address of the Comfort Inn into my navigation system, and headed for what I hoped would be a quick end to the search for Jim McLaren. I thought about calling the local police but decided to wait until I actually confirmed that McLaren was at the hotel. If his car was there, I would get backup.

Those icy fingers danced like crazy up and down my spine. But I ignored them. I had a killer to catch.

CHAPTER SIXTEEN

I PULLED TO THE SIDE of the road just a few hundred feet from the Comfort Inn. I looked at the layout of the building and parking lot. All I had to do was drive through the parking lot, look for McLaren's silver Lexus, and then pull out and wait for help to arrive.

When I get nervous, I find that a stick of gum often helps. I had a package of Juicy Fruit in my glove box. I leaned over and reached for the catch to the glove box.

I never touched that catch. A shot shattered the windshield. I dropped flat on the seat as a second bullet tore into my truck. The engine died, and I could hear steam blowing out of my radiator. I suppose the natural thing would have been to panic, but the natural thing didn't happen. A calm determination to live went through me, and I stayed low as I pulled my 9mm pistol from my belt, chambered a round, and waited, my senses on high alert and a prayer quickly winging its way heavenward.

Time passed as if in slow motion. It seemed like several seconds elapsed before the third round struck my truck, penetrating the door and passing into the fabric of the seat inches from my head. I didn't want to stay where I was; the next round could be closer, or even dead center. But sitting up would be foolhardy, so I stayed and prayed.

The next round passed the other side of my face and entered the glove box. Calmness still controlled my body, but my thoughts were flying all over the place. I wondered if that latest bullet had done any damage to my package of Juicy Fruit. Then I thought how foolish it was to worry about that when my truck was being systematically destroyed. I wondered why I was worried about unimportant things while my very life was hanging in the balance. Of course, I knew that a power far greater than anything on this earth was watching over me. Two more bullets struck the truck, but I was not hit.

Silence suddenly replaced the thunderous barrage of bullets. I waited, annoyed at the unprovoked attack, but I still didn't feel like I should sit up. Then I heard the welcome wail of sirens approaching and thought about the thanks I owed to God and to some good citizen who had called the police. The sirens came right up behind me. A moment later, both of my front truck doors opened at once. I peered up, seeing a police uniform. My anger at the shooter dissipated. "I'm not hit," I called as I wisely laid my 9mm on the floor and sat up. "The shooter was probably driving a silver Lexus," I said. "Jim McLaren. He's wanted for murder in Wyoming. I'm a cop." The wanted-for-murder bit was a stretch, but I was becoming more certain than ever that he had killed my mother.

The Boise officers put away the weapons they'd been holding, and a moment later I was out of the truck, standing on wobbling feet, explaining who I was and what I was doing. A subsequent check of the hotel failed to find any sign of Jim McLaren, although evidence of the use of the fraudulent credit card was right there at the registration desk. The signature was that of Maude Tempest, my late mother. It had been signed, we learned, by a tall woman who looked to be around fifty with long black hair and a lot of makeup. It had been busy at the time, and the woman who had processed the registration hadn't noted much more.

I concluded aloud that Jim McLaren—who was, according to Paige Everest, about six feet tall—had simply dressed as a woman to sign in.

***

I called Chief Thompkins from the police station downtown and told him what had happened. "He was expecting me," I said. "I was set up."

"I'll haul Vernon Bentley in as quickly as I can find him," the chief replied angrily. "I can't believe he got out of jail. That man's got some explaining to do."

"What's done is done," I said. "I'm sure he'll deny everything. One way or the other, I'll need to get another vehicle. I intend to keep after McLaren. I don't suppose he'll be stupid enough to continue to use that credit card."

"Probably not, but you never know," the chief agreed. "Criminals can be extremely stupid. But I think you need help. I want you to back off while I get some help over there. With all that's happened, I think the sheriff will lend me an officer to help out here. He did offer after he realized the problems his detective had caused us. I intend to take him up on it."

"Who will you send?" I asked.

"Who would you like?"

I wanted to say Chaille, but putting her in danger wasn't a pleasant thought. "Whoever you can spare."

"I'm sending Chaille."

"No, I don't think that—" I began to protest.

The chief cut me off. "She can handle herself, Keene. And she's motivated. I think she has feelings for you, and she'll do everything she can to keep both of you safe while making every effort to help you find McLaren. And I know you'll watch out for her as well."

"You know I'd love to have her with me," I admitted. "But I don't want her to get hurt."

"Keene, Chaille is in the building right now. She has already told me that she insists that I let her go."

"But you don't have to," I continued to protest.

"No, I don't, but she made herself clear. If I don't let her go, she'll just quit and go anyway. She's smart, she's pretty, and she's very stubborn."

"Chief, how did she already know I'd had trouble?"

"An officer from Boise called here right after they rescued you. They were just making sure you were who you said you were and that you were working for me."

That made sense. I should have known they'd do that. I would have done the same. "Okay, when will she be coming?" I asked as conflicting emotions of defeat and excitement battled in my head.

"She's on the phone making arrangements for a flight. Like I told you, her mind was already made up. She said she was going with or without my blessing. I'm telling you that you've made an impression on that girl. I don't want to lose an outstanding officer, so she now has my permission."

"Okay, let me know as soon as arrangements are made. I'll get a car and meet her at the airport."

"No, you'll stay put. The officers there are going to arrange a hotel for you. They'll take you there. But you'll need to make sure there is a room for her," he said. "Hold on a second. Chaille needs to talk to me."

I listened as they talked, their voices carrying through the phone. "I can't get a flight for several hours," Chaille told him.

"Then take a patrol car and drive," he directed. "I'll let Keene know." Into the phone he then said to me, "Chaille will be driving. She'll leave right away."

"Okay. But tell her to be careful. I'll watch for her at the hotel, and we'll get to looking again in the morning."

"Keene, I know you will continue to search for him, but unless you get really lucky, the odds are that he'll get away. The description and plate number of his car have been put out in Idaho and the surrounding states. I don't think he'll stick around to give you a second chance at him. On the other hand, like I said earlier, crooks can be real stupid."

So can young cops, I said to myself. I had been stupid, overzealous to get McLaren, and taking chances that the cold fingers dancing on my spine had tried to warn me to avoid. Maybe Chaille's presence would cause me to be much more cautious in the future.

***

It was very late when Chaille got in, but I had reminded her on the phone earlier to let me know when she arrived. She did just that, and I don't remember ever being so glad to see anyone in my life. We embraced. We kissed. We talked. And finally, we each went to our own rooms and tried to sleep.

The first thing I did when I awoke was check to see if, by any chance, McLaren's car had been spotted anywhere. I wasn't surprised to find that it hadn't been. However, as strange as it sounds, the credit card had been used again that morning in Twin Falls. Chaille and I were soon in her patrol car, heading rapidly east on the interstate. When we reached Twin Falls, we went to the convenience store where the credit card had been used to pay for gas and some groceries. The signature on the sales slip appeared to match the one at the Comfort Inn in Boise.

The cashier who had taken the card was off duty by the time we got there, but the manager called her at home. I soon verified that the person who signed was a tall, black-haired woman with a lot of gaudy makeup. The cashier guessed the woman could be anywhere between forty and sixty years of age. When I questioned her about the woman's height, she guessed probably somewhere around six feet.

"He's baiting us," Chaille fumed, echoing my thoughts on the matter.

"I'm sure of it, but we've just got to outsmart him," I said. "And we can't let him get the drop on us like I did in Boise."

Twin Falls was one of the cities that McLaren's employer had reported was on his route. I called Mr. Offerman, told him where I was and what was happening, and asked him if he thought McLaren's employer would give us a list of clients in Twin Falls who had seen McLaren in the past. He said he would get someone working on it and get back to me as soon as he could.

In the meantime, Chaille and I stopped at a restaurant for lunch. While we were waiting for our order to come, I called Chief Thompkins. We'd talked to him earlier as we were driving from Boise to Twin Falls, and as of then he'd been unable to locate Vernon Bentley.

When he answered his cell phone, I asked him if he'd had any success in finding Bentley.

He sighed. "I'm afraid not, but a warrant has been issued for his arrest. The judge who set bail also set some restrictions. Bentley wasn't to leave the county and was to be available on his cell phone twenty-four hours a day. He's clearly in violation of those restrictions; his bond has been revoked and the warrant issued."

"So you think he's left town?" I asked.

"I'm certain of it," Damion said.

"Did anyone check with Hugo Starling?" I asked as Chaille watched me with concern in her eyes.

"He's not around either. Surprise, surprise."

"Do you know what either of them might be driving?" I asked, disconcerted about the two men being out and about in places unknown.

"Bentley's vehicles are at his home, but Hugo's isn't."

"So it's likely that they're somewhere in Hugo's car?"

"That's what we're thinking. It is a 2005 Ford F-250, dark blue, with a heavy custom bumper on the front and a winch," the chief said, adding the license number for me.

My nerves were on edge. It seemed to me like everything was going against us.

I told that to Chaille, and her response was, "We'll get him, Keene. And someone will find Bentley and Starling. Then we've got to figure out if all three of them are somehow involved."

She spoke calmly, her eyes gently calming me. Before long my nerves had settled down, and I was ready to get back to work. She was good for me. I told her so, and it brought a smile that I dreamed of seeing many more times in my life.

A few minutes later, Mr. Offerman, good to his word, had us a list. Even though it was a long shot, we mapped out McLaren's clients on a map we'd picked up at the city offices and began going from one address to the next. We contacted and checked off more than ten names on our list.

It was on the fifteenth visit that we found someone who was helpful. Her name was Jane Parley, a woman in her mid-fifties. Slender and attractive with silver hair, bright blue eyes, and an engaging smile, Mrs. Parley invited us in when we mentioned that we were trying to make contact with an insurance salesman by the name of Jim McLaren. She asked us to sit down and then offered us tea, which we politely declined.

"I was just going to have a cup," she said. "If you don't mind, I'll drink it while we visit."

Mrs. Parley stepped from her neat and immaculate living room into what was presumably her kitchen. Seated close to Chaille on a white sofa, I leaned toward her and whispered, "I wonder what she wants to talk about. She apparently knows McLaren, but she didn't ask us anything about why we were trying to contact him."

"I guess we'll see. With a little luck, maybe she'll tell us that she's heard from him today," she responded softly.

Moments later she returned with her tea on a silver tray and placed the tray on her coffee table. She seated herself across from us, picked up her teacup, took a sip, set it back down, and then looked across at us with those very blue eyes of hers. "I haven't seen or heard from Jim for quite some time." She finally said. Disappointment washed over me, but it was washed away by her next words. "He's a beautiful but wicked man."

"Why do you say that?" I said, giving my partner a quick glance.

Jane smiled. "Because it's true." She paused. "You are a beautiful couple, very much in love, I see. I am a romantic lady, and I enjoy watching young people who are as devoted to one another as you two are."

I felt my face flush and glanced over at Chaille to see hers flush as well. I cleared my throat. "Ah, actually, we're police officers, Mrs. Parley. We are trying to find Mr. McLaren so we can ask him some very important questions."

"You may be police officers," she said with a knowing smile. "But you are also in love. I know love when I see it."

I hoped she was right. After stealing another look at Chaille, who was smiling now, I said, "I am quite fond of Officer Donovan, but we are here on police business."

"Oh, phooey, young man," she scoffed, her smile still in place. "She's not Officer Donovan to you. Don't try to fool me."

Chaille began to laugh. "You're a very bright woman," she said. "Keene and I have only been acquainted for a few days. But we are growing fond of one another."

"You are in love," she said stubbornly. "But let's get on with business. Mr. McLaren, who was once Jim to me, sold us an insurance policy a number of years ago. My husband, God rest his soul, passed away not a year after we bought the policy. It paid nicely, but I had no further need of Mr. McLaren's services. However, he continued to call on me, just to let me know he was concerned about my welfare."

"I'll bet," Chaille scoffed.

Mrs. Parley chuckled. "I like you two young people a lot. And you are clearly familiar with Mr. McLaren and his treachery. You say you are police officers. That means that Mr. McLaren has again done something awful and that you are trying to catch him to make him pay for whatever it is he's done."

"That's right," I said. "But, please, continue with your story."

"Yes, that," she said with a shake of her head. "Well, to keep from prolonging the story unbearably for you two sweet young people, let me simply say that I eventually fell in love with him. He was somewhat older than me but was an attractive and charming man. He walked with a slight limp, something he would never talk about. I must admit it added to his charm. I was a lonely woman after losing my husband, and when Mr. McLaren expressed his love for me and his desire to make me his wife, I accepted."

Chaille offered a dramatic roll of her eyes. "Did you marry him?"

"No, but it wasn't because I didn't want to. I very much desired to be Mrs. McLaren. But one day I got a phone call from a very angry woman claiming to be his wife." For the first time her smile faded completely away. "Can you imagine the shock I felt?"

"Was she his wife?" I asked.

"I'm sure she was because when I spoke with him about it, he hemmed and hawed for a moment, and then he told me that they were separated and that he would soon have a divorce. He still wanted me to marry him. The very nerve of the man," she said with disgust. "I told him I didn't ever want to see him again."

"So is that the last you've had to do with him?" I asked.

There was a moment's hesitation, and then she said, "Well, there was the matter of the credit card."

"What about a credit card?" I again glanced at Chaille.

"Well, a few days after I told him that our relationship was over, I got a bill from a credit card company," she explained. "It was one of my credit cards, but I hadn't used it for quite some time. There was quite a bit of money owed on it."

"How much is quite a bit?" Chaille asked.

"Oh, about $8,000," she said. "So I looked in my purse in the small wallet I keep my credit cards in, and that particular one was gone along with a couple of others."

"Were those others used too?" I asked.

"I'm afraid so. I had to cancel all three of them."

"I'm sure you reported the crime to the police," I said.

She hedged for a moment and then finally said, "Well, no, I couldn't be sure I hadn't just lost them."

"But you did suspect that they'd been taken by Mr. McLaren, didn't you?" Chaille asked.

Jane nodded almost imperceptibly.

"Did you do anything at all about your loss?" I spoke again.

The lady squirmed for a moment, then, looking very sheepish, she said, "No, I was afraid it would get Jim in trouble, and I didn't want that to happen. You've got to understand that I am not a vindictive person. And what I lost was not nearly as much as my dear departed husband's life insurance had paid. And after all, it was Jim who sold us that policy, so I felt a little bit indebted to him."

"How big was the policy?" I asked.

"It was for $300,000. So you see, the money he took from me, if it even was him, was not all that much in comparison."

"How much did you lose on the three cards combined?"

She thought for a minute and finally said, "I guess about $25,000."

"That sounds like a lot of money," I said. "But at least you're still alive."

"Why Officer Tempest, what a strange thing to say!" she exclaimed. "Of course I'm still alive. Why wouldn't I be?"

"It's like this," I said, sitting on the edge of the soft white sofa and staring into her eyes. "He has several ex-wives. Some are dead, and according to local authorities, there were some questionable circumstances in each case. Mr. McLaren is considered a person of interest in each of them, but there's not enough evidence in any of the cases to make an arrest."

For a moment, Mrs. Parley sat there looking stunned. Her smile was long gone. She seemed to have shrunk a little. Her hands were shaking. Finally, she whispered, "But the dead women were all his wives."

"That's right. And I know of one case in which he was actually married to more than one woman at a time. He spent a little time in prison for that," I said bluntly.

Mrs. Parley's face was almost as white as her hair. She seemed at a loss for words. She just sat wringing her trembling hands and choking back little sobs. Chaille and I both sat patiently and waited. I was very curious as to what she would say when she found her voice again. And she did eventually find it. "It isn't certain that he killed any of them, is it?"

"No. If it was, he'd be in prison."

"Could it be just some terrible coincidence?" she asked feebly.

"That seems very unlikely," I said. "But I suppose it's possible."

"I have another question, officers. Did any, ah, um, *lady friends* die that you know of?"

Chaille touched my arm, and when I looked at her, she said, "Let me tell her." She faced the elderly woman once more. "Mrs. Parley, there is one lady he'd been seeing very regularly who lost a lot of money and then died. We believe she was murdered. That's why we're here. The woman who was killed was Officer Tempest's mother."

Mrs. Parley let out a little shriek and then sank back into her chair, her body limp and her eyes closed. I thought she might be having a heart attack, and I sprang toward her. Chaille did the same. But she seemed to be breathing okay, and her pulse was strong. After a few moments, her eyes fluttered and then opened.

"Are you okay?" I asked urgently.

"I could use some water," she said in a very weak voice.

Chaille sprang to her feet and darted into the kitchen. While she was getting a glass of water, Mrs. Parley addressed me, "I'm so sorry about your mother."

"Thank you. I miss her a lot. She was a good woman."

"Do you believe Jim murdered your mother?" she asked as Chaille hurried toward us with the water.

"There's a lot of evidence pointing to him as the killer," I admitted. "But I need to talk to him to see if I can tie up a couple of loose ends. If I can find the evidence I need, he'll be arrested for her murder. We do have a warrant for his arrest but on other charges." Since my mother's card had been used at the Comfort Inn, Chief Thompkins had informed me that the prosecutor had agreed to charge McLaren with the theft of her credit card and a couple related charges. But so far, that was all.

Mrs. Parley accepted the glass of water from Chaille, sipped it for a minute, then handed it back. "Thank you, my dear," she said. "I'll be fine now."

"Can we get you anything else?" Chaille asked. "I know this has been a shock."

"No, but I would like to help you catch him if I can. I've been a fool. He was so sweet to me, so kind and gracious in every way," she said. "I kept telling myself that he didn't steal my credit cards, that someone else did. But deep down I knew. Like I said, I had already figured out that he's a wicked man."

"Mrs. Parley, do you have a phone number for Mr. McLaren?" I asked.

"Yes, I do—two in fact. I have a number to his home in Los Angeles and a cell phone number. Of course, they might not be current. I haven't talked to him in nearly a year."

I was excited at the possibility of being this close. "He may be in Twin Falls right now. Would you mind trying the cell phone number you have?"

"If he answers, would you like me to invite him over?" she asked.

"Only if you're comfortable with it."

"It sounds like he's destroyed a lot of lives. You two sweet young people have brought me to my senses. I would like to help if I can."

"He mustn't know that we are here," I emphasized.

"Of course." She stood up, stepped over to a phone that was hanging on the wall by the kitchen doorway, and punched in a number from memory.

I was tense as I waited. I prayed that he would answer and that he would come to see her. This time, we would be ready for him.

Mrs. Parley held the phone to her ear for a long time. I was about to give up what little hope I had when she said, "Hello, Jim. This is Jane. I've missed you terribly."

CHAPTER SEVENTEEN

I BEGAN TO FEEL SOME anticipation to interrogate Jim McLaren. As Chaille and I listened quietly to the conversation between Jane Parley and McLaren, hope was rising that we might have an early end to our search. We could, of course, only hear one side of the conversation, but from what Jane was saying, it certainly sounded like Mr. McLaren was agreeing to come see her. When he did, he would get a big surprise.

When she finally disconnected, she looked at us with a wan smile. "He's coming," she reported. "I sure hope I'm doing the right thing."

"You are," I assured her. "And remember this, Mrs. Parley. This is America. Here you are innocent until proven guilty. The fact that I *believe* he killed my mother does not relieve us, meaning the police and prosecutors, of proving his guilt. We have to collect the evidence and make our case, but he'll have his day in court."

"Yes, of course. And even though I've struggled with my feelings, I know he did a terrible thing to me."

"What time are you to meet him?" I asked.

"He'll be here in thirty minutes," she said. "But if it's okay, I'd rather not see him at all. In fact, I'll turn my house over to you and leave until he is arrested."

"Are you sure?" I asked. "You can simply wait in another room. It won't take us long to get him in custody once he appears here."

"No, I'll call a friend to come pick me up. I'll give you my cell phone number so you can call me when he's been arrested and taken to jail." She paused. "You two young people be careful." Jane was sober—not the bubbly, happy woman we had met a few minutes ago.

"We'll have the assistance of your local police." I remembered well the lesson I had learned in Boise.

After she left, I called and got the promise of assistance from some local officers. Three men and one woman arrived fifteen minutes later. Together we made a plan, one that would keep all police vehicles and each officer out of sight. One of them, along with Chaille and me, would wait in the house. Others were watching for the silver Lexus a few blocks from Mrs. Parley's house.

We took our places and began the wait. The appointed time came and went. My eager anticipation turned to bitter disappointment. We waited another twenty-five minutes, determined to wait longer if we had to. But we didn't have to.

The officer who was waiting with us in the house got a call on his cell phone. He was shaking his head as he crossed the room toward us. He ended his call and informed us that McLaren wouldn't be coming. A silver Lexus was wrapped around a power pole about two miles from Jane's house. The man survived the crash but was in critical condition. A witness said that another vehicle ran a stop sign. The Lexus tried to take evasive action, which caused it to hit the pole. The other car left the scene and so far had not been located. When the officer told us how long it had taken to get the driver out of the car, Chaille looked at her watch.

"He must have wrecked a little before the time he was supposed to be here," she said.

"Just because it's a silver Lexus doesn't mean it's McLaren," I pointed out. "I'm not sure we should leave quite yet."

But the officer changed my mind when he informed us that the California plates on the Lexus were registered to a Jim McLaren of Los Angeles.

I turned to Chaille. "Let's go to the accident scene first. I'd like to look for the black wig and women's clothes he was wearing earlier. Then we'll go to the hospital and see if there's any chance of seeing him."

"At least he won't be getting away," Chaille said. "One way or the other, we've got him."

There was that, and I felt a little triumph. But frankly, I wanted him to survive. I wanted him to stand trial for what I believed he'd done. I nodded. "Let's go."

The car that had run the stop sign had also been going too fast, according to the witness. Nearby, a teenage girl was upset and couldn't recall much about the other vehicle. All she could tell the officers was that it was blue and that she thought a man was driving.

The Lexus was a total loss. And as I looked at the driver's side, I wondered what the chances of survival were. "This car was moving quite fast when it hit," I thought out loud. "If this pole had been wood instead of metal, it would have been knocked right down."

Chaille agreed with me, as did the officers who were investigating the accident. I requested permission to look inside the car to see if I could find the things he'd been wearing earlier. Permission was given. It took us several minutes to search, the car being in such bad shape, but there was nothing there to indicate that he had been masquerading as a woman.

"It looks like he ditched his disguise," I said with disappointment. "Let's get to the hospital."

As I feared, McLaren was in surgery. The doctors couldn't predict whether he would survive or not. They couldn't even tell me when he might be able to receive visitors. We were at a dead end for now. Arranging with the local cops to take him into custody if and when he recovered, Chaille and I walked out of the hospital. After a moment, I spoke. "We need to call Jane and tell her what happened."

"She'll feel terrible," Chaille said.

"I'm sure you're right, but after we reach her, we need to get right back to work—if we can find anything to do that might actually move the case forward."

"What about the credit card?" Chaille asked after I had talked to Jane. "I wonder what it would take to look through his personal belongings— his wallet and pockets?"

"That's a good idea. Let's talk to the local officers about that," I suggested.

It took a little while, but we finally had the chance to look in his wallet and pockets. I wasn't surprised when the credit card wasn't there. "He ditched it along with the woman's disguise. Either that or they're in a hotel somewhere here in Twin Falls."

We spent some time calling all the hotels in the city. Again, we drew a blank. He wasn't registered at any of them, at least not under his name or my mother's. Late that afternoon, we returned to the hospital to see how our suspect was doing.

He was in intensive care, in a coma, and still in critical condition. After checking on him, we again headed out of the hospital. "I guess there's nothing for us to do but go home," I said as we rode down an elevator.

"We can fly back here if he recovers enough for us to speak to him," she noted. "What are you going to do about your truck?"

"It's still at the police impound yard in Boise. I'm not even sure when it will be released so I can have a body shop take a look at it. I'm afraid there's a lot of damage."

"So what will you drive?" she asked as we started across the parking lot to her patrol car.

"I'll figure something out," I said, discouraged and having a hard time not letting it show.

"Hey, Keene," Chaille said brightly, taking my hand in hers. "Just be glad we got the guy. That's a really big deal. And if he recovers, he won't be going anywhere but to jail. The local authorities will charge him with crimes in relation to the theft of Jane Parley's credit cards. And the warrant we have will get him back to our jurisdiction at some point. In the meantime, we'll continue to build a case against him on your mother's death."

She was right, of course. We decided to head back home. We took turns driving her patrol car, and we had some long, very interesting talks. I learned a lot about her and talked more about myself than I ever had to anyone.

When we got back to Hardy late that evening, we went straight to the police station, where we reported to a very tired-looking Chief Thompkins. After we filled in details of what we'd covered briefly on the phone, he said, "Not a word on the missing cousins." Former detective Bentley and Hugo Starling, owner of the Hardy Café, were still on the lam. "When they're found, there's nothing we can do about Hugo. He has the right to come and go as he pleases. However, the same is *not* true of Bentley. The judge has revoked his bail, and the bond company has joined the search for him."

"I'd go look for them myself," I said, "but I don't know where I'd even begin."

"There's plenty we can do here," the chief reminded me. "Oh, by the way, your brother's body has been released by the medical examiner. You'll need to contact them and tell them what to do with it."

"I'll see what my sister thinks, but I suppose we'll have a local mortuary pick him up."

"That's up to you and your family, but for now, both of you go home and get some rest—and take the day off tomorrow. Since it's Sunday, you two would probably like to attend your church."

"That would be great."

"You'll both be fresh by Monday morning and can get back to investigating," Damion added. "Unless, of course, you need the day to take care of funeral arrangements."

"I have no idea until I can talk to Bree and Grady," I said.

"Since you don't have a vehicle anymore, why don't you let me pick you up for church in the morning?" Chaille offered.

"I'd like that," I told her.

"That's right," Damion said. "You're without transportation. I'm sorry about your pickup. For now, take a patrol car. Thank goodness we've got a couple of old ones that we haven't sold yet. Anyway, you can drive one of them until you can arrange something else."

I thanked him and drove back to the hotel in a Ford that had long since seen its best days. It was quite late, but a surprise awaited me there. When I entered my living quarters, the small living room was filled to capacity.

"Hi, Keene," Grady said, standing up, stepping over to me, and giving me an awkward embrace, the first from either of my brothers in my entire life. "Sorry it took me so long to get here."

"It's good to see you," I said awkwardly.

Bree and her husband, Ron, were also there. Ron and I shook hands, exchanged a few words of greeting, and then he sat down again, looking weary and worried. Bree gave me a hug and then joined her husband on the sofa. Grady and I each found ourselves a chair. "Sean's body has been released," I told them. "We need to decide what to do. I was thinking that we might have a local mortuary pick up and prepare the body for burial."

They all agreed, so I told them I'd make the arrangements even though it was late. I was sure someone would be available at the mortuary. Grady spoke up. "I landed that job in New York. I need to be back there after the weekend, Tuesday at the latest."

"Then maybe we should have a graveside service Monday," I suggested. "That is, if we can arrange for a burial plot and if the mortuary can have him ready by then."

My siblings agreed, and so I got on the phone, made the necessary arrangements, and told the very sleepy-sounding person at the mortuary that we'd meet them the following afternoon to select a casket. After that, we spent some much-needed but awkward family time. We avoided discussion of the murders except for my explanation of what had happened with Jim McLaren.

Bree brought up my need for a vehicle. "Why don't you drive Sean's Corvette?" she asked. "The police don't need it, do they, Keene?"

"Not anymore," I said, feeling distinctly uncomfortable.

I wasn't the only one. Bree's suggestion brought a dark look from Grady. "Actually, I was planning on taking it. I was the closest to Sean, and I know he'd want me to have it."

"Hey, that's okay with me." I held up my hands in surrender, not wanting to see another family argument like we'd had so many of over the years.

Bree, however, snapped at Grady. "That's selfish, Grady," she said, her eyes narrowed in anger. "You don't need it, but Keene does. Besides, you haven't done anything to help, but Keene has worked his tail off for the family."

"I would have if I could," Grady returned lamely. "I've had to deal with getting a new job. And my wife has made my life almost impossible."

Mention of Jean heightened the feeling of discomfort that Grady had stirred up. In an attempt to head off further argument, I said, "Bree, I'm really okay with Grady taking the car. I'll figure something out."

She began to shake her head when Grady said, "I didn't know it was such a big deal. Keep it, Keene. Forget I mentioned I wanted it." He got to his feet. "I need to run. I was going to drive down to Sean's. I know where he kept a key hidden, so I can get in okay. He borrowed some CDs, and I thought I'd go get them. Anyway, I just feel like I need to visit his place to sort of bring myself some closure."

Bree also got up, gave Grady a hug, and said, "So you'll be back when? Tomorrow? Monday morning?"

"I'm not sure," he hedged. "I might spend a little time at Sean's place and come back Monday morning in time for the graveside. There's nothing I can do here anyway."

"Be careful, Grady," Bree said, worry lines creasing her face. "Remember, we could all be in danger."

"Not anymore." Grady sounded confident. "Keene caught the guy who's been after us. We should all be safe now. There is nothing more to worry about."

"What if he isn't the one or if he has an accomplice?" I asked as I also stood up and crossed the room to where Grady was standing next to the door. "We haven't yet ruled out Hugo Starling or Detective Bentley."

"It was McLaren that shot at you. I think that rules out those others." That was so typical of Grady. "There's nothing to worry about, but I will be careful—watch over my shoulder and all that. So I'll see you on Monday morning, if not Sunday night. Keep me a room open just in case I get back Sunday."

"I'll see to it," I promised as Grady made his exit.

Bree and I looked at each other. Her face was grave. "He's the same old Grady," she said. "Thinking only of himself. He blames poor Jean for their breakup, but I'm not so sure it isn't more *his* fault than hers. But at least he came. All three of us are here now. That's a positive thing."

"That's true," I agreed. "I just wish he'd have stayed and visited and picked up his CDs on Monday before he leaves for New York."

Ron gave me a ride to the sheriff's impound yard several miles from Hardy, where the Corvette was being held. I drove it back to the hotel and parked it in the slot where I usually kept my truck.

***

The following morning, Chaille showed up right on time, looking like a million bucks in a blue dress that brought out the best in her complexion. She smiled brightly when I greeted her in the lobby. I gave her a kiss, letting it linger just a moment. There was no question that I was smitten.

There were a lot of questions from ward members and even more expressions of sympathy. I found that I was drawn to the people of the Hardy Ward. They made me feel like one of them. There was also no shortage of looks of approval whenever Chaille and I happened to be standing next to each other. The Everest women—Paige, Tess, and their mother—all made a point to greet both of us after the meetings with smiles of approval. After Tess walked away, I realized that if I hadn't already fallen for Chaille, I might have considered dating her. She was both sweet and very attractive. And yet there was something in her eyes that bothered me. Something wasn't right with Tess. Maybe all this mess with the hotel was simply worrying her. She had been close to my mother.

Chaille must have followed the direction of my eyes; she poked me in the shoulder and said, "Yeah, she's good-looking, isn't she?"

I nodded in agreement but said, "I probably need to be getting back to the hotel."

The grin faded. "Oh, I was hoping you would consider coming over to my place and having dinner with me. I put a roast in the oven before I left to pick you up."

"I'm not in a hurry," I said quickly. "I'd love dinner at your house."

The smile returned. "That's great, Keene. Let's go, then."

The afternoon was so pleasant that I didn't even look at my watch as the time passed. Along with her other talents, Chaille was a great cook. We visited, went for a short walk, visited some more, and had banana splits, which she prepared as carefully as she'd prepared dinner. We even shared a kiss or two. It was nice just spending time with her that was not job related.

I was as relaxed as I could possibly be, my family tragedies at the back of my mind. We held hands as we left her house for the ride back to the hotel. I reluctantly let go when my cell phone began to ring. The call I took shattered the peacefulness of the afternoon.

"Keene, is Chaille there with you by any chance?" Chief Thompkins asked.

"Ah, yes, she's right here," I said, expecting to hear a chuckle of approval from our boss.

He did not chuckle. He just said, his tone extremely serious, "You two need to know that Jim McLaren has disappeared from the hospital in Twin Falls."

CHAPTER EIGHTEEN

I WAS STUNNED. HOW COULD Jim McLaren have escaped from the hospital when, the last I knew, his very survival was not certain? I signaled for us to return inside Chaille's little house and whispered, "Jim McLaren's not in the hospital." As her face registered shock that must have mirrored mine, we headed back to her front door. She slipped her key into the lock, and I continued my conversation on the phone. "Chief, do they have any idea how he did this?"

"Not a clue. The officer who was on guard was found unconscious in the room, and there was simply no sign of McLaren. The IV and tubes had been removed. He was simply gone."

"Did the officer regain consciousness?" I asked as my partner's face continued to show bewilderment.

"Yes, but he remembers nothing. The last thing he recalls was from the day before. He doesn't even remember coming on shift. The nurses say the last time they noticed him he was sitting outside the room looking bored with no hint anything was wrong. They have no idea how or when the guard went in McLaren's room or why he was unconscious."

"And the cops have no idea what happened?" I asked. "Just a second, Chief. Let me put my phone on speaker." I did that as we entered the house and Chaille shut the door behind us.

"They think the officer may have been drugged. Tests are being conducted as we speak," Damion said.

"We're burying my brother tomorrow or I would head there right now. But maybe we could change our—"

The chief cut me off. "You need to take care of your family matters first, Keene. Chaille, they would like one of us to come though. I could send Payton, but you're more familiar with things over there. Could you go? I know I promised you the day off, but if you left within the next half hour, you could be there before eight. From here to Twin Falls is only about a four-hour drive."

"I can be on my way in twenty minutes. I need to run Keene back to his hotel, pack an overnight bag, and gas up my patrol car."

"You're a gem," he said. "I knew I could count on you."

Chaille packed her bag while I waited, then we talked on the way back to the hotel. I thought aloud, "Is it possible that he had help getting out? We still don't know where Hugo and Bentley are."

"That was my thought. Although," she said, giving me a sideways glance, "I suppose McLaren could have made a miraculous recovery, taken the cop out, and simply left."

"Wearing what?" I asked dubiously. "His clothes were a mess after the accident."

"You're right," she agreed. "So we probably should assume that Hugo or Bentley or both helped him."

The thought was disturbing. We were back to square one: not having spoken to McLaren and knowing that we couldn't find the other two. I continued, "I frankly think that the three of them are in this together, but we can't rule out the possibility that it could be any one of them acting alone or a combination of two of them or even another accomplice we don't know about yet. We need to keep an open mind."

Chaille pulled up in front of the hotel but didn't shut the engine off. She was anxious to get on her way. It scared me. I wished I was going with her. Shaking my head and taking hold of her hand, I said, "I'm sorry, Chaille. I should be going with you. If the chief will let me, I'll join you by tomorrow evening if you are still in Twin Falls."

"I'd like that," she said with a warm smile.

"You be really careful," I said. "Don't let anything happen to you." I felt my voice choke up, and I took a minute to clear my throat. "I'll miss you."

She was the one that choked up this time. She squeezed my hand. "Ditto that, Keene. I'm kind of getting to like being around you." She leaned toward me, and our lips touched briefly. With that, she leaned back, pulled her hand free, and put the car in gear.

I got out, shut the door, and said more to myself than her since the windows were closed, "Go safely, girl. I need you in my life."

She gave a little wave and a quick smile, then she was gone.

I stood there for a moment, feeling empty inside. I wanted desperately to be with her right then, but I knew that I had to be here for Grady and Bree, to see that the graveside was a fitting tribute to our brother and to give them moral support. Grady was right about one thing. He had been much closer to Sean, and this was probably harder on him than I realized. Bree had also been closer to Sean than I had. I'd always been the kid brother to be kicked around, especially by Sean and Grady.

"Where's Chaille?" Bree asked as I stepped into the apartment a few moments later. "I thought that she'd come in for a while since you both have the day off. I'm assuming you had lunch together."

"We were having a good day until Chief Thompkins called," I said bitterly.

Bree gasped and a hand came to her mouth. Her husband rose quickly from the sofa. "What's happened now?" she asked. "Please don't tell us something happened to Grady. He just refuses to take this whole thing seriously."

"It's not about Grady," I said. "Jim McLaren is missing. He somehow got out of the hospital."

Bree gasped again. "Did Hugo and that Bentley guy help him?" she asked astutely. "I thought he was in pretty bad shape."

"So did I, and they don't know how he did it. They don't even know if he had help." I explained what details I knew and then added, "They needed an officer to go up there. The chief sent Chaille since I couldn't go due to the graveside service for Sean."

"Oh, Keene, we could change that," she said. "I don't want Chaille to get hurt. I can tell she's beginning to mean a lot to you, and I like her a lot myself. She's a great girl. I'll arrange things here if you want to call her and have her come get you."

"The chief won't hear of it." I shrugged. "He said that family comes first. And he's right. Grady has his new job to think about. He was right, you know, when he said he was closer to Sean than either of us."

"He's also selfish. I feel so sorry for Jean . . . and their baby. I'm just sick at the way Grady has treated her."

"Maybe it's not all his fault," I said, defending my brother out of family loyalty. "He claims it may not even be his baby, remember?"

"I remember, but I still think it's mostly his fault," she ranted angrily. "But he's our brother, and I guess we need to be concerned about his job. After all, I'm sure he'll be ordered to pay alimony and child support. I know he says he will, and I hope he means that, but if an order is in place, he'll have no choice. So he needs a good job for Jean's sake and for the baby's."

"I told Chaille to be careful and that I would go meet her after we got Sean properly buried," I informed her.

"And you'll take Sean's Corvette," she said in a tone that left no room to argue. "You'll be safer in that than in an old clunker the chief has you driving. And when you guys are together up there, doing whatever it is you need to do to help find McLaren, you can both use the Vette. I'm sure that McLaren, if he's even up to watching for you, won't be looking for a red Corvette. Nor do I think that Hugo and Detective Bentley would be looking for it either."

I had a troubling thought that I didn't mention. I wasn't sure that there wasn't another dirty cop in the sheriff's office who could be keeping track of the progress of Sean's case. If so, he might know that the Corvette had been released to me. That was definitely an unsettling thing to consider.

Sooner or later, Bree would probably think of that, but I wasn't going to worry her with it now. "That's a good idea," I said. "I'll drive it over to Twin Falls."

We were all antsy, wanting to do something. But there wasn't really anything we could do. I did call Chaille a couple of times. She called me once, and when my phone rang at dusk, I thought she was calling to tell me she had arrived and was checked into a hotel. I was wrong.

The call was from Grady. "These people are crazy," he shouted into the phone. "They shot at me, even hit me once, but it's not too bad, just skimmed my left arm. My rental car's in bad shape."

"What happened and where?" I asked in alarm as I put the phone on speaker so that Bree and Ron could hear.

"I went to a local café for something to eat. When I came out, I got in the car and started back to Sean's house. Suddenly, something shattered my rear window. I knew it was a bullet. More followed, and I just ducked, trying to keep from wrecking. I made it to the side of the road okay, steering with my left hand, and ducked down so I wasn't as exposed. It was one of the last bullets that hit my arm. Whoever did it passed me as I was stopping the car. They put another bullet into my car as they went by."

Bree was holding her mouth with both hands. Ron was gritting his teeth and holding her protectively. I was thinking with a sinking stomach how closely that mirrored what had happened to me. "Did you see whoever did it?" I asked, almost sure what his answer would be.

"No, I was too busy ducking. They nearly killed me, Keene. I should have taken your advice more seriously," he wailed.

"Did you call the cops?"

"Of course I did. They took the car as evidence. They also made me go to the hospital, but all they did there was patch me up and let me go."

"Could you tell what kind of gun was used?" I asked. "Was it a pistol or a rifle?"

"They used one of each, according to the cops. So I think there had to have been two shooters," he concluded. "I've never been shot at before. I'm still shaking."

"Where are you?"

"I'm at a hotel. The cops wouldn't let me go back to Sean's house."

"That's smart actually. They won't know where to find you this way." Bree said

"What are you doing about a car?" I asked. "Do you need me to come down and get you?"

"No, the rental company is bringing me a replacement. Thank goodness I had insurance on the car. They were really quite good about it," he explained, a little calmer now.

"Will you be able to be here by noon for the graveside?" I asked.

"Of course I'll be there," he said. "Don't worry about me. I'll be more watchful now. But, Keene, who would have done this? That McLaren guy's in the hospital, so it couldn't have been him. Could it have been that cop and the café owner?"

He had already reached the same conclusion I had although he didn't yet know about Jim McLaren, so I guessed I better tell him. "It could have been, but we just learned that McLaren somehow left the hospital. They have no idea how he did it. We have a cop going that way to help the Twin Falls officers. I'd go myself if we weren't burying Sean tomorrow."

"Yeah, and it's lucky you aren't burying me too. This thing's getting scary," he said.

It had been scary for some time. I was glad he was not hurt badly, but I was also relieved that he now knew that the danger was real. "Little brother," he said, "you be careful when you go to Twin Falls. And tell that lady cop to be careful too. I suppose she's the one going up?"

"She is, and when I go, I'll go in an unmarked car. It should be safer that way."

"Are you taking the Vette?" he asked. "That would be best. It's fast if you need to make a getaway or something. If I'd had it today I might have been able to get away from whoever was shooting at me."

"Maybe," I said, not giving much credence to that. He still wanted the Vette; that was clear. Apparently, Bree was thinking the same thing, for she was shaking her head vigorously while tears streamed down her face.

Grady finally ended the call. "I'll see you guys in the morning. And tell Bree not to worry. I'll be okay."

Telling Bree not to worry was like telling the earth not to rotate on its axis. She was pale and sobbing. Her husband was a strong man, and he kept trying to reassure her that everything would be okay, something none of us could say with any kind of certainty. Things were far from okay right now, and I couldn't see how they would be much better in the near future.

"What do you suggest we do?" Ron asked after I'd put my phone back in my pocket.

"I'm not sure you and Bree should stay here any longer. You'd be safer in a hotel or even a little motel out of town somewhere," I suggested.

"That's not going to happen," Bree said resolutely though trembling. "We'll just stay right here in the hotel. We can get Paige or her mother to get groceries for us."

I tried to argue, but my suggestion was met with the same stubborn refusal to budge that she'd used when it came to who would get the Corvette. Finally, I relented. "Okay, but you need to keep a gun with you at all times."

Ron nodded. "I bought a pistol after I got here. I would have brought one with me, but I was sure they wouldn't let me bring it on the plane. I'll keep it right with me, and I'll keep Bree with me as well."

"Good." But my thoughts were racing, and another worry struck me. "What about your kids? These guys, whoever they are, seem to know a lot about us, where we are and where we will be. Are you sure the kids are safe with your parents, Ron?"

Bree's gasp and the way the blood drained from his face were all the answer I needed.

"I'll call my folks right now and have them take the kids somewhere safe," he said.

"Okay, you do that, but I'm going to call the police down there or, better yet, have Chief Thompkins call them. He'll probably have more luck in impressing upon them the seriousness of the situation." I pulled out my phone, located Damion's number in my contacts, and punched the Call button.

At the same time Ron was calling his folks, I was explaining things to Chief Thompkins.

He was happy to oblige. "I'll call right now, and then I'll call the police that are investigating Grady's shooting. They may be able to tell us some things that Grady may have missed. I'll let you know what I learn. In the meantime, Keene, I want you to call Chaille."

"That was my next call," I told Damion. "And then, if it's okay with you, I'll call a couple of the officers with the Twin Falls police. I want them to keep an eye on Chaille as well."

"Thanks, Keene. We'll get these guys." That last was an attempt to reassure me, but the reassurance I needed came from inside me. I was determined to find them, whoever and wherever they were.

"I've been wondering," I continued after a short pause, "if we're missing someone. You know, if there's someone else besides McLaren, Starling, and Bentley."

"I was thinking the same thing. I know it seems unlikely, but I can't get that drunken fool Alvin Cramer out of my mind. He took an awful chance lying for Bentley. Maybe he's involved."

"But he's in jail," I reminded the chief. The silence was just long enough that the hair on the back of my neck stood up. "He got out?"

"I'm afraid so."

"How did he manage that?" I asked.

"The judge wouldn't set his bail very high, said he wasn't a flight risk. Someone paid his bond for him."

"Do we know who?"

"I'm afraid not. The bond just appeared at the jail in the mail—cash. There was a note saying it was for his bail. They released him before the sheriff or I heard about it," Damion said.

"Could it have been Hugo or Bentley?" I asked.

"I suppose so, or someone they had do it for them," the chief admitted.

"Has anyone been watching him since he was released?"

"He was at the bar that night, but I haven't seen him since, and neither has Payton." That statement didn't cause the hair on my neck to lie back down. I mentally added another conspirator to my list. Damion spoke again, "We better get to making those calls. And I suppose we better give them all a description of Alvin Cramer. I have no idea what he might be driving, but I'll find out."

After hanging up with the chief, I called Chaille. She was as worried as the rest of us about the attempt made on Grady's life.

"I'll be careful," she promised after I'd told her about Alvin Cramer. "I'd like to get my hands on that creep."

"You wait for me or at the very least for the Twin Falls cops if he shows up in that area," I said. "I plan to call them as soon as I finish talking to you."

"That won't be necessary. They're here with me right now. We've been comparing notes. Would you like to talk to one of them?"

I did, and I was assured that they would make sure Chaille was okay.

A few minutes later, as I was packing an overnight bag, Chief Thompkins called me back. "Okay, Keene, the cops that are looking into the attempt on your brother couldn't add much. I suspect, however, that it was our friends, Starling and Bentley. I also suspect that Alvin Cramer somehow made his way to Twin Falls and helped McLaren get away. It's entirely possible that the two of them know each other. Of course, it's not such a long drive that Bentley and Starling couldn't have gone to Twin Falls. But we need to keep Cramer in mind. Did you warn Chaille about him?" Before I could answer, he added, "Of course you did."

"Chief, I plan to leave for Twin Falls from the cemetery as soon as we finish there. I'll be driving Sean's Corvette," I told him. "I'm going to take an overnight bag out to the car in just a minute. I want to be ready to roll as soon as the graveside service is over."

***

As I put the bag in the trunk, I noticed something that the deputy who'd searched the car had apparently missed. It was a small piece of notebook paper, crumpled up, looking quite inconspicuous, and yet something no one should have missed if there was something written on it. I reached for it but then jerked my hand back. Now wasn't the time to get careless. I hurried to the patrol car the chief had lent me, got a pair of gloves, slipped them on, grabbed my camera, and then went back to the Corvette. I first took several photos, and then I picked the note up, straightened it out, and read the words that were written on it.

CHAPTER NINETEEN

THE NOTE WAS WRITTEN IN sloppy, almost childish handwriting. The two sentences it contained were not childish. After what had happened, they were chilling. The note read: *Sean, I'll meet you at your hotel room tonight. I'm sure we can come to an understanding.* That was it. There was no signature. There was nothing indicating what might happen if "an understanding" was not reached. I slipped it in my pocket, locked the car, and headed back to the hotel, angry that some cop had been so careless. This note should have been processed and sent to the lab.

As soon as I was inside, I called the chief again. "Who searched the Corvette?" I asked, unable to mask my anger.

"I'm not sure. It was someone with the sheriff's department. Why, did they miss something?"

"I'll say they did," I fumed. "They missed a critical piece of evidence. It's a note that I found crumpled up in the trunk."

"What does it say?" Damion asked.

I read the note to him, and he said, "I'll be right there, Keene. You're right, this could be a golden find, and it should have been found earlier."

Bree and Ron had listened to the exchange, and when I clicked off, Bree said, "Could it have been Detective Bentley that did the search?" she asked.

"I thought of that," I responded. "But this isn't something he would leave, at least not if it might point a finger at either himself or, more likely, Hugo Starling."

She nodded in agreement.

The chief was soon there. I met him in the lobby. "The sheriff's on his way too," he said. "He's not happy that one of his guys might have missed this."

***

The chief gave me a form accepting custody of the evidence. When the sheriff arrived, he filled out a second one as the sheriff received the note. Both men felt, as I did, that this note could be crucial to solving my brother's murder and convicting the murderer in a court of law.

The sheriff promised to find out which of his people had searched the car—not that anything could be done about it now. The argument could be raised that the note had been planted in the trunk of the Corvette after the search was completed. That argument might be weak if the sheriff could show tight security of his impound lot. Then again, the chief pointed out, it could have been put in there after I parked the car at the hotel. "It's not likely but could be argued in court," he concluded.

I didn't for a second believe that was the case, but it was a problem. "It's still a lead for us." I shrugged.

It had been a day of highs and lows, and it was all rolling about in my mind when I finally got to bed late that night. The time I'd spent with Chaille—peaceful, romantic, and relaxing—kept getting pushed aside by thoughts of Jim McLaren's escape and the attempted shooting of my only surviving brother. But the worst thought of all was the one that kept rising to the surface and keeping me awake with worry. Chaille was in Twin Falls, where danger could be lurking. I wished more than ever that I was with her.

I did finally fall asleep. When I awoke to the sound of the alarm on my phone, I groaned and rolled out of bed. After shaving, showering, reading my scriptures, and eating a quick bite of cereal, I headed toward the front of the hotel, planning to give the Corvette a more thorough daylight search. I hadn't seen anything of Bree or Ron. I assumed they must have been even later than me in going to sleep. The worry and tension was taking its toll on both of them. Like me, I expected that they were concerned about security at the grave site. The sheriff had promised to have officers in the vicinity, but that didn't do a lot to alleviate their worry.

Paige Everest was at the front desk. Her eyes were slightly dull from the long night on duty. But her smile was bright when she saw me. "Hi, Keene. How are you this morning?"

"I'm fine," I replied. "And you?"

"I'm really good. I'm just so glad you caught that awful Mr. McLaren. I feel so much safer having him locked up."

I suppressed a groan. She clearly hadn't heard all the bad news from Sunday afternoon and evening, and I wasn't about to mention it to her now. "Who relieves you this morning?" I asked, both to change the topic and because I honestly wanted to know.

"My mother," she said. "Thanks again for giving her a job. She needed something to get her out of the house a little bit."

"You're welcome, Paige," I called as I stepped out the front door. Once outside, I headed around to the back. My patrol car was parked where I'd left it, but the Corvette wasn't. In fact, the Corvette was gone. It had vanished. I had to fight off a wave of panic. Someone had stolen it. Who could that someone be, and why would they have taken it? My first thought was that there was more critical evidence in it that someone didn't want found. That thought was followed with a mental picture of Hugo Starling and his cousin Vernon Bentley, the crooked ex-cop.

I shook my head and just stared at the empty parking stall. Now I would have to take the old patrol car to Twin Falls. Reluctantly, I pulled my phone out of my pocket and prepared to disturb poor Chief Thompkins again. I thought the call was going to be sent to his voice mail when he finally answered. "This is Damion," he said, clearly very tired. I assumed I'd woken him from a sound sleep, and I felt guilty. But I needed his help, so I forged ahead.

"Chief, this is Keene. I'm sorry to bother you, but I have a problem at the hotel."

"What now?" he grumbled. He was probably getting tired of the Tempest family's problems.

"Someone stole Sean's Corvette. I'm standing in the rear parking area right now, and it isn't here. It was parked right beside the patrol car you lent me, but it's not there now."

My announcement did wonders when it came to bringing the chief fully awake. "That's crazy," he said. "I'll be right there."

While I waited, I wandered back to the front entrance and nodded at Paige as I started past the registration desk.

"Keene, what's wrong?" she asked. "You look really stressed."

"I guess you could say I am," I said. "It seems my brother's car has been stolen."

"You mean the red Corvette?"

"That's right. Have you seen my sister or her husband?" I changed the topic.

"Not yet." She sighed. "Will it never end?" Gone was the tired smile from a few minutes ago.

"I guess I better find them and let them know what's happening," I said and headed for the apartment.

***

The three of us were standing together, looking in dismay at the empty parking stall where a beautiful red Corvette should have been, when the police chief showed up. He was followed shortly by a deputy named Roger White. There really wasn't much to be done. We did search the area around the parking spot. The only thing we found was a deep scratch all the way across the front of the old patrol car the chief had lent me. His face went red with anger. "This was uncalled for," he ranted as he traced the unsightly line with his finger.

The deputy was thoughtful as he watched Damion. Finally, he spoke. "I remember a few years back when this happened to one of our patrol vehicles. It was Vernon Bentley's unmarked car. It was getting old, and he'd been pestering the sheriff for a new one. He got one after that. I always thought that Bentley did it himself, but I had no proof so I didn't say anything. But this sure makes me wonder."

What Roger had just said made sense. The chief agreed. "I can't help but think that he and Hugo Starling are around here somewhere. They've probably taken the Corvette just for spite."

"Or maybe they heard I was going to be driving it," I ventured. I turned to Deputy White. "Who would you say was Bentley's closest friend in the department?"

"That's easy," he said with a disgusted chuckle. "A guy by the name of Renny Criswell. The two are as thick as thieves. Renny shaves his head just like Bentley. He's not too tall but is getting quite heavy—flabby, I'd say. Sort of worships Bentley in a way. By the way, the sheriff told me about the note you found last night. That search was conducted by Renny. He's not known to be too thorough. When I told the sheriff it was Renny who did the search, he said that Renny would be following his buddy down the road if he wasn't careful."

"Let's go have a talk with Deputy Criswell," Chief Thompkins suggested, his face still flushed.

"He left on vacation right after he finished the shift when he searched the Corvette," Roger said. "He's out of town. He said he was going with some fishing buddies. He left his wife and kids at home."

"Are you sure of that?" I asked.

He shrugged his shoulders. "Well, no, it's just what he said he was doing."

"Did he mention who any of the buddies were?" Damion asked.

"Not that I recall. He and Bentley usually went on trips like that together."

The chief and I exchanged glances. Then I asked, "You say Criswell sort of worships Bentley?"

"Oh yeah. Sun rises and sets on Bentley as far as Renny is concerned," White said.

Bree and Ron had been standing near us, holding hands and looking very troubled. Bree spoke up. "Deputy, would Renny do something illegal if Bentley asked him to?"

Roger nodded his head and chuckled. "He'd do anything for the guy." Then he frowned. "He'd key a patrol car for him. Or steal a car for him. Stupid guy would probably kill for him if Bentley told him it was important."

I spoke up. "Someone tried to kill my other brother last evening."

Roger nodded his head slowly. "I was just emphasizing how tight those two are. But as much as I hate to say it, if Bentley made it a condition of continued friendship or something like that, then I suppose it could be possible."

"Another person of interest," the chief said blandly.

I still had more questions. "I would guess that Renny's not terribly bright. Could he have picked up the note I found, thought it was of no value, and thrown it back in the car?"

"Yeah, that's about right," Roger said. "I don't know why he was asked to search the car. I suppose his sergeant wanted him out of his hair for a while. The sheriff wasn't happy about it. He doesn't care for Renny. He *liked* Bentley until all this stuff happened, but he's never held much stock in Renny. Maybe we ought to talk to the tow truck driver. I understand he was there when Renny was doing the search."

"Is *he* reliable?" I asked, exasperated.

The chief snorted. "Not so you'd notice it. Nobody likes to use him, but he's on the rotation at dispatch, and when it's his turn he gets the call. His name's Karl Cramer."

Alarm bells went off in my head. "Is he related to Alvin Cramer?"

"As a matter of fact, he's Alvin's nephew," Chief Thompkins acknowledged. "Maybe we could go talk to him."

"I'm afraid I don't have time," I said. "I'm sorry."

"I meant Roger," Damion clarified. "I know you have lots to do. By the way, what are you going to do about driving to Twin Falls after you finish at the cemetery?"

"I don't know," I said glumly.

"You can take that old patrol car." He nodded at the scratched vehicle.

"I guess I'll have to." I wasn't excited about the idea, but I didn't have much choice at this point. "Will you be listing the Corvette as stolen?" I asked.

"I already did. I had all the information at the office from when it was impounded. I stopped and got it entered on my way here. That's why it took me a little longer than I'd planned."

***

When Grady met us at the mortuary an hour later, he ranted over the theft of the Corvette. "I should have taken it," he said.

Bree laughed mirthlessly. "Are you saying they couldn't have found it if you'd had it?"

"I guess you have a point. I just hope they don't do something to my new rental."

We did what we had to at the mortuary and then drove back to Hardy. We had a few other tasks to complete before the noon burial. I rode with Grady to the cemetery, following right behind Bree and Ron. Grady was moody and sulking, so we didn't talk much. He did say that he'd be heading for New York as soon as the burial was over. "And I suppose you'll be heading for Twin Falls," he added.

"Yes, and it looks like I'll have to drive that old patrol car."

He made no comment, but I thought I saw a smirk cross his face. He really didn't want me to have Sean's Corvette. As for what I wanted—my trusty Ford F-150, repaired and running, was at the top of my list.

We arrived at the cemetery with no more conversation. We weren't there long, but I was a little more choked up than I'd expected to be. The words of Ollie Brown kept swirling around in my head. Had Sean actually loved me? My sadness was nearly overwhelming when I thought of what might have been.

When we left, Grady bid us good-bye and headed south, saying that he'd catch Interstate 80 and head east. I rode with Bree and Ron back to the hotel, and later than planned, I was on my way to join Chaille in Twin Falls.

The old patrol car was running fine, so I figured I'd be okay except that I was quite certain our enemies knew I'd be driving it. An hour into the drive, Chief Thompkins called me. "Is the car running okay?"

"Purrs like a cat," I said cynically. "But I feel like a sitting duck. I'll be fine. I'm keeping a close eye out for any potential trouble." Not that it would be easy to see it coming, as I'd already learned from my experience—and Grady's—being shot at.

"Have you heard from Chaille?" he asked.

"I talked to her when I left town," I reported. "She's working with the local cops. It seems that McLaren did have help. One of the nurses remembered seeing a doctor she didn't recognize in the hallway near his room. They checked closer this morning, and no one knows who the doctor was. They also checked their surveillance cameras. It showed the man helping McLaren out of the building. Nobody recognized the man, and several people looked at the video. They're guessing it was one of our growing list of persons of interest who was simply dressed up like a doctor."

"How is the officer doing who was supposed to be guarding McLaren? Did they figure out what happened to him?" he asked.

"Chaille says he's fine. He'd been drugged. I suppose it was by the fake doctor."

"The reason I called, Keene, is to tell you about our interview with the tow truck driver," Damion told me. "He said he did see the note. Apparently, Renny picked it up, looked at it, and dropped it back on the floor of the passenger side. Renny apparently didn't think anything of it. The tow truck driver also read it, and he wadded it up and dropped it in the trunk, where Renny was poking around then. Neither man, according to him, commented on the note to the other."

"In your opinion, Chief, do you think that either of those guys could be involved?"

"I'm not ruling them out, that's for sure. I shared my suspicions with the sheriff, and he was not happy, to say the least. He doesn't like Renny at all. I think he's looking for a reason to fire him."

"Chief, I've been thinking a lot while I've been driving. Things have happened all over the place, but whoever shot at Grady also could have been in Twin Falls. The time between the two events and locations would fit with time to spare," I reasoned. "I still think that whatever is happening is being done by Hugo and Vernon. McLaren is involved too, but even though he got out of the hospital, the doctor told Chaille that he wouldn't be able to do much. His life is no longer in danger, but he is still in serious condition."

"You may be right, but I'm not convinced Deputy Criswell isn't somehow helping. And the same with our drunken friend, Alvin Cramer."

"What about the other Cramer—Karl, the tow truck driver?" I asked.

"I'm not ruling him out entirely, but I don't think he has anything to do with it. He's just a big dumb guy who's lazy and drinks too much."

"Would he do something that was illegal but fairly easy if the money was good?" I asked.

"No doubt," the chief replied. "Do you have something specific in mind?"

I did, but it was probably a long shot. "I left the car locked last night, and I can't imagine a thief busting it up to get into it—the alarm would have gone off. I sort of figure that whoever took it must have had a key. And since the tow truck driver had the car in his custody for a while, I just wondered if he somehow got a copy of the key."

The chief seemed to consider this. "Maybe I'll go have another talk with Mr. Cramer."

Ten minutes after I hung up with him, I got another call. It was the voice I adored. "Hi, Keene," Chaille said when I answered. "We found Jim McLaren."

CHAPTER TWENTY

"IS HE IN CUSTODY?" I asked.

"Sort of," she said. "He's in the morgue."

"He's dead?"

"More than just dead. He was murdered. Someone bashed him on the back of the head and threw him into the Snake River. A boater found his body washed up on a sandbar."

My head was spinning. I couldn't imagine why anyone would kill McLaren. That was what had me confused. I said so to Chaille.

She paused, then, "Unless someone thought he might have a loose tongue."

Chaille was a smart woman. Just one of the reasons I was so attracted to her. I was not happy that McLaren was dead, even though he'd tried to kill me and had very likely taken my sweet mother's life. I was not happy because I might never be able to find out *for sure*. I wanted closure, not lingering doubts.

"Is there anything more we can do in Twin Falls?" I asked her.

"I don't think so," she said. "I'm filling the officers here in on everything we know about Hugo Starling, Vernon Bentley, Alvin Cramer, and Renny Criswell. Are there any others they need to know about?"

"Yes," I said thoughtfully. "Tell them about Karl Cramer, Alvin's nephew, the tow truck driver. He hasn't disappeared like the others, but I can't help but think he knows something he isn't telling the chief. Maybe he'll break down, and Damion will learn something more from him before we get back to Hardy."

"Okay, I'll mention him too, and then I'm heading home."

"I guess I can just as well turn around too." But I wasn't ready to do that just yet. I was worried about her. "On the other hand, I think I'll keep coming. We can meet somewhere, and then I'll follow you back to Hardy."

Chaille took a moment to respond. But she finally said, "That's sweet, Keene. It's not necessary, but sweet."

"It's okay with you, then?"

"Of course it is. We can meet and have dinner before we drive the rest of the way back to Hardy."

***

That's exactly what we did.

We took our time over dinner, enjoying one another's company, but we also discussed the cases we were working on at length. At one point, I expressed a thought that had occurred to me. "Chaille, what would you say if I told you I needed to go to Los Angeles?"

"I'd say I'd miss you," she replied with a long face. "Why do you want to go there?"

"I don't *want* to," I said. "I *need* to."

She reached across the table and took hold of my hand. "Why do you need to? McLaren obviously won't be going back to Los Angeles—except in a casket."

"That's right, but McLaren has a house there. I'd like to search it. Who knows, he might have kept some kind of evidence that he didn't think anyone would ever see."

Her face brightened. "Yes, that makes sense. What a good idea."

I pulled out my iPhone and dialed Sergeant Tom Brolin's number.

"Hey, Keene, what's happening, my friend?"

I briefly filled him in.

He moaned into the phone. "Oh, Keene, this isn't good. You and your family are in extreme danger."

"And the only way to overcome the danger is to take out the source of it," I said grimly. "I need to come down there, Tom. I'd like to search Jim McLaren's house."

"And you'd like me to work on obtaining a search warrant?" he asked perceptively.

"That's why I was calling," I admitted. "I'll fly down during the night. I can be there in the morning."

"I'll have the warrant ready," he said. "I think I can arrange to help you do the search. I could get others as well, but I suspect that you'll want to do most of the looking. You'll most likely know what you're looking for when you see it. Someone else, even me, might miss it. But I'd like to help."

"That would be great," I said. "I'll let you know what time I'll be getting there. I'll rent a car when I get to the airport and drive—"

Tom cut me off. "You won't need to rent a car. I'll pick you up. We'll conduct the search, and when you're ready to go, I'll take you back to the airport."

"I appreciate that, Tom," I said. For the next few minutes, we talked about what the affidavit for the search warrant needed to say, and then I ended the call.

I held Chaille in my arms beside her car after we'd left the restaurant. I wanted desperately to stay with her, but we had separate cars, and time was of the essence. We finally shared a sweet kiss, got in our respective cars, and headed east.

About thirty minutes later, the chief called. "I got nowhere with Karl Cramer. Well, I can't say that exactly. That he didn't admit to anything would be more correct. But he knows something. He was sweating like a hog, kept shifting his eyes, refusing to meet mine, and he kept telling me that he had work to do."

"Was he more nervous on some of your questions than others?" I asked.

"I was about to mention that," Damion said. "The answer is yes. Karl was more worried when I asked him what he knew about the Corvette than at other times. He denied everything. Says he didn't have a key, was in bed all night asleep, and he couldn't imagine who might have taken it."

"Is he married?"

"He doesn't even have a girlfriend anymore. He lives alone. No one can vouch for where he was last night."

"So, Karl's a dead end," I said, discouraged.

"No, I wouldn't say that. I'm not through with him yet. With enough pressure, I think he'll tell us something. I just need time and something more for leverage."

"Okay. Chief, I need to fly to LA tonight," I told him. "My friend Tom Brolin with the LAPD is working on getting a search warrant for Jim McLaren's home."

"That's a good plan, Keene," he encouraged. "Would you like my secretary to make flight arrangements for you?"

"That would be great."

"Then consider it done."

I wanted desperately to ask him if there was any chance that he could let Chaille go with me, but I knew better. I realized how tight things were for him. As it was, he and Payton were burning the candle at both ends. Following my conversation with him, I called my sister to let her know what was happening. She told me that Grady had promised to call when he got to New York. "He's scared, just like I am, Keene. I think he's glad he has an excuse to be in New York. He says he'll feel safer there, and I'm sure he's right. At least, I hope he is. He had a terribly close call as it is."

"Have you talked to Jean?" I asked.

"A couple of times, actually. I didn't think that Grady would tell her about the shooting, so I did. Their marriage might be over, but I'm convinced more than ever that it's more our dear brother's fault than it is hers. She loves him, Keene. I'm sure of it. I thought she was going to fall clear to pieces when I told her. I called back later just to see how she was doing."

"And how was she?"

"Better," Bree said. "In fact, she'd been thinking about everything. She says she'd rather be here with us than at her place alone. She's trying to work things out so she can come in the next few days."

"I guess that's good. It would probably be better to have her closer," I said. "After all, she is a Tempest whether Grady likes it or not." I then told Bree of my plans. She was supportive.

"Just make sure you talk to me and Ron before you leave Hardy," she concluded.

I followed Chaille into Hardy a little before ten that night. Our return trip was uneventful. We drove straight to the office; Chief Thompkins's secretary had completed the arrangements for my flight to Los Angeles as promised. The chief handed me a packet with the flight information and then said with a grin, "I'm afraid I can't let you go alone. Deputy White is on loan from the sheriff for as long as I need him. So you and Chaille go get ready to leave."

Chaille let out a happy squeal, and the chief said soberly, "Don't act so happy. I just want someone to keep an eye on Keene's back."

"You know I'll do that," she said, taking me by the arm and snuggling close.

"And he'll watch yours," he added. "Now you two get going. You're going to have to make good time in order to catch your flight."

"Thank you, Chief Thompkins," she said with a slight blush. "You have no idea how much I appreciate this."

"Oh, I think I do," he said with a smile. "Now get going, you two."

Thirty minutes later, I had checked with Bree and packed a slightly bigger bag. I was ready for Chaille to pick me up at the hotel, and she didn't make me wait. She drove up right on time. I slipped in beside her, leaned over for a quick kiss, and we were off.

***

We were both exhausted by the time we were finally on the plane a few hours later. Chaille, lucky for me, snuggled against my shoulder and fell asleep. I drifted off occasionally during the flight, dreaming of the woman whose pretty red hair cascaded down the front of my shoulder. Holding her hand had become almost second nature, and we were doing just that when we got off the plane, each of us with a carry-on bag in hand, and Tom Brolin met us.

"You didn't tell me you'd found a girlfriend," Tom teased as he took Chaille's bag. "I take it this trip is both business and pleasure."

I grinned at him. "You're looking good, Tom, for a man who took a bullet not that awfully long ago. And by the way, I would like you to meet Chaille Donovan—*Officer* Chaille Donovan of the Hardy Police Department. She's sort of my partner right now."

"Yeah, it looks like it," he said, still grinning. Then he turned serious. "Okay, so we have work to do. I have the search warrant. Would you two like to stop for some breakfast before we go to McLaren's house? I'm guessing you're both hungry."

He guessed right. We left LAX, and he took us to a pancake house that was on the way to McLaren's home. We ate quickly since we were anxious to get started. I was hoping for a big break in the case from the search of McLaren's home and property.

It was shortly before ten when we turned onto the street we were looking for. I was seated in the front with Tom. Chaille was in the back-seat, leaning forward, her head between us, listening to us and watching ahead. Suddenly, she said excitedly, "Keene, look! There's a red Corvette."

I spotted it immediately even though it was nearly a block away. It was parked in the driveway of a very nice frame house. Tom saw it too, and he pressed the accelerator. "That's about where McLaren's house should be."

I'm not big on coincidences. What were the odds of a red Corvette being parked near the home of one of our suspects, albeit a deceased one? The Corvette started to move just as a large moving van pulled away from a house across the street, blocking both the driveway and the street. The Corvette was parked sideways, so we were looking into the passenger side window and couldn't see the driver as we sped up. We were in a marked LAPD cruiser, and he'd seen us. The driver jumped out of the car and fled on foot without any of us getting more than a fleeting look at him. We couldn't even be sure of the color of his clothes. For that matter, we couldn't even be sure it was a man.

The large moving van had the street so effectively blocked that Tom couldn't get the patrol car past it. I jumped out, shouting back at Tom and Chaille, "I'll try to catch him," and began to run. I caught a couple glances at the fleeing figure, but it was only that—a couple glances. Behind me I could hear more footsteps. I took a quick look back. Chaille, her red hair streaming out behind her, was running faster than I would have thought possible.

I reached an intersection, looked both directions, and couldn't see anyone. Suddenly, a white car sped out of a driveway to my right. It was moving fast; it clipped a car parked on the street, ran a stop sign, and sped out of sight.

I stopped, dropped my hands to my knees, and took deep gulps of air. Chaille ran up behind me. "Did he get away?" she asked, breathing hard.

"In a white car," I said. "From up there." I pointed, and we both forced ourselves into a jog. Standing in the driveway was a large woman. She was looking around in puzzlement. "Are you missing your car?" I asked as we approached. "We're police officers. Someone just drove out of your driveway in a white car."

"My name is Lois Carry. It's my new Accord," she said. "It's gone. My husband will kill me. We just got it yesterday."

"We'll see if we can find it," I said, even as I was pulling my phone out and dialing Tom's number.

The woman was talking rapidly. I heard her say to Chaille, "I forgot my purse. I just ran back inside to get it."

"Was the car running?" Chaille asked.

"Yes. I was only inside for a couple of minutes," she wailed. "My phone rang as I was getting my purse. I answered it, but I didn't talk long."

However long she talked was too long. I stepped away from Chaille and Lois when Tom answered. Chaille had her arm around the lady's shoulder and was steering her toward the house.

"Did you get him?" Tom asked.

"I didn't even get more than a glimpse of him," I said. "He stole a white Accord, brand new. It'll have temporary tags and damage to the right front fender." I glanced at the house and read off the number to Tom. "I'm not sure of the street name, but it's close to McLaren's street. I only ran about four blocks before he stole the car."

"I'll call this in while I come to your location."

We'd only seen one person, but that didn't mean another wasn't nearby. Tom picked us up, and we kept our eyes peeled as we returned to Jim McLaren's house. We left the escaped Corvette/Accord thief to the local authorities.

When we entered the house, we took a quick look at things. Whoever had driven the Corvette had broken into the house through the back door. Inside, things were not too badly disturbed. Tom spoke first. "It looks like we were not long behind the guy."

"I wonder what he was after and if he got it or if it is something that will help us if we can find it," I said hopefully. "Before we begin, though, I'd like to pull the Corvette into McLaren's garage. I don't want to lose it again. And besides, it'll need to be searched too. Who knows? Maybe the thief left something that will help us identify him—or them."

"I'll get a forensics crew on the way," Tom volunteered. "At the least there will be fingerprints."

"I better wear gloves then," I noted. "Do you have any in your car?"

"I'll get them for you."

Once the car was secured, we left the key in the ignition. The key, I noted, was an original, not one that had been made up by our tow truck driver or anyone else. It was identical to the one I had back at the hotel in Hardy. I ruminated on that while I made a cursory search of the interior. I found no baggage of any kind, and there was nothing to indicate who might have been driving it.

Finally, I went inside to join the systematic search while we waited for the forensics team to arrive. We worked together, since we were not, at this point, in a particular hurry. We began in what was clearly Jim's office. I began with his desk while Chaille began going through the first in a series of file cabinets. Tom said he'd keep an eye on the forensics people and help them make a detailed search of Sean's Corvette.

Having checked everything on top of the desk, I had barely begun to sift through the first of five drawers when my cell phone began to ring. It was Chief Thompkins. I hadn't even thought to call him about the Corvette yet, and I felt a little foolish. "It's Damion," I told Chaille before I answered.

"Oh, we should have called him," she said with a little frown.

I nodded then spoke into the phone. "Hi, Chief."

"Have you had a chance to begin the search yet?" Damion asked without any preamble.

"We just started," I replied. "We got delayed."

Before I could mention why, he continued. "I just finished another session with our favorite tow truck driver. I got lucky when I went to his house the second time. I could smell burnt marijuana. From there, I soon located some meth as well. Deputy White was with me. We arrested Karl, took him to the office, and began to put the squeeze on him. I was afraid that he'd want to lawyer up, but we got lucky again. He's not that smart, and he's scared to death. He admitted stealing the car, but he refused to tell us who he delivered it to, where he left it, or whatever. Who knows where it is now? Even though he knows who took it, he won't say a word more."

"I know where the Corvette is," I said without fanfare.

CHAPTER TWENTY-ONE

"Say what?" the chief asked, sounding quite puzzled.

"I found the Corvette. It's here in LA at Jim McLaren's house."

I'm not sure Damion believed me. "But I just told you that Karl Cramer admits he stole it. It couldn't be down there."

"But it is. Believe me, Chief. I know Sean's car when I see it."

"How did it get there?" he asked. "I mean, I'm sure it was driven, but do you know by who?"

"I don't. He got away," I said. I told him about our foot chase and the second stolen car. "So we are beginning to search the house now, and a forensics team will be going over the Corvette in detail. I hope we find some prints that will lead us to whoever drove it down here. I think it had to be either Hugo Starling or Vernon Bentley. Frankly, from the way the guy ran, I'd say it wasn't Hugo. He could never have run like that. Bentley is the more likely bet, but I'd guess that Hugo's in the area, at a motel or something."

"If those guys are the ones who shot at Grady, then I must say that they do get around."

"That's true, but it is entirely possible," I said thoughtfully. "Or there are more than these two involved."

"There's still the older Cramer—Alvin—but I see him as a drunk, not a killer, although one never knows, I guess. We need to be open-minded. Do you have any idea what the thief was looking for in McLaren's house?" the chief asked.

"No, and if he happened to have found it, we may never know. I'm just hoping we find something to tie things together a little better."

"I'm guessing you will, Keene. You're doing well," he said. "Now, I think another visit with Mr. Karl Cramer is in order. Maybe a little bluff would pay off. He doesn't need to know that you only have the car and *not* the driver."

I liked that idea and told Damion so. I concluded, "Now I better get back to work. We have a lot of looking to do here."

As I ended the call, I again began to sift through the dead insurance salesman's desk. Chaille was still working on the top drawer of the first file cabinet. After filling her in on my conversation, we both quietly pursued our tedious work. While my fingers searched, my mind wandered. Somehow, I couldn't get past the feeling that I was missing something. But think as I might, I couldn't come up with anything else.

The phone on Jim's desk began to ring. Startled, I stopped my search and looked at it.

"Do you think you should answer it?" Chaille asked.

"That's what I'm wondering," I said as I looked at the digital display. It said *Christy Haynam*. "Another wife or girlfriend?" I asked, not expecting an answer, just thinking out loud.

"It can't hurt to find out." Chaille stepped up beside me, and I reached for the phone.

"Hello," I said as Chaille put her head near mine so she could hear both sides of the conversation.

"Jim, darling," a feminine voice said. "I've missed you. Why haven't you returned my calls?"

I was thinking rapidly, trying to come up with something to say. Finally, even though it was lame, I answered, "I've been very busy, Christy." I used her name, hoping that by so doing she might take a little longer to discover that she was not speaking to Jim McLaren.

"You're always busy," she said in a pouty voice. "I've left a dozen messages on your cell phone the past few days. I only called this number because I was getting worried. I didn't really expect you to be there. I thought you were supposed to be in Montana or Wyoming or someplace."

"I had a change of plans," I said.

"Well, my darling, I'm just glad I caught you there. Me and you, we really need to talk. If we're going to get married next month, we need to make some plans."

Chaille gripped my arm tightly as I spoke. "I know that, but I do have work to do."

"That's what you always say when you don't have time for me," she retorted. I guessed I was doing pretty well at my little imitation. I prayed that I could keep it up. She was still speaking. "There's something else I need to talk to you about."

Chaille and I glanced at each other. She was having a difficult time hiding a smile. Into the phone I said, "What's that, Christy?" I would have used a term of endearment—*honey* or *dear* or *sweetheart*—but if I used the wrong one it could tip her off that I wasn't her *darling*, so I stuck to her name.

"I lost one of my credit cards," she said. "And someone's been using it. They've spent over three thousand dollars already. What should I do, darling?"

"Have you called the credit card company?"

"Not yet. I wanted to talk to you first. I knew that you'd know what's best."

"Yes, that's true," I said. "Why don't you come to my place and we'll work it out."

"Oh, my darling, do you mean it?" She sounded excited.

Yes, I meant it, all right. I told her so. "But just so I can begin some work on it, why don't you give me the card number."

"Just a minute," she said. "I have to look at my latest statement, the one that nearly gave me a heart attack. Hang on, and I'll be right back, darling."

I heard her lay her phone down, so I put my hand over the one I was holding and said to Chaille, "Can you believe that guy? I wonder how many more poor women he has suckered. I'm guessing we've barely scratched the surface."

"I hate to speak badly of the dead, but he was a horrible man," she said.

Christy came back on the line. "Here it is." I wrote as she read off the information to me. When I had it all, she asked, "Did you lose your cell phone? You always have it with you."

"No, I dropped it," I said. "It broke, and I haven't had time to get a new one."

"Jim, are you all right? You don't sound quite right," she said.

I couldn't blow this now. "I've had a rough three or four days. I've been a little under the weather," I said. "I don't know what's wrong with me, but I'm sure I'll be fine by the wedding."

"I'll come right away," Christy said. "I'll help you feel better."

"I'll have a big surprise for you when you get here," I said on a sudden impulse.

"Really, darling? That's so sweet of you. I love you so much. Oh, I guess you'll have to give me directions to your home. I only have a post office box number for you," she said. "I need your street address."

I read off McLaren's address, and then I asked, "How soon can you be here, Christy?"

"I'll leave right away. Let's see, it's what, just over three hundred miles, I think. Driving I can be there in seven or eight hours. Will that be okay?" she asked.

I agreed that it would. "And remember, I'll have a surprise for you."

After I hung up, Chaille said, "That was mean." But she was smiling as she spoke.

"What was mean?" I asked.

"You told her you'd have a surprise for her."

"It's true, isn't it?"

"Yes, but, well, she'll be devastated."

"But she'll still be alive," I said as anger at the dead insurance man rose inside of me. "Now, I gave her this address, but we don't know where she's coming from. I'd have asked her, but I'm sure that would have tipped her off. After all, I'm sure McLaren has been to the poor woman's home enough times."

"I don't suppose he would have it on his Rolodex?" she asked.

"I'll look. And while I do, would you mind calling one of those cops in Twin Falls? Find out if Christy Haynam's credit card is in the belongings they're holding."

She called and I looked, but I came up with nothing. Chaille was on hold when I finished, so I went back to searching the desk drawer I'd begun with.

Chaille had more success. After she'd disconnected, she explained that they not only had the stolen credit card, but they also had an appointment book that had been taken from the wrecked car. In it they found the name and address of our latest victim. They also had McLaren's cell phone. She showed me the address she'd written down. "I guess not all of his girlfriends and wives are from out of state," she said as I looked at the address in the northern part of the state.

We both went back to work on the search. I tried to open the next drawer, but it was locked. That piqued my interest and I mused, "This drawer is locked. I'll bet we find something of interest in it if I can get it open."

"It can't be too hard," she said. "I'll bet he has some tools in his garage. Probably all we need is a screwdriver or something to pry with."

I suddenly pulled her close and stole a little kiss. She looked up at me and smiled. Her lovable smile was all the encouragement I needed, and I leaned back down and deepened the kiss. After a little battle between heart and brain, my brain won out; we were here on a job. We parted reluctantly and went together to the garage, where the forensics team was hard at work on the Corvette. I explained to Tom what we'd learned and that a fiancée of the late Mr. McLaren was on her way here.

"I'd like to be here when she comes," he said with a grin.

"She told us she'll be here in seven or eight hours. You're more than welcome to wait with us," I said.

"Boy, will she ever get a surprise," Tom said, shaking his head. "This guy was a real piece of work." He helped us find a large screwdriver and then accompanied us back to the office. It only took a moment to force the drawer open.

I began to explore the contents. I picked up a journal with a hard red cover. I opened it—and whistled.

"What is it?" Chaille leaned over my shoulder trying to get a better look.

"I've heard that a lot of criminals like to keep a record of their conquests. Jim McLaren was one of those, it appears," I said as I set the notebook on the desk.

Tom and Chaille watched while I thumbed through the first few pages. Every other page had a name at the top, a photo, a date, and a few paragraphs. Each entry turned out to be a *set* of two pages. The name and photo were on the left page, but the writing continued on to the right-hand page. I didn't take time to read anything, simply turning back to the first page so I could do a thorough gleaning for information. Even though I was anxious to find my mother's name, which I assumed would be near the back, I wanted to look at the book one set of pages at a time.

The first name was beside a date from twenty years ago. The woman had been McLaren's first wife, and the date was the date of her death. He'd written: *She was the first. She died on the date above after twenty-five years of marriage. The only way she failed me was in not producing children. But I forgave her. She certainly tried. We had twenty-five good years together.* On the opposite page, following some brief memories, he'd continued: *If she hadn't gotten sick and died, she might have been the only one in my life. But she made me promise the day she passed away that I would not live the rest of my life alone. I loved that woman, so I did what she asked. Since then, I've been very lucky in love.*

A small color photograph of a pretty woman who looked like she was in her late fifties was pasted on the page. Beside it was another small photograph of a young couple. There was more writing on the facing page. We all agreed that the handsome young man in the picture was Jim McLaren around forty-five years ago and that the young woman was the girl he'd married back then. From the things he'd written, it appeared that he'd truly loved her. But it also appeared that he'd snapped after her untimely death. I turned the page with interest, more anxious than ever to get to my mother's page, if it was there, and I was almost certain it was.

The next page contained a name, an address in South Dakota, a photograph, and more writing. This woman looked a lot like his wife.

"This creeps me out," Chaille commented from behind me.

"I'm guessing it gets worse," I said as I began to read what he'd written on this page. Once again, he'd expressed love for this woman and recorded the date he'd married her as well as the date she'd died. There was no mention of the cause of her death. He did include something very interesting. He'd recorded the information that had been taken off a credit card in her name. Then there was a notation about how much he'd spent using that card. Near the end of the second page, he'd written: *She never did realize I was stealing from her, the poor, sweet woman.*

Page after page, we read of women who'd been sucked in by Jim McLaren's sweet tongue, deceitful promises, and loving ways. Some he'd married, some were dead—as we already knew—some were still out there somewhere, but every one of them had unwittingly contributed to his wealth. Of those who were dead, there were only brief sketches of the events surrounding their deaths. He took no credit for any of them dying, but in some cases he did write that they'd pressed him about their missing finances and that he'd had to terminate his relationship with them. But that was the closest he came to admitting responsibility for their deaths.

His journal had some pages that were not yet closed out. One was about our friend from Twin Falls, Jane Parley, who'd helped lead to Jim's end, and another about Christy Haynam, who was right then driving toward us to claim her surprise—a devastating surprise. I turned the page, my stomach in my throat.

CHAPTER TWENTY-TWO

WE HAD FINALLY REACHED THE last entry. I looked almost in horror at the picture of my beloved mother pasted there. Bile rose in my throat. My hands were shaking as I began to read. Tom, who had lost all interest in the forensic search of the Corvette, and Chaille, who was glued to my side, read along with me. Chaille reached over and took hold of my hand. Her tender action had a calming effect, and I was able to swallow the bile and read.

As in each previous case, except for his first wife, McLaren's first comments about my mother were glowing, but gradually, I could detect anger creeping in. At the end, he referred to what he'd stolen from her using her credit card. He made no mention of the money I was certain he'd been bleeding away from the proceeds of the hotel, money Tess Everest had alerted me to. Then he made mention of one of Mom's sons causing him problems and of how angry that made him. He didn't name the son that had interfered, but the three of us agreed that it must have been Sean and that he had died because of his involvement, whatever it was.

I looked up from the page. "I still don't think McLaren could have killed Sean himself, but if he and Hugo had been partners in that robbery, then it only makes sense that Hugo was still his partner in a way. I think he was directly involved in the murder. How do you two see it?"

They both agreed, but Chaille asked, "Then how is Vernon Bentley involved?"

"Could there simply have been money in it for him?" Sergeant Brolin suggested.

"That could be it," I said, rubbing my aching eyes. "He might have been promised a share of the loot from the bank robbery if he'd help them gain ownership of the hotel."

"If the money is hidden there," Chaille offered. I looked at her, and she quickly added, "Which I think it is."

"I think that's a distinct possibility," I agreed. "But then again, maybe there's something we don't know about Vernon Bentley, something we're missing."

I looked back down at the page, almost afraid to read on. But I forced myself. The last words almost made my stomach lurch. *She didn't have to die. All she had to do was marry me. I loved that woman. If only her son had stayed out of her business, she'd still be alive. I am grieved.*

I closed the book, dropped my head in my hands, and sobbed softly. Chaille put her arms around me, saying nothing. I was aware of Tom Brolin stepping away and saying quietly, "I'll go see how the forensic team is coming on the Corvette."

After a long time, I straightened up. "I'm sorry, Chaille. I'm not usually this emotional."

"You have the right to be," she soothed, tenderly stroking my back. "Should we go back to searching? I have a feeling there's a lot more to be found in this creep's house."

I turned and faced her. For a moment, our eyes were locked, then I reached out, and she melted into my arms. With feelings that came from the very depths of my soul, I said, "I am so grateful you're here." After that, neither of us spoke as our lips became otherwise occupied—pleasantly, comfortingly occupied.

When I finally turned back to the desk and once again looked into the drawer where I'd found the journal, I spotted a large manila envelope. I picked it up and felt my heart race. I opened it up and dumped its contents next to the journal. Little rectangles of plastic scattered across the desk. Credit cards—several dozen *stolen* credit cards.

I thumbed through them, recognizing names from the journal. I searched for the one that had been in my mother's name, one he had obtained without her knowledge, but as I expected, it wasn't there. He'd been using it in the days before his death.

Also missing was a card with the name of Christy Haynam. That one was in the evidence room of the Twin Falls Police Department. I supposed there could have been a second one, but there wasn't.

"I found something, Keene," Chaille said from across the small office. As I turned, she blurted, "So have you, it looks like."

"Yes, a bunch of stolen credit cards. What have you got there?"

"A letter from your brother," she said, holding it up with a gloved hand. "Sean?"

"I'm sure, but it isn't signed, and it's typed."

I left the pile of credit cards and stepped over to Chaille. It went from her gloved hand to mine. I looked at it, read it, and then carried it over to the desk, where I placed it with the growing collection of evidence. The letter had been short and succinct. My brother had told Mr. McLaren in very plain language that he was not going to get the hotel and unless he quit trying there would be serious consequences.

"Is there an envelope in there?" I asked as I walked back to Chaille and pointed into the open file drawer.

"No, just the letter. It was in a folder labeled *Interfering People.*"

"Is there anything else in the folder?"

"Yes, but this is the only thing I pulled out."

"Let's see what else is in there," I suggested. Chaille pulled the entire file out, and we went over to the desk and spread it open.

The next letter in the folder, again without an envelope, was from an attorney. This time, however, there was letterhead at the top of the page with the lawyer's full name, address, and California bar number. We read it quickly. It was an official-sounding document telling Jim McLaren that unless he agreed to an immediate divorce from a Joyce Stone, a name from the journal, a lawsuit would be filed and the police notified. It was dated over five years ago. At this point, I didn't see where that letter had much significance as far as our current investigation was concerned, but Chaille made a note to consider calling the lawyer later.

We laid that letter on the desk and proceeded to the next paper. It and three more were from relatives of various wives and girlfriends threatening to make trouble. "It's not worth the time right now, but at some point, we may want to compare these notes with the list of women in the journal. It would be interesting to see if there is a correlation between the women who are deceased and these demands from family members for Mr. McLaren to back off," I said.

Chaille nodded and picked up the next paper. She began to read it as I laid more letters down on the stack next to the folder.

"Keene," she said, something in her voice catching my attention, "you're mentioned in this."

I took it from her and read. This letter, unlike the previous one from my brother, was signed. Well, it wasn't exactly signed, but *Sean Tempest* was typed where I would have expected a signature. Again, the letter was short, but it was to the point. *Mr. McLaren, my mother tells me that she thinks you're considering doing something to my little brother. Don't try anything. I'm warning you. We've hired protection for him. Keene works part-time for the LAPD. They, like my mother and me, will not tolerate any kind of harassment against my brother. Leave him alone!*

I looked at Chaille and said, "I always thought Sean hated me. And maybe he did, but he also defended me. He admitted to Ollie in the bar that he cared about me. I'm feeling guilty now for the way I whipped him that night at the hotel. I probably could have been gentler. Why couldn't he have just let me know that he cared a little bit?"

"He was a tough and angry guy," Chaille said. "Maybe he didn't know how to tell you, so he just went on treating you the same way he had when you were young."

Tom Brolin came in from the garage a moment later. I showed him the letters. "Hmph," he snorted. "My healing shoulder and your shot-up truck tell me that Mr. McLaren didn't take to the warning very well."

"But we know one thing," I said. "Sean didn't dump McLaren in the Snake River. And since he didn't, there's someone else out there who is a killer. And whoever it is, they want both Grady and me dead, and probably Bree as well."

Chaille added, "I can't see where it could be anyone but Hugo Starling and Vernon Bentley."

I didn't disagree, but something was still bothering me, nibbling about the edges of my mind. I said nothing about that, but I did say, "I sure wish someone would catch those two."

"In time," Tom said. "They'll slip up. Now, about the Corvette, Keene. It was pretty much clean, as you know. No luggage, no personal papers. Not even any gas receipts. But there were fingerprints, and they successfully lifted a bunch. They'll process them in the morning. They're busy the rest of today. LA has lots of crime. We had a double murder a little while ago. The crew's headed there now."

"Don't forget that some of the fingerprints will be mine," I noted. "I appreciate their help, and yours."

Along with Sergeant Brolin, we bagged the evidence we had found so far. Then we again began to search. We hadn't made any more discoveries by the time my phone rang.

"Keene," Chief Thompkins said, "are you having any luck?"

"As a matter of fact, we are." I told him what we'd found as I stepped out of the office.

"You guys are doing well," he said. "Keep at it. Deputy White and I have been discussing things. And with what you just told me, I think we're on the right track. I think a thorough search of Sean's house might be helpful. Perhaps he kept correspondence from McLaren. With permission from you and your siblings, we could search it."

"Go ahead. It sounds like a good idea. If I could be there, I'd help," I said.

"You two have your work cut out for you down there," he said. "Should I check with Bree and Grady too?"

"I'll call Bree and get right back to you if she has any objections, but I'm sure she won't. I'll try calling Grady, but I'm sure he won't care. Anyway, he can be hard to reach," I answered.

"Can you let me know within the hour? We could begin later this afternoon."

I agreed, we disconnected, and I called Bree. It took several minutes to bring her up to date on the latest developments. When I'd finished, I asked her if she had any objections to Chief Thompkins searching Sean's house. As I suspected, not only did she not object, but she was anxious to have it done. "I'll try to call Grady," I told her, "and get his feelings on it."

"It won't do you any good," she said. "I tried to call him earlier, just to make sure he was okay. I got a recording. It sounded like he made it just for the two of us. He said he was under a lot of stress with his new job and wouldn't be checking his messages for a day or two."

"Is the recording for us or is it for Jean?"

"I never thought of that," she admitted. "I expect you're right. Jean did tell me she'd called him a couple of times and that he'd told her not to call back. He might be making sure she doesn't bother him. It breaks my heart. I wish those two could work out their problems, whatever they are."

"I'll try calling him anyway," I said.

Bree was right; all I got was the message she'd described. With a shrug, I called the chief back and gave him the go-ahead.

I'd been making my calls in Mr. McLaren's living room. So when I was done, I rejoined Tom and Chaille in the office. "Any more luck?" I asked.

"Yes. I found a stash of letters from women. They were in a locked file drawer. Sergeant Brolin used the screwdriver again. They're on the desk," Chaille responded. "We thought we'd wait to go through them until you had finished making your calls."

"Thanks," I said. "Let's do it now."

We began riffling through the papers. "This guy didn't throw things away," Chaille marveled a few minutes later. "I think he must have kept every letter he got from his girlfriends."

Indeed, there was an assortment of them. We perused each one. Mostly they were love letters of the mushy variety. But some were from angry women, ones who felt jilted. "I'm surprised he kept some of these, as angry as some of them sound," Chaille said, showing me a particularly bitter letter. "I also wonder why he didn't put them in the interfering persons file."

"Probably because they were angry but hadn't taken it beyond that. They may not have gotten others involved, at least not when he filed these letters," Tom guessed. "Anyway, there are a lot of letters here. They wouldn't have fit in that other folder."

"I guess McLaren was an equal opportunity hoarder," I said, trying to lighten my own mood. It didn't work. And it only got worse when I finally found a letter from my mother to Jim.

I handed it to Chaille without reading it. "You read it," I insisted. "And then tell me what it says."

She took it from my hand without a word and began to read. The color drained from her face. Her hand trembled a little bit. Twice she looked up from the letter and caught my eye, shook her head, and went back to reading. When she finished, she said, "Keene, I can't tell you what it says. You'll have to read it for yourself, but why don't you sit down first."

I was more worried than ever as I followed Chaille's advice and sat down at Jim's desk. Then she handed me the letter. I looked at it with apprehension. The letter was not at all what I'd expected. The tone of my mother's letter was one of anger. She berated McLaren for making light of her concerns about money being deliberately bled from the business. From her words, it wasn't too difficult to figure out what Jim must have told her. She wrote that it was hard not to believe he had something to do with it; I could picture him adamantly denying any involvement.

It was clear that he was trying to place the blame elsewhere. About an unknown credit card in her name, he must have told her that she'd just forgotten getting it, for she wrote: *I did not forget getting a new card. I am very careful about such things. Someone opened it in my name. Surely it wasn't you.*

Without looking up from the letter, I mumbled to Chaille, "She more or less accused him of applying for a credit card in her name. That alone may have cost Mom her life."

Chaille murmured her assent, and I kept reading. Suddenly, the words on the page seemed to slap me. *I know that the proceeds of the hotel are down, way down. But I resent your telling me that I needed to look closer to home for the source of that problem. And to think that when I told you it wasn't anyone from here in Hardy and it certainly wasn't my family, you had the gall to tell me that I needed to look at Tess Everest! What a horrible thing to say about a sweet young woman. I am still angry over that. And to think that when I told you I would trust her with my life, you would say something so cruel—trusting her with my life as well as with my money could cost me both. How horrible of you, Jim. I don't want to ever see you again. Don't come around at all. You are not welcome here anymore.*

The letter went on for a few more lines, but there was nothing more that concerned me, just my mother saying good-bye to someone she'd come to care for. It was sad.

I put the letter down on the desk, took a deep breath, and without looking up, said, "I've been thinking that I was missing something. I hate to even think it, but, well, how close are you to Tess?"

"We're good friends," Chaille said. "If you're suggesting that she could have had anything to do with either the theft or your mother's death, then I'd have to say you're crazy."

"I hope I'm not crazy." I stood up.

Tom Brolin had been standing a few feet from us. But now he stepped over and pointed to the letter. "May I?"

"Of course," I said. He picked up the letter and began to read. I spoke once more to Chaille. "I'm not saying that Tess is involved, but do you think it would hurt to check her out a little closer? I mean, you know, see if she's made any large purchases lately or if she has some large savings accounts somewhere."

Chaille's face grew hard. "It can't be," she said. "Tess is honest, and she's good. And isn't she the one who helped you see what had been happening?"

"Yes, and she's been a great help, so would it be fair to her *not* to disprove this accusation—absurd as it is?"

For a moment, Chaille just looked at me, her eyes flashing, and then her face softened. "I'm sorry, Keene. You're right. She has the right to have her name cleared. Who knows, Jim might have said similarly horrible things about Tess to others."

"Who's Tess Everest?" Tom asked, looking up from the letter.

"She's our accountant. She was my mother's, and now she's mine," I answered.

"And you both think she couldn't in any way be involved?"

"There's no way," Chaille said firmly.

"As we were just saying, she's the one who alerted me to the fact that someone had been bleeding my mother dry. Only after Jim quit coming around did things pick back up," I said.

"I see." He put the letter down. "I know an investigator who's skilled at finding hidden, laundered money. Would you like me to give him a call?"

"Yes," Chaille said without hesitation. "We must clear her name as soon as we can."

"I'll get right on it," he said. "Give me a little more information about her."

We told him what we could. To my surprise, Chaille knew Tess's birth date and where she had gone to college. I told him what little I knew, including who her boss was. Finally, Tom said, "This will give us something to start with. Just let me take this from here. And don't either of you feel guilty. Good police work includes clearing the innocent as well as finding the guilty. You two get back to searching, and I'll get on the phone. Remember, you're expecting a guest in a few hours."

We went back to work. Two hours later, we'd finished our search of the office with no more significant discoveries. We turned next to the master bedroom. We had barely begun to go through the dresser drawers when I got a call. It was Paige Everest, and she was upset.

"Tess is gone!" she wailed.

CHAPTER TWENTY-THREE

"What do you mean, gone?" I asked as my mind raced, considering all the possibilities. To Chaille, I whispered, "Tess is missing." Alarm registered on her face, and then her hand flew to her mouth.

"She's not at work and she's not at home, and no one knows where she is." The distraught girl was rambling. "We were planning to go to dinner before I went on shift at the hotel. But when I called her to tell her that Mom wanted to come with us, the receptionist said Tess had left the office at noon and hadn't come back."

"Did that seem to surprise her coworkers?" I asked.

"Yes," Paige said. "She had a meeting scheduled with a client at two o'clock and another at three. She missed both appointments. We've been trying to call her cell phone, but it just keeps going to voice mail."

"Paige, you need to calm down." I could hear her hyperventilating over the phone.

"What should I do? I can't go to work," she sobbed.

"Where are you now?"

"I'm at home. Mom's sitting here with me. She's about to fall apart."

Not unlike Paige herself. "You two stay right there," I said. "I'll get someone to meet you there. And don't worry about the hotel. I'll have my sister take care of it."

"Thanks, Keene. Tess's got to be okay. She's just got to."

As soon as I'd ended the phone call, I dialed Chief Thompkins's cell. He answered right away. "Are you still at Sean's?" I asked.

"Yes, and we've already found something interesting," he replied.

"You'll have to tell me about that later," I said. "Right now we've got to have someone get over to the Everest house in Hardy. Tess has disappeared."

Apparently, my news took precedence over his, for he said, "How did you learn this?"

"Paige called. She and her mother are distraught," I said. "Tess has been gone since noon, missed two appointments, doesn't answer her cell phone, and hasn't made contact with anyone."

"Okay, clearly Roger and I can't go there right now, but I'll call Payton and send him over immediately. Do you know anything about what's going on with Tess?"

I hesitated, not sure how much to mention of the allegations we'd discovered in my mother's letter. My hesitation was apparently too long, for Damion asked, "Keene, there is something, isn't there? Tell me."

So I told him.

"That's impossible," he said after I'd finished. "She's as honest as the day is long."

"I know, but we can't just ignore it. I already put an investigation into motion regarding her personal finances."

"Okay, good. Keep me advised, and I'll do the same for you. Right now I'll get Payton on the move."

After completing the call, I dialed my sister's cell phone.

"Are you guys finding anything else down there?" Bree asked. "I need something to do before I go nuts and drive my husband nuts as well."

"Okay, I'm calling because there is something you can do," I said.

"Does it involve leaving the hotel?" she asked. "If so, I don't think we should do that."

"You stay in the hotel. But here's what I need for you to do. And Ron can help you."

"Okay, we'll do whatever you need, Keene."

"Paige Everest can't come in to work tonight. I need for you and Ron to run the registration desk."

"What's the matter with Paige?"

"Tess, her sister, is missing," I said. "We hope it's nothing, but Paige, as you can imagine, is terribly upset."

"Oh, Keene, when will it ever end?" she moaned.

"We're making progress," I said, although I honestly didn't think we'd learned much about anyone other than the dead insurance man.

"Can you tell me more?" Bree asked.

"Not right now. I'm really busy. But I'll catch you up when I get a few minutes."

"Okay, I guess that's all I can ask."

"Do you know what to do at the desk?"

"Not really, but Byron Row is working. He can fill us in before he goes off shift," she said. "We'll take care of the hotel. You don't have to worry about it. I'll be waiting to hear from you."

I thanked her and ended the call. Then I turned to Chaille. "The chief started to tell me about finding something in Sean's house. I'm going to call him back and find out what it is."

But before I could make the call, my phone rang. Bree's voice greeted me. "Keene, Ron just reminded me that there's a letter here for you from Tess."

"Do you have it right there with you?"

"Yes, Ron just handed it to me. We thought you might want to know what's in it," she said.

"Yes, please open it," I said urgently.

I waited for a moment. I could hear paper tearing as Bree opened the envelope. Then she said, "Would you like me to read it? It's just a sheet of notepaper, folded up."

"Please," I said, the curiosity building so fast I thought my head might explode.

There was a rustle of paper, and then Bree said, "It's really short, Keene. She says she needs to meet with you as soon as you can, that there's something she needs to tell you. And she says she's sorry."

"That's all?"

"That's it. It must be pretty important."

"Yes, it must. Thanks, Bree."

"I'm sorry it wasn't more helpful," she said.

I was afraid that it could mean a lot more than Bree could imagine. "Yeah, well, it was worth opening," I said. "Thanks again."

I immediately phoned the chief back. "Is Payton on his way to the Everests'?" I asked.

"He's there," he said. "And I'm worried, Keene. Could something have happened to Tess?"

"I don't know," I said as I wiped the sweat from my forehead. "This is so unexpected. Tess left a letter for me at the hotel. She wrote that she wanted to meet with me right away."

"That's not good. Too many people are vanishing lately. I don't like the feel of it." Then he abruptly shifted the subject. "Keene, we've been looking at Sean's guns. Do you know anything about how he took care of them?"

"I have no idea," I told him.

"We inspected them closely," Damion said. "They're all clean except for two. He has an old .45 semiautomatic pistol and a .30-30 rifle that have been fired. Neither has been cleaned since their use. I don't suppose you'd have any idea which guns he used the most."

"Nope. Remember, Sean and I weren't exactly close."

"I'm just covering all the bases," the chief said. "Okay, so here's the kicker. Slugs have been recovered from Grady's car. He was shot at with both of the calibers I just mentioned."

"Are you suggesting that he was shot at by Sean's guns and then they were returned to the house?" I asked, puzzled at such an absurd thought.

"It's worth pursuing," he said. "I'm sure you don't mind if we take the guns into evidence and have ballistics run on them. That's all it will take to either prove or disprove their use in the attempt on Grady's life. And while we're at it, we'll check for fingerprints; although, I suspect that if they were used, they will have been wiped clean. But it's worth a try."

"Have you found anything else?" I asked.

"No, but if we do, I'll let you know."

Chaille looked as worried as I felt when I told her what Tess had written. Out of loyalty, we both avoided pointing fingers at her. But as I continued the search of Jim McLaren's house, I hated the thoughts that were running through my mind. I kept telling myself that Tess was loyal to me and to my family and that she couldn't possibly have done anything wrong. The matter of Sean's guns was something else, and Chaille and I speculated about that to each other. The most obvious conclusion, if the ballistics matched, would be that the person or persons who tried to kill my surviving brother did so with weapons *borrowed* from Sean's house. What purpose that served was unclear. In fact, it didn't make any sense at all.

***

The doorbell rang. "It's still a little early for our visit from Christy Haynam," I said, glancing at my watch. "I wonder who it could be."

Tom Brolin, who had been on the phone orchestrating an investigation into Tess's affairs, chuckled. "I'll get it," he said. "I thought you two might be as hungry as I am. I ordered pizza."

"Good idea," I said. "I'm famished."

"So am I," Chaille agreed.

We ate and then resumed our work. The next time the doorbell rang, I answered it. Standing there looking very puzzled was an attractive woman of about sixty with short black hair. She was dressed in designer clothes. She had the look of wealth from her shoes to her hair. In the driveway was a sleek blue Cadillac.

"I'm sorry," the woman said. "I must have gotten the wrong house. I'm looking for Jim McLaren?"

"Are you Christy Haynam?" I asked.

"Yes, and who are you?" she asked, her eyes squinting with suspicion as she took a half step back.

"My name is Keene Tempest." I pulled out my LAPD ID. "I'm a police officer. Please come in. This is Mr. McLaren's home."

Chaille and Tom came into the room from the spare bedroom where we had been searching for the past hour. "Sergeant Tom Brolin and Officer Chaille Donovan," I said, pointing to them. "We need to talk to you."

"But . . . but I'm meeting my fiancé, Jim McLaren," she said as her eyes wandered around the living room. The puzzlement on her face was growing more pronounced by the second. "There's some mistake," she said. "Jim's house is very large, very expensive. It's not a small house like this."

"But you've never actually been there," I stated.

"Well, no, but he told me all about it. Where is he? I just talked to him a few hours ago." She was still standing at the doorway.

"Please, ma'am, come in and sit down. There are some things we need to talk to you about."

She stepped tentatively through the door, and Tom slipped past her and pushed it shut. "I talked to Jim a few hours ago," she repeated. "He said he had a surprise for me. He also said he was not feeling well. There is a big mistake here. I need to call him." She pulled out a small folding cell phone.

"Is it *Mrs.* Haynam?" I asked.

"Yes, I'm a widow."

"It was me that you spoke with on the phone," I told her as I took hold of her elbow and gently guided her to a chair on the far side of the room. She sat down at last, and I did the same, as did my two colleagues.

"I'm sorry to have deceived you, but we're investigating a series of crimes and very much wanted to meet with you."

"I can't imagine why," she said with a pouty face as she smoothed her short dyed hair. "I seldom come to LA, and I am certainly not a criminal. But somebody is. Somebody stole my credit card, but then I guess you already know that if it was you on the phone this morning."

"Jim McLaren has been using your credit card."

Her pout turned to one of utter astonishment. She clasped her hands over her chest. "I can't believe that. Where is he? I want to talk to him. He'll straighten this out."

"I'm afraid he won't," I said as gently as I could. "Mr. McLaren is dead."

Mrs. Haynam gasped, and her hands flew from her chest to her mouth. "That can't be!" she protested loudly. But then she started to cry.

We gave her time to work some of the grief and shock out of her system before I continued. "Jim McLaren was a criminal, and his crimes finally caught up with him. He was murdered in Twin Falls, Idaho."

"He loves . . . loved me," she protested, her voice now subdued. She shook her head slowly and began wringing her hands. "You must have the wrong man."

"No, we have the right man. Let me show you something." As planned, Chaille pulled on a pair of gloves and retrieved the journal from the home office.

She slipped beside Mrs. Haynam and knelt on the floor. "I am going to show you something," Chaille said. "But this journal is evidence, so I can't allow you to touch it." Chaille opened the book to the two facing pages that were devoted to Mrs. Haynam. The pages spoke clearly for themselves. She read it as Chaille held it. Tears again filled her eyes.

Finally, she asked, "What is on the other pages?"

Chaille glanced up at me, and I nodded. She then flipped randomly to another page. Mrs. Haynam scanned down through it without a word. Then Chaille flipped to another page and one more.

"He was married to some of these women," I said. "And at least once he was married to more than one at the same time. He did a short stint in prison for bigamy a few years back." I looked at Chaille. "Officer Donovan, please show her my mother's page."

"Your . . . your . . . mother?" she stammered.

"Yes. He stole from her as well, but she never married him. She's dead now. Murdered," I said, the words coming out much more harshly than I had intended.

"Oh, I'm so sorry. Did . . . did . . . Jim do it?"

"We don't know for sure, but there's evidence pointing in that direction. Unfortunately, he died before we had a chance to talk to him. He might have been able to clear up the matter of my mother's death."

Mrs. Haynam's face was as white as a sheet. "I'm so very, very sorry. I honestly thought he loved me," she said in a shaking voice. Then her eyes narrowed. "He was living a lie."

"I'm afraid so." I nodded. "Now, the reason we wanted to see you is to see if you can help us in some way. We believe that some other men have helped him. Did he ever mention the names Hugo Starling or Vernon Bentley?"

She slowly shook her head. "Not that I recall. I don't think so."

"I have pictures of them here," I said. I'd brought the pictures into the house for the purpose of letting her see them. I didn't have much hope, but it was worth a try.

I showed her former Detective Bentley's picture first. She shook her head. Then I pulled out the one of Hugo Starling. She stared for a moment, and then her eyes began to grow wide. "That's Ervin Stuler. He was going to be our best man. He and Jim are—were—good friends."

Chaille and I exchanged a meaningful glance. The connection between Hugo and McLaren had been firmly established.

We talked a little while longer before Mrs. Haynam left to find a hotel for the night. My partners and I discussed what we'd learned. In sum, it strengthened our theory that the money from the robbery was hidden somewhere in the Tempest Hotel. We also theorized that Hugo didn't want to share the money with Jim McLaren, strengthening the theory that Hugo was Jim's killer, or at least one of them.

My mother's death could have been orchestrated by either Hugo or Jim or both simply because she stood in the way of their gaining possession of the hotel. Since we now knew that Hugo and McLaren were still in touch, McLaren could have financed Hugo's attempt to buy the hotel. And finally, we decided, Sean may have died at their hands because he somehow found out what they were up to. The note in the trunk of the Corvette may have been written by Jim or Hugo or someone working with them, like Vernon. I felt encouraged that we were going to get to the bottom of all of this yet. But I also felt an increased urgency as the lives of myself, my sister, and my remaining brother were still at risk.

We decided to search a little longer. About an hour after our visitor left, my phone beeped, indicating that I'd received a text message. I pulled the iPhone from my pocket and was surprised to see that the text was from Tess Everest. I quickly opened the message and read:

Keene, I've done something terrible. I had to leave town. Don't try to find me. It will only bring more pain.

CHAPTER TWENTY-FOUR

CHAILLE AND I WERE BEYOND stunned. "I'm telling you, Keene," Chaille insisted, "Tess is not capable of doing something terrible."

"But she admits it right here," I said, shaking my phone. "So I guess she is capable. The question I have is what it is that she did."

"I just can't believe it, Keene," Chaille persisted.

"Then why would she tell me not to look for her?" I pointed out.

Chaille shook her head but suddenly shook her fist fiercely. "Keene, she said that she needed to talk to you in the letter Bree read you. She *wants* you to find her. That's what she really wants."

"But that's not what she said," I insisted.

"I know her very well, Keene. She's smart. She used her cell phone," Chaille said, looking thoughtful. "We can find out where she is by tracing the phone. And I'm betting that she knows that, that she's counting on it."

"Maybe, or maybe not," I said, running my hand through my hair. "But you do have a point. We can trace her whether that's what she wants or not. Let's get on it."

Tom Brolin was sticking with us, and for that I was grateful since he had the ability to tap the resources of the LAPD. We didn't even have to ask him. He was already making a call. He got someone on the line and then asked, "Keene, what's Tess's cell phone number?" I gave it to him, and he relayed the information. When he'd completed his call, he said, "They'll go to work on this right now while the text message is fresh."

"Thanks, Tom," I said. "I don't know what we'd do without you."

"Hey, I'm part of this, Keene," he reminded me. "I took a bullet meant for you, and I take that personal. We'll get these people. I hope your accountant isn't involved, but if she is, we'll find out."

"I think I'll try calling her," I said, looking at Tom for confirmation.

"It can't hurt," he agreed.

I tried, but all I got was voice mail. I fought off the disappointment I was feeling. I tried again a couple of minutes later with the same results. Then I sent a text. There was no response.

Once again I bothered my boss, the chief of police in Hardy. "Damion," I said when I got him on the phone. "Are you still at Sean's house?"

"We are," he answered. "And we found something I was going to call you about."

"What is it?" I asked eagerly, hoping it was something that would help—and not incriminate—Tess. I desperately wanted for her not to be involved, although I was very much afraid that she was.

"Sean had a letter from Jim McLaren. It was in the pocket of a sports coat that was hanging in his closet," the chief said. "Would you like me to read it to you?"

"Of course," I said as I thought about the letter from Sean to Jim that Chaille had found in Jim's interfering people file.

Chief Thompkins said, "It reads as follows: *Mr. Tempest, I want to be very clear on something. Your mother loves me. I love her. We plan to marry. No one is going to stop that from occurring. Your little brother, however, apparently thinks otherwise. You better get him under control or he will pay for it. Do I make myself clear?*"

"That letter makes no sense. I didn't even know about McLaren."

"But apparently he thought you did," Damion countered.

"But Mom never once even mentioned Jim, let alone marriage to the creep. And I talked to her every few days," I argued.

"My guess is that he knew she talked to you regularly. Maybe she was resisting his advances, and he simply assumed it was because of you," the chief suggested.

"Okay, that makes sense," I admitted. "But I'm not sure it helps us a lot. However, we have found some things here that do help. We met with a woman by the name of Christy Haynam. She also planned to marry McLaren, and she identified the picture of Hugo Starling as the man who was going to be the best man at their wedding. He was using an alias."

Chief Thompkins let out a whoop. "Wow," he said, clearly excited. "That's the break I think we've been looking for. Great work, Keene. Now if we can just find Hugo and Vernon."

"Chief, there's something else you need to know. It's about Tess Everest."

"Payton's been meeting with her mother and sister. They're distraught, but frankly I think her disappearance probably has nothing to do with our case," he said. "They said that she'd been writing to a young fellow from Utah. They say she denies it, but they're convinced that she's quite serious about him. They admit that she simply might have run off to see him, that he might have been pressing her to come."

"That's not it, Chief. I wish it were."

"Why do you say that? What is it you know that I apparently don't?"

"She texted me a few minutes ago." I told him what the text said, and the line went silent. "Chief, are you there?"

I heard him clear his throat, and then he finally spoke. "I don't know what to say, Keene. And despite what she told you, we've got to try to find her."

"We're on it," I said. I told him Sergeant Brolin was using the vast resources of the Los Angeles Police Department to assist us in the effort.

***

We searched the house until ten that night, but we didn't find anything else of significance. Tom went home after Chaille and I had retrieved our bags from his car and packed them in the Corvette. We set out to look for a hotel for the night. Instead of flying back to Hardy, we decided to drive the recovered car back. We planned to leave early the next morning.

We had dinner in the restaurant on the main floor, and shortly before midnight we were in our rooms. I was brushing my teeth when my cell phone began ringing.

"Keene, it's Tom. I'm sorry to call so late, but I figured that if they could get *me* out of bed, I could do the same to you." The statement was accompanied by a light chuckle, but I could tell that whatever he was about to tell me wasn't something I would laugh about.

"Who are *they*?" I asked as my recent dinner began to stir unpleasantly about in my stomach.

"Actually, I've heard from both the officer that was looking into Tess's finances and the one who was attempting to trace her cell phone," he said.

"And?" I prompted.

"First, Miss Everest is in Arizona. She has done some major driving since she left Hardy."

"Where in Arizona?"

"She's at a little resort called Jacob Lake, not too far south of Kanab, Utah."

"I know where it is. I've been there," I said. "I hope she's still there."

"Her car, a Chevy Cavalier, has OnStar. They're helping us track her. Right now she apparently has a room there," Tom said.

"Then that's where I'm heading," I said with sudden determination.

"Tonight?"

"Yes, tonight."

"Are you going to fly?" he asked.

"Sort of," I said. "I'm taking Sean's Corvette."

"I take it you are taking Chaille."

"She'd never let me go without her, and frankly I don't want to," I said. "Now, what did your other officer say, the one looking at the money angle?"

"Yes, that," he said slowly. "This is not good news, Keene." I waited. After a short pause, he went on. "She's been getting money from someone—possibly Hugo Starling."

"She does his accounting," I said, unfazed. "I would have expected that."

"Fifty thousand dollars?" he asked calmly.

I was no longer unfazed. "She told me Hugo didn't have the money to buy the hotel. Fifty thousand would have made a good down payment," I said.

"So either she lied or she got the money from someone else. What you need to do is find out why she lied and why someone was giving her that kind of money."

"Okay, I better get moving." I sighed. I could feel the desire to sleep pressing down on me.

Almost as though he could read my mind, Tom said, "Be careful driving, Keene. Don't fall asleep and wreck that beautiful car and hurt that gorgeous girl of yours."

I dialed Chaille's cell phone. It took her a while to answer. When she finally did, she sounded groggy. "What's up Keene? I was already in bed and asleep."

"I'm leaving for Arizona in a few minutes. I know where Tess is."

"I'm coming with you," she said, the grogginess vanishing like magic.

"I was hoping you'd say that," I told her. "You can help keep me awake."

She started to ask a question, but I said, "We can talk on the road. Let's pack as quickly as we can. We need to get there as soon as possible. I hope I don't get stopped for speeding. I'll come by your room in three or four minutes."

When I tapped on her door, she opened it immediately.

***

A few minutes later, Chaille entered our destination into the navigation system while I filled the gas tank. When we hit the road, we knew that it was just over an eight-hour drive to Jacob Lake. "I can do it in less," I said. "I hate to speed, but this is cop business, and the sooner we catch up with Tess, the better."

"Should we call Chief Thompkins?" she asked after we had been on the road for fifteen or twenty minutes.

"I've bugged him enough the past few hours. Let's let him sleep. We'll call when we get there." A minute later I spoke again. "Why don't you try to sleep? I'm wide awake now, but I might need you to spell me later."

"You'd let me drive this car?" she asked with a tease in her voice.

"Just sleep." I smiled. "Then we'll see."

She leaned across the console and kissed me lightly on the cheek. Then she let the seat back and tried to do what I'd asked. After about half an hour, she finally fell asleep. I couldn't have slept now if I'd tried. My mind was in high gear. I was mentally reviewing everything we knew about the case. Tess's involvement was a wild card in the whole thing. Hugo and Jim were bad guys. There was no doubt about that. But why Tess would help them was beyond me—unless . . .

I shook my fist in the air. Maybe she'd seen or heard something she shouldn't have and the terrible thing she'd done was keep it to herself. Or perhaps she'd confronted whoever the money came from, and she got paid to keep her mouth shut. Of all the alternatives I could think of, that one seemed the more likely of a litany of unlikely crimes. If that was all it was, I could help her.

As I continued to think things over, a very disturbing thought came to me. I ran it around in my mind for a minute or two. It was awful. It wasn't possible. I tried to dismiss it, but it wasn't going to be easy. I had allowed seeds of doubt to sprout, doubt about our theory of the case. I shook my head, but the doubts persisted. I drove on, disturbed, angry over my own thoughts, and worried sick.

For two more hours, I drove. Beside me, Chaille stirred from time to time. But she was sleeping well, and even though I was getting tired, I didn't disturb her.

When I finally knew that I had to stop or I'd fall asleep at the wheel, I looked at the time on the car's digital display screen. It was four in the morning. I'd been making good time. If I could keep up the pace, I could be at Jacob Lake by seven o'clock or a little before. Surely Tess wouldn't have left yet if we could get there by then.

I pulled off the freeway, checking my gas gauge. I was okay still, but I saw a station ahead and decided to fill up, just to be on the safe side. As I pulled up to the pumps, Chaille woke up.

"What's going on? Where are we? What time is it?"

"One question at a time, please," I said with a smile. "I'm getting sleepy and needed to walk around for a minute to get my blood stirring again. So I decided to gas the car up."

She glanced at the clock on the dash and said, "Keene, you should have woken me up sooner."

"I've been fine until now. And I'll be okay again in a few minutes."

"I'll drive while you sleep for a while if you'd like," she said.

"Are you sure?"

"Yes, I've had several hours of sleep. I can drive now and be fine."

"Okay."

***

In a few minutes we were back on the road with cold drinks and some snacks.

I sipped at my pop for a minute, wide awake again. I chewed on some chips and watched the profile of the woman who was becoming an inseparable part of my life. She glanced over at me in the dim interior of the Corvette and said with a smile, "I thought you were going to sleep."

"I'd rather look at you," I said.

"There's plenty of time for that later."

"Is that a promise?"

"Yes," she said firmly. "That's a promise."

With that sweet thought, I managed to fall asleep. When I woke up, two hours had passed, and I was considerably refreshed.

"Would you like me to take over the driving again?" I asked.

"If you'd like to."

I drove hard for the next hour and pulled into the parking area at Jacob Lake just after seven. "Would you know her car if you saw it?" I asked Chaille.

"Yes, but it's not here."

"I'll go see if she's checked out already," I said. It didn't take long to discover that Tess had been gone for ten minutes.

"She left already," I said as I got back in the car and fired up the powerful engine.

"We didn't pass her, so she must be headed south, toward the North Rim of the Grand Canyon," Chaille reasoned.

I gunned the car as soon as I'd reached the highway, and we were soon a red streak flying through the beautiful Kaibab National Forest. We had only gone a few miles when Tom called. The reception was poor, but I was able to hear him say, "She's driving south, Keene."

"So are we," I told him. "Keep me posted if you can."

I didn't catch his answer as we lost the signal. I was sure he'd do the best he could. I handed the phone to Chaille and said, "You keep the phone in case he calls back. I need to concentrate on my driving. We've got some ground to make up."

I drove hard, glad I had a car that was made for speed. Thirty minutes later, having passed several cars, Chaille suddenly pointed. "Up there, Keene. That could be Tess."

I slowed down and gained on the white Cavalier at a more reasonable rate. The car had Wyoming plates. "That's her," Chaille said. "Thank goodness."

"Then all we have to do is get her to pull over. I'll pull alongside her, and you signal for her to stop. I can't imagine that she'd even think of trying to outrun us."

It took a little while on the curvy road before there was a spot where I dared pull up beside her. When we were directly opposite of Tess, she looked over, her mouth dropping wide open in recognition. Chaille pointed to the side of the road, but Tess shook her head. Chaille pointed again, and I pulled slightly ahead of Tess. I guess she realized that if she didn't stop I'd force the issue. So she pulled off the road at a wide spot, and I stopped behind her.

She got out of her car, looking crushed and sad. We both got out and approached her. "Are you going to arrest me?" she asked.

CHAPTER TWENTY-FIVE

"For what?" I asked.

"For what I did." She began to sob, and Chaille put her arms around her. "I am so sorry."

"Tess," I said, trying to be gentle, "I . . . we don't know what you did. Would you like to tell us?"

"You don't know?" she asked. "Then why did you come after me?"

"We came because we are concerned about you, Tess. You're our friend. And your family is concerned as well," Chaille said.

Tess looked confused. "How did you find me?"

"That's what we do, Tess. We're police officers. Come on, let's find some place to talk," I suggested.

Her face hardened. "I don't want to talk. I did something I shouldn't have, and I don't want to talk about it."

"Tess, you have to. People's lives are at stake, and we need to get to the bottom of all this," I said, trying not to get angry.

"Yes, people's lives are at stake, including mine," she said with sudden bitterness. "Please, just let me go."

I shook my head. "It's not going to happen."

"You can't force me, not unless you arrest me," she said stubbornly.

Cars were passing, making it hard to hear. This wasn't working. I prayed silently for inspiration. Some came as I remembered what I'd thought about during the night. "You're in danger," I said. "But running won't help. We can protect you, Tess, and you have my word that we will."

"Mine too," Chaille chimed as she continued to keep her arms around her friend's shoulders.

"You don't know . . ." She hesitated for a moment, and then she asked, "Can we go someplace where we can talk?"

That's exactly what I'd asked her only moments ago, but I didn't remind her. I simply said, "Let's find a café somewhere and ask for the most private table they have. Then we'll talk."

"I'll follow you," she said as her eyes turned to the Corvette. Suddenly, she had a shocked look on her face. "Where did you find that?" she asked. "I thought it was stolen."

"It's a long story," I told her, surprised that she hadn't noticed it until now. I figured she must be scared out of her mind. "We'll talk about it over breakfast."

"I'll drive you," Chaille said. "We'll follow Keene. Where do we go?" she asked as her eyes focused on mine.

"Back to Jacob Lake," I said. "That's going to be the easiest."

Forty-five minutes later we pulled back into the parking area at the Jacob Lake Inn, having traveled much slower on the return trip than when we'd been pursuing Tess. We went into the restaurant, were shown to a private corner booth, and accepted menus and water.

I was in no hurry to question Tess. I was hoping that by just sitting there and quietly visiting, she would relax. But she was ready to get on with it. "So what do you want to know?" she asked.

"What the terrible thing was that you did," I answered. "First, though, does it have to do with the $50,000 you put in the bank?"

"What are you talking about?" she asked, looking quite shocked.

"We've been doing a little checking since you took off yesterday," I admitted. "We found that someone paid you that amount in cash."

"It's simply not true," she said adamantly. Just from the look of shock on her face it was hard not to believe her.

"The money's in your account," I countered.

"Which account, my savings or my checking?"

She had me there. I didn't know. I admitted as much. She pulled her iPhone from her purse and began to work with it. Finally, she said, "Here's my checking balance. Less than $2,000." She turned the phone so Chaille and I could see what was displayed on the screen.

A minute later she had her savings account opened. It held just over $30,000. "Those are the only accounts I have," she said. "So where is the $50,000?"

"I'll see if I can find out," I said. It was my turn to pull out my iPhone.

I called Tom Brolin, who said, "You found her?"

"That's right. We're back at the Jacob Lake Inn. She's here with us now. She says she doesn't know anything about the $50,000. We've checked both of her accounts, savings and checking, and she doesn't have that much money," I reported.

"I'll call you back in a few minutes with the details of the money," he said. "Also, I have the results of the fingerprints." He told me what they had found. After the thoughts I'd had during the night, I wasn't surprised. I said nothing about it to Chaille. I needed to think about it some more.

While we waited, we ordered our meals, and then I said, "We'll get to the bottom of the money thing, Tess, but why don't you tell us who you are afraid of."

She sat quietly for a moment, her hands in her lap and her eyes on the table in front of her. Finally, she said very quietly, "It's quite simple, really. I found a copy of a letter that your mother had sent to someone. She'd inadvertently enclosed it with some papers she'd given me. I didn't think much about it until after Sean was killed. Then I thought I should send it to the person it was addressed to. So I mailed it. I should have just left it alone, but I didn't know. That was the terrible mistake I made. He threatened to kill me. But I don't even know what it said. I never read it. I didn't think it was any of my business. *I* haven't done anything illegal, but this guy did something very, very evil. He confronted me on the phone, thinking that I knew, and before he finished shouting at me, I did know." She trembled with fear even as she sat there with us, two armed police officers who cared about her.

"When did he call you?" I asked. She told me. It fit with the time I noticed her odd behavior.

"He called me again at the office yesterday. That's when I ran. I had to."

"Who was it, and what exactly did he do?" I asked.

She looked around, the fear on her face growing. Then she leaned forward just a little bit, and we leaned toward her. Then, speaking so softly that I had to strain to hear, she told us who and what. Chaille gasped and grasped my arm.

I remembered the disturbing thoughts I'd had during the night as I was driving, the thoughts I'd been reminded of only moments before when Tom had told me about the fingerprints. It was like a light had come on. I didn't have it all figured out, but I had a pretty good idea that I knew what had happened . . . and what was still happening.

"Keene, are you all right?" Chaille was watching me.

The truth was that I was not all right, but I knew what had to be done and that it had to be done quickly. "I'm fine," I fibbed. "I had a feeling about this." That second statement was true.

"You did?" Chaille asked. "You didn't mention it to me."

"It was while I was driving during the night that it just sort of hit me," I said. "And Tom just told me whose fingerprints they found in the Corvette." I looked across the table at Tess. "He won't touch you, Tess. I promise. We'll keep you safe. Will you ladies excuse me for a minute? I need to make some calls. I'll be right back."

They both watched me as I slid out of the booth, their faces full of apprehension. I moved quickly away, left the restaurant, and walked over to the Corvette. Then I called Chief Thompkins. "Chief," I said when he answered his phone. "We have Tess. We're in Jacob Lake, Arizona."

"Has she told you what she did?" he asked.

"Yes, but she hasn't committed any crimes. She's a victim, not a criminal, and she's running scared—for good cause," I added. "We need to step up our efforts to locate the missing fugitives."

"Okay, Keene, tell me exactly what is going on," the chief ordered.

I did, and he said nothing for a moment. Finally, he spoke. "Have you warned your family? If this is true, the danger now is more critical than ever."

"I'm pretty sure it's true. Do you have any idea where Starling, Bentley, Criswell, and Cramer are?"

"Not a clue. And to make matters worse, it seems that Alvin's nephew Karl has disappeared."

My stomach twisted. "Karl, who admitted to stealing the Corvette but who we know for a fact didn't take it to Los Angeles? I'm pretty sure I know who did," I said.

"I wish you were wrong," the chief replied.

So did I. But I was sure I was on the right track, appalling as it was.

"What are your plans now, Keene?"

"I've got to get Tess someplace safe, someplace where no one can track her. I'm not sure yet where that will be, but I promised to protect her, and I have got to do that," I said, praying that it was possible.

"Then what?" the chief asked.

"Then I'm coming back to Hardy. I have a killer to catch."

I called Bree and spoke to her briefly. "We found Tess," I reported. "She's safe, and she hasn't done anything wrong. She's in danger, terrible danger, and she ran in an attempt to save her life. I'll call Paige and see if she and her mother can resume work."

"We're doing okay," Bree said. "We can handle it longer if we need to."

"I want you out of there today—this morning. Bree, go someplace and don't let anyone but me know where you are. Have your parents move your kids too. Things have gotten much worse."

She gasped. "Keene, what's happening?"

As I told her what we'd learned, she began to sob. "This can't be," she said.

"But it is. Where's Jean?"

"She'll be here this evening."

"Can you call her?"

"Yes, we've been talking regularly."

"Then do it. Don't tell her exactly what's happening, but make sure she knows that she can't come to Hardy yet. In fact, why don't you and Ron arrange to meet her someplace and hide out together until I give you word that it's safe to come back."

"Keene, this is horrible." She tried to get her emotions under control.

"Yes, it is, but we have to deal with it. Will you call Byron Rowe? Tell him you have to leave, and put him in charge until I get there. I'll call Paige and her mother and have them come back to work as well. I'll tell them to report to Byron."

"Okay. I will," she agreed.

"Good, and Bree, one other thing: leave your cell phones at the hotel. Buy new ones. Have Jean do the same. She can mail hers to the hotel. In fact, she needs to mail hers to the hotel. Call me later from a pay phone with the numbers."

"Why, Keene? I don't understand."

"We traced Tess's cell phone. You could be found the same way."

"Oh." She paused. "Keene, we'll do exactly as you say. But you also need to be careful. You need to get a new phone too."

"No, I want to be found," I said. "I'll be fine."

"I love you, Keene. I had no idea what a great guy you were. I'm sorry." She began to sob once more.

"I love you too, sis. Now call Byron and then get out of town."

I next tried calling Grady, but as was usually the case, I got only voice mail. I left him a short message, saying simply, "Grady, it's Keene. Call me. It's very important."

Next I called Paige. She answered so quickly that it made me wonder if she'd been sitting at the phone just waiting for my call. "Have you found Tess yet?" she asked, the fear emanating from her voice.

"Yes, Paige, and she's fine. She's not in any trouble, but she is in a little danger," I told her, trying to minimize the terrible reality of the situation. "There's nothing for you to worry about because Officer Donovan and I are taking care of her."

"Is she with you now?" Paige asked.

"Yes, but I think it's best if you don't talk with her yet. Just take my word for it that she's fine," I said. "Now, I have a favor to ask you."

"Anything, Keene. I am so grateful to you for finding my sister."

"I need for you and your mother to help with the hotel again. My sister and her husband have to leave for a few days. The rest of the staff will be working; Chief Thompkins and the other officers there will keep an eye on you. Byron Rowe will be in charge until I get back. Bree is talking to him today. He'll coordinate your schedules. You will not be working nights for a while, nor will your mother. Byron will take care of that. I'll make sure a police officer checks by every so often. But don't worry. We've got things under control." That wasn't entirely true, but I didn't want to scare her, and I needed her help.

"We'll do it," she promised.

After I ended the call, I returned inside and sat down. My breakfast was waiting for me. It didn't look very appealing now. I was afraid I'd lost my appetite, but I knew I needed to eat, so I forced myself. The three of us talked as we ate. Suddenly, Tess said, "I have a confession to make."

My stomach lurched. *What now?* I wondered. "Go ahead," I said after swallowing a mouthful of eggs.

"I hoped you'd find me," she said. "I know I didn't act like it when you stopped me, but deep down I hoped you would."

Chaille smiled. "We had a feeling about that. We're grateful we did."

"Not as grateful as I am," she said. "But I'm terribly afraid now. You'll keep me safe, won't you?"

"You have our word," Chaille promised.

At that moment, Tom Brolin called me back. "What have you got, Sergeant?" I asked.

I listened to him for a minute while he outlined his news. "Okay, thanks," I said and disconnected.

Neither woman had resumed eating; their eyes were on me. Tess began to wring her hands. Chaille simply placed one of hers on mine. "What did he say, Keene?"

I didn't keep them in suspense. "I learned that someone—they don't know who yet—opened an account in your name at a bank in Cheyenne and put the money in it. It could have been any of our several suspects. An investigator in Cheyenne will be receiving several faxed photos of those suspects, and then they'll try to determine if someone at that bank recognizes any of them. We can only assume someone was hiding money by putting it in an account in your name that you didn't know about. Or perhaps someone was trying to throw suspicion on you about the money missing from the hotel. At any rate, that doesn't really matter now. You have done nothing wrong, and we'll catch whoever did."

We finished eating, and I told the two women that I needed to go back to Hardy but that they were to find someplace safe to hole up until it was safe to return to Hardy.

"Tess," I said. "I'll need to borrow your cell phone, and you'll need to get a new one. Use a public phone to call me and tell me what the number of your new phone is. And I'll also need yours, Chaille. Same thing: get a new one, call me from a public phone, and give me the number."

"Why?" Chaille asked.

"We were able to use Tess's cell phone to figure out where she was. If we can do it, so can others. They might be using my phone or yours to trace us."

"But what about you?" she asked. "If you have all three phones, they'll surely be able to find you."

"That's what I want," I said. "But I hope to be back in Hardy before then."

Both women looked at me for a moment and then at each other. "Are you sure?" Chaille finally asked.

"I *do* have a plan. Chaille, you and Tess take her car. It has OnStar so you'll have to get another car as well as new cell phones—just cheap, temporary ones. Then go a long ways from where you leave her car before you find a hotel to hide in."

"What do we do with her car?" Chaille asked.

"Store it somewhere and rent a car. If it gets traced to where you leave it, it won't matter because you won't be anywhere near there," I explained. "When we have this case wrapped up, we'll get the car back."

Chaille said to Tess, who was looking at me doubtfully, "Keene's right. We better get on our way."

"You'll need to drive south from here. We don't want you running into someone who is looking for you," I said. "We are on US 89A here. You'll meet up with US 89 in a few miles. Go there and then drive to Flagstaff. That would be a good place to ditch the car, rent a new one, and buy phones. Then you decide where you want to go from there, but wherever it is make sure it's a good distance from Flagstaff. You should be fine, since I'll have both of your phones. If he is very sophisticated, which I'm quite sure he is, he'll think we're all traveling together."

"But what about you?" Chaille asked again. "What if you meet him somewhere?"

"I'll have a faster car, and I'll be watching for him anyway. Don't worry about me. I'll be okay, Chaille," I said, touched by the emotional, concerned look she was giving me.

Tess interrupted. "We better get moving," she said as she handed me her cell phone. "I need to visit the restroom, and then I'll be ready to go."

She started away, and Chaille turned to follow her, but I caught her arm. "Chaille, there's something else I need you to do."

She smiled feebly and then leaned into me. "Whatever you need, Keene."

"Good. Here's what I want you to do." I gave her some detailed instructions and asked, "Have you got all that?"

She nodded her head gravely, and then she turned her face up toward mine. I kissed her intensely, and then she said as she handed her cell phone over, "I'll go find Tess. I'll be praying for you, Keene. Please, please take care of yourself for me."

CHAPTER TWENTY-SIX

I REALIZED THAT I MIGHT be overestimating the skills of the killer with all the precautions I'd taken, but I felt that it was better to err on the side of caution. After all, two innocent women's lives were at stake.

Having gassed up at Jacob Lake, I was ready for a long, fast drive. My goal now was to make it back to Hardy in one piece. That meant I couldn't afford to fall asleep. It also meant that I had to avoid a confrontation with my enemy, or enemies, somewhere between here and there.

I'd spent several years alone since I'd moved out of my parents' home. But I'd never really been lonely. I was lonely now. I missed Chaille with an intensity that I didn't know it was possible to feel. I wondered if she also was missing me. I hoped she was. I envisioned a beautiful future for the two of us.

Bree called when I was a hundred miles north of Kanab. She'd already taken the precaution of getting a new phone. "We'll be meeting Jean at the airport in a little while."

"Good. What about your kids?" I asked.

"Ron's folks are great. They're doing exactly as you asked. They'll be okay. I just wish the children could be with us."

"I hope it won't be too long," I said. "I'll let you know when it's safe to come back."

***

I drove until I was simply too tired to continue, then I pulled off the road and parked the car out of sight in the trees. Still being very cautious, I set the burglar alarm on the Corvette and then hiked two or three hundred yards. I wanted to be a safe distance from it but close enough to hear the alarm if it went off. I found a large, thick pine tree with low-hanging branches. I set the alarm on my phone for three hours and then made my bed on the soft pine needles beneath the tree. Despite my worry, my loneliness, and the grief I carried in my heart, I was soon asleep.

***

I woke up to the screaming of the Corvette's alarm. I grabbed my 9mm pistol from the holster on my belt and headed toward the car. I took a roundabout route, walking quietly, my ears and eyes alert to every sound and motion. The unearthly sound of the alarm made it hard to hear other things, so I had to be cautious, but it also meant they couldn't hear me. This wasn't where I'd wanted to have a showdown or make an arrest, but I guess it wasn't going to be my choice. I'd been found—or at least Sean's red Corvette had been.

When I was close enough to see the car through the branches, I could make out two unfamiliar figures. One was sliding an unlocking rod down the passenger side window of the Corvette, but he wasn't having any success. I hoped that he didn't give up in frustration and smash a window out with a rock. The other burglar appeared to be standing guard a little ways back in the trees not too far from a dark blue late-model pickup. But he wasn't doing a very good job of standing guard. I slipped behind him and brought my pistol down on his head. I caught him with my empty arm as he slumped back, and I laid him quietly on the ground. He'd been holding a small revolver, which I picked up and slipped into my pocket. Then I moved toward the other man. He had a shaved head and wore a tight-fitting shirt that showed an abundance of muscle.

I didn't see any way to get close to him like I had the other man. And the alarm was blaring so loudly that I wasn't sure he'd hear me if I hollered a command to freeze. So I simply did the next best thing and fired a round from my 9mm into the radiator of the pickup. Steam immediately blew out, but not any faster than the bald muscleman moved away from the Corvette. Angry, I fired another round into the ground in front of him. He stopped, turned, and started to run. Another bullet sprayed up dirt in front of him. This time he stopped, and I stepped out where he could see me, pointing my pistol at his midsection and shouting as loud as I could, "The next one goes through you if you so much as move a muscle."

He stood frozen in place, all but his eyes, which were roving about. "You're all alone," I shouted as I stepped closer. "Your buddy's down and out. Put your hands high, where I can see them." He complied, anger and hatred written across his face. With the pistol held steady in one hand, I fished the Corvette keys from my pocket and pushed a button, shutting off the infernal racket. I didn't need the noise anymore to mask my approach. And the second man was certainly giving me his attention after the shots I'd fired.

The silence that settled on the forest was almost menacing, matching the look on the face that glowered from beneath the shaved head. I put the keys back in my pocket, watched the man for a moment, and then stepped closer. "You should learn not to take things that aren't yours," I said through clenched teeth. "Step over to your truck and assume the position." He knew exactly what I meant, and I soon had him with his hands on the hood and his feet spread far apart. I stepped closer, pulling handcuffs from my belt.

"Keep one hand and your forehead on the hood and put your right hand behind your back," I ordered. "If you make one false move, I will plug you, so don't try anything."

I sensed that he was not about to let me handcuff him.

I was right.

As I reached forward, ready to snap one cuff onto his wrist, he suddenly spun. And I kicked him in the knee. The kick put him down, but he struggled to get back to his feet, his eyes shooting me with deadly looks. I didn't have time for this, so I clubbed him over the head with my pistol, and he joined his partner in la-la land.

I dragged him to the truck and propped him up against the left rear tire. I made a fast search of their truck, and with rope I found there, I tightly bound the would-be thief. After searching him for weapons, I turned my attention to the other man. He was still out cold. I patted him down then propped him against the right rear tire and bound him tightly.

I was pretty sure that my shot to the radiator had disabled the pickup, but to be certain, I took the knife I'd found on the bald man's belt and slashed all four tires. I gathered up the weapons I'd found—three more pistols, two rifles, and five knives—and put them in the trunk of my car and then took time to find the men's identities. I wrote down their names along with the make, model, and license number of the truck. Finally, I checked both men over carefully. Reassured they wouldn't die before someone could get to them, I got in the Corvette, drove back to the highway, and headed north again.

I hadn't recognized either man, and their names didn't ring any bells. I assumed that they were simply trying to steal the car, though they could have been hired by my suspects. I stopped at the next town, went to a pay phone, and made a call to the local sheriff's office. I did not identify myself. I simply told the dispatcher that two men had tried to steal my car and had also tried to attack me. I gave their names, the information about the truck, and then said, "You'll find them bound, leaning against the truck." I described the location, put the phone down, and hit the road again. I was reasonably sure that action would be taken. But just to make sure, I stopped at the next town and called from another pay phone. I was assured that the men had been found and that they'd been wanted for bank robbery. The truck I had damaged was stolen. I was asked to identify myself. I explained who I was and why I had been unable to remain at the scene. "I'll get with you later to give you a statement," I said. "But right now, there are lives at stake, and I've got to go. Please don't mention my name. If you need confirmation, call Sergeant Tom Brolin on the LAPD." I gave them his number and then put the receiver back and sped north, satisfied that I'd taken out a pair of bad guys but regretting that they weren't the ones I was after.

Bree called me, just to check in. I assured her I was safe, and then she assured me that they were okay. I tried again to call Grady, with the same negative results. I worried and waited for a call from Chaille. It was with relief that I finally heard from her about thirty minutes later. She gave me hers and Tess's new numbers and assured me that she was following my instructions to the letter and that she would continue to do so. She asked how I was doing, and I told her I was fine. I kept my run-in with a couple of bad guys to myself.

I couldn't go much longer with so little sleep, and so, once again, I had to figure out how I could safely get a few hours of sleep. I was almost to Salt Lake City by then. After thinking for a few minutes, I devised a plan.

I checked in at the Radisson Hotel downtown and parked in the underground parking. I put the cell phones in the hotel safe, and without even going to the room, I called a cab from a phone in the lobby. I had the cabby take me to a store, where I bought a cheap cell phone. From there, I rode to the Little America Hotel several blocks away, checked in there, and, carrying my luggage, went to my room.

I showered and shaved and then sat down at the head of the bed and began to make calls. I made sure everyone who needed it had my new phone number. Then I reached for the room phone and ordered dinner. While I was waiting for my meal—the first I'd eaten since that morning at Jacob Lake—I watched the local news. The lead story was about two men who had been taken into custody in a remote area of Southern Utah. I listened with interest, grateful that the police had honored my request and kept my name from the press.

I set the alarm clock on the nightstand for 3 a.m. and went to bed. I slept soundly and awoke when the alarm went off. I was much refreshed. I called for a cab and had it deliver me to within about a block of the Radisson, where I'd left the Corvette. I exercised extreme caution as I approached the hotel. I didn't see anyone or anything suspicious, and within minutes, I had picked up the cell phones, checked out, and was driving the Corvette out of the parking area. Traffic was light as I hurried north on Interstate 15.

***

The first thing I did when I arrived in Hardy a few hours later was stop by the police station, where I sat down with Chief Thompkins. While we were there, he got a call from the police in Cheyenne. They had identified the person who had created an account in Tess's name and then deposited the $50,000 into it. I was not terribly surprised to learn that it was former Detective Vernon Bentley. When the chief had finished the phone call, we discussed that name. It made sense, but I knew that the former cop was not working alone, and I realized that what Tess had told me and my own disturbing thoughts had been right on point. I knew who had killed both my mother and Sean, and I knew why. Now it was a matter of forcing hands, gathering evidence, and making arrests.

There were a lot of details that still needed to be sorted out, such as exactly where the $50,000 had come from. But that wasn't the most crucial detail. I needed evidence that put the killer with both my mother and Sean when they'd died.

I finally went to the hotel. Joy Everest was on duty, and when she saw me, she rushed around the counter. "Mr. Tempest," she said urgently, "are you sure my Tess is okay?"

I smiled at her, hoping to put her at ease. Then I said, "She's just fine, Mrs. Everest. She's safe, and she hasn't done anything wrong."

"But I heard she said that she'd done something terrible," Joy pressed, obviously worried.

"She did nothing wrong," I reiterated. "She did make someone very angry, but it's not something she did intentionally. Believe me, she'll be okay."

"Thank you, Mr. Tempest." She was near tears. "You're a good man. You remind me so much of your mother."

I smiled at her again. "I appreciate the way you and Paige have helped out here."

"It's the least we can do," she replied. I started away, but she stopped me. "How much longer is this terrible situation going to go on?"

Looking her directly in the eye, I said, "I hope not too much longer. But honestly, I don't know. It'll be over sooner than it would have been without your daughter's help. Thanks to her, I am focused in the right direction now."

Her eyes grew wide. "How did she do that?"

"When it's all over, I'll tell you—but not now. Thanks again for what you're doing."

I entered my living quarters. Some of Bree and Ron's stuff was scattered about, evidence that they'd left in a rush. I was grateful they were gone, for it could get dangerous here again. I just prayed that I could survive and help bring justice to my mother and brother.

I sat down on the sofa, exhausted. The next thing I knew, my cell phone was ringing. I shook off the sleep and answered it.

"Keene, it's Grady. I'm sorry it took me so long to get back with you. I've been really busy."

"I'm sure," I said. "So where are you?"

"I'm in New York, of course," he answered a little crossly. "But I think I need to come back there. Not that I want to get shot at again, but I feel like we need to stick together as a family until we get this whole thing resolved."

"That would be a good idea. I think you should, but I don't want you to lose your new job."

"There's no danger of that now," he assured me.

"That's good to hear. By the way, we got the Corvette back."

"You did? That's good."

He didn't ask how or where we recovered it, and I didn't volunteer the information. "When will you be getting here?" I asked.

There was a pause, and then he finally said, "Tomorrow evening. I'll come directly to the hotel."

"I'll look forward to seeing you," I said evenly. "Be careful."

"Oh, I will. No one's going to get a shot at me again. By the way, why isn't Bree answering her phone? I've been calling her, and all I get is voice mail."

"Kind of like we get when we call you," I retorted a bit sharply. "This whole affair is getting her down. She's been staying inside day and night. She even has her groceries brought in. I'm so angry at the way Sean's murder has affected our family."

"Yeah, me too," he said. "Tell Bree I'm coming tomorrow night. I'll see you guys then."

As soon as he'd ended the call, I checked the time. I'd been asleep on the sofa for several hours! I'd needed the sleep, yet it felt like wasted time. There was much to do.

Tom Brolin and I had been in touch regularly ever since I'd left Jacob Lake. I'd asked him to make several inquiries for me. Of course, it was his and his colleagues' efforts that had led to the discovery of Vernon Bentley opening an account in Tess's name at a Cheyenne bank.

"Tom," I said. "Thanks for what you've been doing. I especially appreciate your efforts to clear Tess's name."

"I'm glad we could do it," he said.

I'd asked him to put the department's considerable resources into locating our suspects using the most modern electronic means. They'd had some success. They didn't know where any of them were at that moment, but they knew where some of them had been fairly recently, and with luck, they'd catch up with them soon. There was one—the one I was most interested in—that they hadn't been able to track. I suspected that he'd taken the same precautions I'd asked my family and friends to take.

"I'll let you know if I hear more," he said. "And by the way, the authorities in Southern Utah are grateful for your help in capturing their two fugitives." He chuckled. "That was good work, Keene." The call ended, and I thought of Chaille. I missed her, and I prayed that she was still following my instructions. I was sure she was. She was smart, she was honest, she was thorough, and she was loyal. I adored the girl. I had talked to her just before I fell asleep on the sofa. And I had dreamed of her.

It would be dark in an hour. There were a few little tasks I needed to complete before then. I set about doing them. When all was finished, I sat down on the sofa again. But this time I didn't go to sleep. I couldn't afford to. I felt danger close by. I might be wrong, but I had a feeling that I wasn't.

Darkness settled outside. I turned the lights on. I waited, my stomach in knots. Time was crawling by. I got up and moved around the room. I'd laid a trap, a trap that may or may not work. Only time would tell. Another hour passed. I did little sitting, mostly pacing the small apartment, my mind and senses alert.

There was a knock on my apartment door. I'd been expecting that, even hoping for it, but my heart jumped in my throat anyway. *This could be it,* I thought as I checked my pistol for the tenth time. I put it back in my holster and stepped over to the table at the far end of the room. I clicked a button on the small digital recorder that I'd hidden behind a stack of books. I moved toward the door, took a deep breath—trying to keep my hands from shaking—and opened it.

"Fancy me getting here so fast," my brother's killer said.

CHAPTER TWENTY-SEVEN

THE PISTOL HE WAS HOLDING in his gloved hand was big, and it had a factory-made silencer on it. I was looking at the face of Deputy Sheriff Renny Criswell. That wasn't who I'd expected. I was not, however, confused. Renny, as he'd been described to me, wasn't as tall as the man holding a gun on me. Renny kept his head shaved, but the hat this man wore hid that. I kept my face steady. Hatred shot from his eyes. "Some people just never learn, do they, little brother?" he said.

"Hello, Grady," I said, my voice steady and even. "I've been expecting you."

"Sure you have," he said, peeling the skintight Renny Criswell mask off with one hand. "That's why your gun is in your holster and mine is centered on your puny little chest. You said Bree was here. Where is she? In one of the bedrooms? Bree!" he called out loudly. "Please come in here. There are some things that you and Keene and I need to talk about."

"Bree isn't here. I sent her away."

His head slowly swiveled back and forth. "Too bad. I'll have to take care of her later."

"Why? She hasn't done anything to you."

"I hadn't planned that at first, but I could see that she felt close to you; she defended you. She even wanted you to have the Corvette. But never mind. I'll get her too. Or should I say that Renny will?"

"Grady, I was hoping we could talk," I said calmly, facing down his anger and hatred.

"You're a cop," he said with such venom in his voice that I wondered what had happened in his life to make him hate police officers so badly. "I'll talk to you, but shouldn't you read me my rights first?" It was just a game to him.

"You're right." I recited the Miranda warning.

"Okay, so ask me your questions, then," he said, his hate-filled eyes boring into mine. "Not that it'll do you any good to hear my answers. You'll never be able to testify. You see, little brother, I've come here to shoot you. And this time I will not miss."

"Why would you want to do that?" I asked.

"I wanted this hotel so I could sell it. I had a buyer all lined up, and I needed the money, but then I found out Mother was planning to give the place to you."

"Was your buyer Hugo Starling?"

"So you figured it out. I expected you would. He'll still buy it once it's mine," he sneered.

"Where did he get the money to buy the place?"

"His good buddy Jim McLaren was going to help him."

"What happened to Mom?" I asked.

"She wouldn't listen to reason. She even hired somebody to protect you down there in LA. But I almost got you anyway. She was very stubborn, so I poisoned her. But if it'll make you feel any better, she didn't suffer." He chuckled then, the most devilish sound I'd ever heard.

The blood in my veins turned to ice. Confession number one had just been recorded. I still needed more. "She never told me she planned to give it to me," I said. "In fact, it isn't even mine. It belongs to all of us. I'm just managing it."

"Liar," he spat at me. "She was giving it to you, and you put her up to it."

"Sorry, Grady, but you've got that wrong. I never wanted this place. I still don't."

"Liar," he repeated. He must have enjoyed calling me that.

"But why did you go after Sean?" I asked, baiting him. "What did Sean do?"

"I used to think he hated you as much as I did. It turns out I was wrong. He was a drunk and he didn't treat you very good, but he would have given his life for you." He chuckled once more, a dark and mirthless sound. "Fact is, I guess you could say he did. He was just lucky *you* didn't kill him first. Who would've known you're so good with your hands?"

"I didn't want to hurt him," I said. "When he swung on me, I just reacted. But I had no idea he didn't hate me."

"Which is why you left him in jail when I wanted him out."

"Why did you want him out?"

"So I could kill him," he said coldly.

"Why? He'd always been good to you, Grady."

"That was true to a point, but when he supported Mom's decision to give you the hotel, he turned his back on me. He knew I wanted it. I hated him as badly as I did you after that. If he would have let you just stay in LA like you wanted to, I could have taken over the hotel, and then I would have figured out a way to take over everybody else's shares. I had to make you both pay. I made Sean think McLaren was after you; he helped Mom hire that agency in LA."

"I didn't want this place, Grady. I still don't."

"Liar." He sure liked to say that. Of course, I'd much rather he call me names than pull the trigger on that large pistol he was holding.

"Could we sit down?" I asked.

"I won't be here long," he said. "And I'm sure not fool enough to let you get close to me. But let me finish telling you about Sean. I sent him a note, asking to meet him in his room here at the hotel. I told him we could work things out. He believed me, the fool."

"So you killed him?"

"Yes, and you would have been next, but my friend Detective Bentley had a better idea. He said he could pin Sean's death on you. That would have been great, wouldn't it? You going to prison for something I did."

Confession number two had been recorded.

I changed track, trying to keep him off balance. "What did Jim McLaren ever do to you?" I wanted every one of his vile crimes recorded. I hoped I had time enough to get it before he made his attempt to get me.

"He wanted to marry Mom and take this place," he said. He laughed more of that devilish laugh of his. "I played him for the fool. He thought I was on his side, and then when Mom died, I made him think he did it accidentally. He was running scared, but after a while he figured out what I'd done. I'm not sure how, but he did and was fool enough to tell me so. I was content to let you take him down for it. But after the fiasco in Twin Falls, he had to be eliminated before he talked."

"Was it you that shot at my police car in Los Angeles?" I asked. I wanted this all on my recorder.

"Thought I'd got you that night." He clicked his tongue.

"You shot a good friend of mine," I told him.

"His bad luck."

"No, yours. He wants you arrested. You don't know the LAPD. They take it personally when someone tries to kill one of their own. They've been a big help. They even discovered that it was Vernon Bentley who opened the account in Tess Everest's name after you found out she had a letter that would point fingers at you. What I'd like to know, Grady, is where you got the $50,000 that you had Bentley hold for you."

"From Jim McLaren. I told you I'd played him for the fool. He was quite willing to give me money to keep my mouth shut," he said with a chuckle. "He was good at getting money from all his lady friends."

"So you knew about that?" I asked.

"Of course I did. I've been busy, little brother. I've made so many trips to Idaho and California that I'm tired of it. Who do you think forced McLaren into the power pole then took him from the hospital and finished him off? He'd outlived his usefulness. That's where I was when I said I was going to Sean's house." He chuckled, an ugly sound. "You thought Sean and I were so close. Not hardly. After that, I did go to Sean's for a little while. Yes, little brother, I've been busy, and I know lots of things."

"How did you get to be friends with Detective Bentley?" I wanted to keep him talking.

"Well, it's like this. I met Hugo first, and I learned that he wanted the hotel. He introduced me to both Jim and the detective. Bentley and I just sort of hit it off," he said.

"Birds of a feather," I commented dryly.

"We do think a lot alike," he agreed.

"What would you say if I told you that Tess never even opened the copy of the letter Mother wrote to you, the one Tess forwarded?"

"I'd call you a liar. Of course she knew what it said. Mother should have never written that letter."

"Actually, Tess didn't open it. She only sent it because it had your name on the envelope, but you go and threaten to kill her for mentioning it." I shook my head sadly. "You had nothing to fear from her."

"I guess I still have to clean up that little loose thread too. I can't have her shooting off her pretty little mouth."

I made no further comment on that. "So who shot at you when you went down to Sean's house to see what you could steal?" I asked instead. "You know, after you got back from Idaho."

There was no change of expression on his face when he said, "I did it myself. Cops are so stupid. I figured right when I assumed that none of you would ever suspect me if I got shot at. I even used Sean's guns. I created the setup, and it worked perfectly. The only downside was that I had to shoot myself to make it look real. But of course, I did myself the least damage I could. It wasn't easy to twist my arms to make it work, but I managed." He laughed again. It was all so funny to him. "You got lucky in Boise, kid. I nearly got you then. After Bentley got fired and couldn't pin Sean's death on you, I knew I had to take care of things myself. I had you in my sights, but you got lucky again. You have led a charmed life, little brother—until now."

"Where's Alvin Cramer?"

"He doesn't even matter, nor does his fool of a nephew. Karl got the Corvette for me." He chuckled that ugly sound of his then added, "That's a nice car. Sean owed it to me. No way was I letting you have it." He paused for a moment. "I understand Karl can't be found either."

"That's right."

"Well, this may disappoint you, but I didn't do anything to them. And if you weren't about to die, I'd tell you to go after Vernon Bentley and his friend Renny Criswell about the Cramers. They are pretty bloodthirsty—for cops. Of course, I was careful coming in here, just in case anyone saw me, they'll think it was Deputy Criswell. And when they examine this gun they'll find his fingerprints all over it. It's his pistol."

"You think you've thought of everything, don't you?" I said.

"I've covered my bases," he bragged with an evil smile. "And now time's up, little brother. You can take all this precious knowledge with you to the grave."

"Just one more thing, Grady," I said, holding my hand out toward him, my palm facing forward.

"Okay, one more thing," he agreed with another of his awful smiles. "Let's call this the condemned man's last request."

"You didn't quite cover things as well as you think. I had you figured out. Do you know there's a gun pointed right at the back of your head? Don't even flinch, Grady, or you will die where you stand."

I sincerely hoped, for my sake and for Chaille's and Damion's that he wouldn't flinch. But he did, and it was my poor greedy brother's last act.

Damion stepped into the room from the door that had been slowly opening while I was stalling Grady. Chaille had followed my instructions perfectly. She had left Tess in a hotel and driven home and met the chief. She stepped in right after him.

I was in shock. I had tried hard to convince myself that Grady would surrender, but he hadn't. I had hoped that the three of us could arrest him without any fanfare once we had him surrounded. I had been so wrong. All the tension I'd been hiding the past few minutes refused to stay bottled up inside me for another second. I began to cry, feeling like a weak fool. But the beautiful person who comforted me didn't let on if she thought it was a weakness that made me less of a man.

EPILOGUE

CHAILLE AND I FLEW TO New Mexico to escort Tess home, even though with Grady's death, we felt the danger was past.

Hugo showed up in New York, where Grady had never applied for, much less obtained, a job. Hugo was arrested, and two days after our return, he was extradited back to Hardy.

Under my intense questioning, he finally admitted that the money from the bank robbery was, in fact, beneath the floor in one of the rooms of our hotel. It seems that Grady had learned that fact from McLaren, Hugo's partner in that long-ago robbery. At that point, my brother's quest to get the hotel had intensified to the point that he was willing to commit murder to reach his goals.

Renny Criswell showed up. He returned from Canada a week after Grady's death. He'd finally gone on the hunting trip he'd been rumored to have gone on when his best friend, Vernon Bentley, had been fired by the sheriff. The sheriff had enough to fire him, but he was never charged with any crimes.

As for Vernon Bentley, he has never been found. I believe that he knows if he's ever caught he'll be facing a very long prison sentence and chose instead to leave the country. Perhaps he'll eventually be found and have to answer for his crimes.

Finally, the Cramers, both uncle and nephew, have not been seen again. We expect they won't be, although Renny Criswell never did confess to having done anything to them as Grady had alluded. Someone must have, but I don't know who. Grady had denied it in his rambling account to me of his crimes. Maybe Bentley, wherever he is, knows something about it. I guess that's one mystery that will have to remain a mystery.

We sold the hotel after recovering the hidden loot from below the floor. Insurance had long since paid off the bank that Hugo and Jim had robbed, so the money was ours as the owners of the hotel. I didn't want a dime of it. Neither did Bree. We gave it all to Grady's widow—she needed it worse than we did.

After asking the love of my life to marry me, I submitted my resignation to Chief Thompkins and accepted a job as a detective with the sheriff's department. I would have liked to stay with the Hardy Police Department, but I needed full-time work, and Damion didn't have the budget. I left with his blessing. I loved police work, but to this day I pray that I have handled the worst case I'll ever be confronted with.

Chaille, after a few months of marriage, left police work. What she really wants is to raise a whole bunch of redheaded, Irish-American kids, all with the last name of Tempest.

ABOUT THE AUTHOR

CLAIR M. POULSON WAS BORN and raised in Duchesne, Utah. His father was a rancher and farmer, his mother a librarian. Clair has always been an avid reader, having found his love for books as a very young boy.

He has served for more than forty years in the criminal justice system. He spent twenty years working in law enforcement, the last eight as the Duchesne County Sheriff. For the past twenty-plus years, Clair has worked as a justice court judge for Duchesne County. He is also a veteran of the US Army, where he was a military policeman. Clair has been personally involved in the investigation of murders and other violent crimes. He has also served on various boards and councils, including the Justice Court Board of Judges, Utah Commission on Criminal and Juvenile Justice, Utah Judicial Council, Utah Peace Officer Standards and Training Council, an FBI advisory board, and others.

In addition to his criminal justice work, Clair has farmed and ranched all of his life. He has raised many kinds of animals, but his greatest interest is horses and cattle. He is also involved in the grocery store business with his oldest son and other family members.

Clair has served in many capacities in the LDS Church, including full-time missionary (California Mission), bishop, counselor to two bishops, young men's president, high councilor, stake mission president, Scoutmaster, High Priest group leader, and more. He currently serves as a High Priest instructor and single adult advisor.

Clair is married to Ruth, and they have five children, all of whom are married: Alan (Vicena) Poulson, Kelly Ann (Wade) Hatch, Amanda (Ben) Semadeni, Wade (Brooke) Poulson, and Mary (Tyler) Hicken. They also have twenty-three grandchildren. Clair and Ruth met while both were students at Snow College, and they were married in the Manti temple.

Clair has always loved telling stories to his children and later to his grandchildren. His vast experience in life and his love of literature have always contributed to both his storytelling and his writing.

This book is Clair's twenty-fourth published novel. He would love to hear from his fans, who can contact him by going to his website clairmpoulson.com or can find him on Facebook.